IN THE
DAMAGE
PATH

IN THE
DAMAGE
PATH

A Nut Cracker Investigation

Katherine Ramsland

LEVEL
BEST BOOKS

First published by Level Best Books 2023

This novel is entirely a work of fiction. The names, characters and incidents portrayed in it are the work of the author's imagination. Any resemblance to actual persons, living or dead, events or localities is entirely coincidental.

Katherine Ramsland asserts the moral right to be identified as the author of this work.

Author Photo Credit: Noelle Means

First edition

ISBN: 978-1-68512-395-6

Cover art by Level Best Designs

This book was professionally typeset on Reedsy.
Find out more at reedsy.com

For my first readers: Sue, Sally, Dana, and Ruth.

Praise for Books by Katherine Ramsland

For *Damage Path*

"No one understands the criminal mind like Katherine Ramsland, and *In the Damage Path*, starring her determined and brilliant Annie Hunter, is another winner. Sinister, captivating, and propulsive—I could not turn the pages fast enough! Not for the faint of heart, but Ramsland, a talented storyteller, does not flinch at reality—and the authenticity of this gripping novel will haunt you long after its final pages. Ramsland is a force of nature—passionate, brave, and relentless. True crime fans will be riveted, and no reader will ever look at the psychology of crime and the science of investigation in the same way. Do not miss this!"—Hank Phillippi Ryan. *USA Today* bestselling author

"Ramsland wastes no time capturing the reader's attention and taking us on a complex investigative journey. Annie Hunter and her team deploy unique and creative methods to find the bad guys—not only is this series a great read but you will also learn some cutting edge investigative techniques along the way."—Joe Pochron, retired law enforcement, Digital Forensic & Insider Threat Lead—Big 4 consulting firm

For *I Scream Man*

"I was intrigued by the first sentence. All true crime fans will be fascinated, then hooked immediately as they immerse in the culmination of the lead character working crimes that haunt her. Annie Hunter is the perfect mix of brilliance and successful field application, much like Ramsland herself. No one conveys the kind of intellect and mystery in a book like Katherine Ramsland." — Laura Pettler, forensic criminologist, author of *Crime Scene Staging Dynamics in Homicide Cases*, and owner of Laura Pettler and Associates

"Intense, dark, and full of twists and turns, Katherine Ramsland's debut novel I SCREAM MAN will keep you flipping the pages nonstop until you're done. With a hurricane bearing down on them, forensic psychologist Annie Hunter and her team of sleuths must wade deep into the world of sex trafficking to rescue her kidnapped daughter and several other children, who are victims of a corrupt juvenile detention system. The suspense grows with the strength of the hurricane as she turns to a shaman and a medium for help, unsure who to trust in a hunt for evidence that will cripple the network. I highly recommend this book and I look forward to more from the author."—Lori Duffy Foster, author of *Never Broken*

"A thoroughly entertaining and captivating read. *I Scream Man* has all the elements of a great mystery and crime drama, with some paranormal phenomena and a threatening natural disaster adding to the intrigue. As a retired Internal Affairs Investigator and now Private Investigator, I found the storyline and the characters compelling, and relatable. As often happens, what on the surface seems like a simple case is found to be entangled in realms others don't want you looking into. Knowing who you can trust, and who can provide legitimate information, is key, and Annie Hunter possesses that asset. She has assembled a team I would love to work with or share a glass of wine. I look forward to reading more of The Nut Crackers' adventures."—Susan Lysek, private investigator

"Missing children get under Annie Hunter's skin. A brilliant forensic psychologist, she is familiar with the secrets and shadows that hide inside the mind, but her search for the disappeared sets her on a propulsive, suspenseful ride through a world more dangerous and mysterious than she expected, especially when it gets personal. Gritty crimes, paranormal explorations, spine-tingling adventures—this twisty thriller grabs hold of the reader and never lets go. *I Scream Man* is the start of an outstanding series featuring Annie and her colorful team of investigators, and I'm anxiously awaiting the next installment."—Ruth Knafo Setton, award-winning author of *The Road to Fez*

"Forensic psychologist Annie Hunter leads her team of crackerjack but quirky investigators through an exceptionally convoluted and precarious case involving missing children, the paranormal, and unfinished business that begs for resolution. Author Katherine Ramsland, a renowned expert on forensic psychology, skillfully uses her extraordinary insight into the human mind, and a razor-sharp knowledge of crime-solving forensics to bring to life *I Scream Man*, a cleverly plotted thriller."—Lee Lofland, Author of *Police Procedure and Investigation, a Guide for Writers* and founder of the annual Writers' Police Academy

"As Katherine Ramsland leads us down a murderous path that keeps getting darker and more complex, there are many twists and surprises. She uses her unique real-world expertise and experiences to craft intriguing characters and a story that will keep you turning pages well past bedtime. And the thrill ride to the end is one you'll not soon forget."—J. D. Allen, Shamus Award-nominated author of the Sin City investigation series

For *Darkest Waters* collection

"New or classic cases, no one writes with the insight of Katherine Ramsland. Period." — Gregg Olson, *New York Times* bestselling author

For *The Mind of a Murderer*

"Dr. Ramsland writes with a clarity of prose and elegance of style that makes her the envy of forensic commentators and establishes her as a genuine authority in her field."—Host of *Most Evil*, Dr. Michael Stone

For *Ghost: Investigating the Other Side*

"The best book of its kind I've ever read."—Dean Koontz, *New York Times* bestselling author

"Ramsland is a master of foreboding."—*Publishers Weekly*

Chapter One

The young brunette opened her eyes. She seemed surprised at the pile of sand that trapped her. She looked left. Then right. Her hazel eyes widened. She couldn't budge. Her nostrils flared.

"No, no! Help me!" She tried to move. Sweat oiled her nose. "Oh, my God! I can't get out! He's coming! He'll kill me!"

I cringed. Buried in sand. What a nightmare! I paused the video at her open mouth and glanced at Ayden Scott, my agency's investigator. In a collared blue shirt, he looked professional today, less like a beach bum. "What is this? Do I really need to see it?"

Ayden raised a blond eyebrow and redirected me with his head to the laptop screen. "Keep watching."

I hit *play*.

"Tommy!" the girl yelled. "Don't do this. I want to *be* with you. I love you!" She spat out sand. Her expression froze, as if she saw this 'Tommy' approaching. "No! Don't! Please don't! Not *that*, please! No more sand!"

Off screen, someone snorted. The trapped teen pressed her red lips in annoyance. The clip ended.

I sat back. "That's it?"

Ayden nodded. "That's it. Fake. The person filming it blew it."

"So, Sand Girl is play-acting? Like she was buried alive by a serial killer?"

"Yup. There's more on *NicKnac* if you wanna see 'em."

I shook my head. "She said Tommy. Did she mean *our* Tommy?"

"The same. He's getting quite a fan base."

I turned Ayden's laptop screen away. I normally love research, but this

1

one hurt. "Tommy," the killer these girls adored, had once snatched my best friend, Hailey Harper. She'd been just thirteen at the time, a year younger than me. Tommy Ray Bruder had picked her up on his Harley. I was there. I'd never forget his flirty dark eyes and trimmed mustache. Girls think cute guys can't possibly have wicked intent. Hailey and I were that naive. When Bruder removed his helmet to offer us a ride, his wavy brown hair had looked boyish. He'd focused on Hailey. She'd gotten on. He'd sped away, and she was gone. A search commenced, but the case went cold. I'd been devastated. I'd blamed myself.

Ayden grabbed a cinnamon scone from the plate I'd set out. "You going to the trial, boss?"

I nodded. "I want to catch that psychologist, Maura Reynolds, after she testifies. She discussed Tommy Bruder on a podcast. Maybe she can help us. Plus, it's a unique trial."

Ayden winked. "Your thing."

"Yes, my thing. And thanks to my expertise on suicide, I got a reserved seat. Killing two birds with one stone, I guess."

He cocked his head with a knowing look.

"I won't get sidetracked. Dr. Reynolds is relevant to our current investigation. That suicide case is secondary."

"Bet they'll hire you."

"They have their experts. I'm just an observer. You know better than anyone that finding Hailey's my priority."

Over the past twenty years, I'd searched for her. That's partly why I established my agency, the Nut Crackers, named for the twisty "hard nuts to crack" that we investigate. Recently, I'd gotten closer to my goal.

I'd pieced together Bruder's past to locate possible places he'd taken his victims. I still had aggravating gaps but also better leads. In the process, I'd bumped against crime groupies like 'Sand Girl' in this video. And they weren't just wacky sideshows. Their antics contaminated the trail. These drooling Bruder fanatics could thwart my progress. Some listened to my podcast, *Psi Apps*, where I'd vilified Bruder and displayed my dismay over his dim-witted devotees. They'd left nasty comments on my website, even death threats. One Bruder-kook in particular, Carly Krebs, often taunted me on her own podcast, *Killer Hooks*.

They baffle me. How do they get so inured to the horror of murder? Why do they joke that murder tales soothe their daily stress? Some as young as my nine-year-old daughter wear T-shirts emblazoned with "Choke me, Ted" and "Eat me, Jeffrey." They seek to swoon like Victorian virgins in gothic fiction from a vampire's bite.

On video media sites like *NicKnac*, I'd watched a fan of Ted Bundy drag herself across a floor, as if he'd just bludgeoned her with the crowbar he used on his actual victims. She'd acted ravaged. She'd even tattooed on herself a replica of his savage bite mark. She'd also dyed her hair black and sported vintage 'seventies clothing to resemble Bundy's victims. From true crime books, she'd mastered every detail. She'd even purchased envelopes offered as Bundy's from murderabilia sites. On camera, she'd pressed a seal against her lips to "absorb his essence" from where he'd licked it.

And now, on Ayden's laptop, I'd just watched the same bent devotion play out for Tommy Bruder. I motioned to the laptop. "Get on the *Killer Hooks* website. Krebs was supposed to make some big announcement today."

I got up to fill our coffee mugs. "Maybe Sand Girl got her idea from Krebs' rumor that Bruder buried girls alive. I think Krebs started that just so she could pin her nickname on him."

Ayden looked up. "You mean 'Captain Kidd'?"

"A play on words. A pirate with buried treasure, and kids are his prey. Krebs likes to use shock and awe, even disgust, to hook listeners."

Ayden scanned the website. "Same stuff here. Claims she's identified more than two-dozen victims. Brags about her uptick in followers. Thanks her chat partner, BH." He squinted.

I sat down and tapped the table. "BH is for Bleeding Heart."

Ayden rolled his eyes.

"Krebs has devoted several episodes to Bruder. She thinks she owns him."

Over the past two decades, Bruder had been a minor killer, unknown and languishing in his cell. He'd pled guilty to a single murder in Tennessee. On paper, he was just a run-of-the-mill loser. But podcasters seeking their own signature investigation had decided he was linked to several cold cases. He was an "undiscovered" serial killer. That claim gave them better purchase in a crowded marketplace.

I leaned toward Ayden. "Two days ago, something changed. Krebs hinted at an announcement. If she has something truly explosive, Bruder's gonna get media attention like never before. That's bad for us. These slinkers—"

Ayden snorted. "Slinkers?"

"Sloppy thinkers. The amateur sleuths who've linked Bruder to more unsolved cases, with no corroboration. Krebs claims she's confirmed the links, but she won't say what she has. Claims he has victims in multiple states, from New York to Florida. By her reasoning, if he *could* have abducted them, he *did* abduct them. She wants to solve them. If she can turn Bruder into a significant predator, she raises her online profile."

Ayden pointed at the screen. "Got it. The big announcement." He turned his screen toward me, pressed a key, and sat back as an audio came on.

Chapter Two

Krebs sounded excited, even breathless. "Over the past month," she said, "I've received several communications from Captain Kidd. I kept it secret, because I wasn't sure. He didn't like what I've been saying. He made some claims, and I checked them out. And now I literally think he might not be a killer at all. He says he was framed for the murder that put him in prison. Just like Captain Kidd being falsely accused of piracy!"

I nearly fell off my chair. I pointed at the screen. "Turn it up!"

Ayden increased the volume.

BH chimed in, as if on cue. "But, like, Bruder confessed."

Carly had a comeback. "And there's such a thing as a false confession. He said it was coerced. He was scared."

"And you believe him?"

"I didn't at first. I thought he was trying to get me to back the eff off because I was so close to the truth. But now I think I'm literally wrong. I even have proof. All this time, we've been trying to pin crimes on him when we should've been trying to *clear* him. So, now I have a new mission."

"To free Captain Kidd?" BH sounded flat, as if trying to remember what she'd been told to say.

"Yes, to show the world that Mr. Bruder is innocent, *literally,* and see that he gets compensated for this terrible miscarriage of justice. He's lost twenty years of his life! And I'll launch a real investigation that identifies the killer who's literally responsible for the list of abductions and murders I've collected."

She assured her fans she'd keep them informed, and invited them to write on her comment area. I could just imagine the reactions she'd get. And I could guess the reason she'd changed her position: Bruder had gotten to her. He was a good-looking guy. No doubt his letters had triggered a *frisson* that made her feel special. She'd staked a claim on his crimes, and now she had *him*.

The clip ended. I sat back. "I can't believe it. And she'll probably find a scummy lawyer to help."

"She's got a link here for a fund-me account. Just hit the button and send in your money."

I frowned. "I wish I'd started this a year ago. Even a month ago. All this attention to Bruder just muddles things."

"You weren't ready a year ago." Ayden picked up a large envelope. "And you might change your mind when you see this. Carly wouldn't like knowing this, but she's actually helping us." He removed several 8x10 color photos and placed them on the table. "She posted these images."

I leaned in. The photos displayed colorful tattoos covering a man's muscular back. I nodded. "I've seen them. That's Bruder."

"You've seen, Watson, but you haven't *observed*."

I rolled my eyes. "Okay, Sherlock. What am I missing?"

He picked up a pen. Using it as a pointer, Ayden lightly tapped one photo that showed a green and purple alligator tattoo. The snout pointed up and the tail curled around a kidney dimple. "See this shape here on the gator?"

I nodded.

"It follows the tail. I think it's the outline of a county where Bruder lived as a kid."

I scanned it and shrugged. "What makes you think so?"

Ayden flashed a smile, showing white teeth made brighter by his tan. "In an obscure prison newsletter, I found an interview with Bruder's former cellmate, one Pete 'the Panty Thief' Nemeth. Adding two and two from what he said and what we know gave me an idea."

He pulled up a map on his laptop. I don't question Ayden's sleuthing strategies. Despite his gig-work approach to life and his fondness for fun in the sun where we both reside on North Carolina's Outer Banks, as an investigator, he stays the course like a sniffer dog with heart. And he delivers.

Ayden continued. "We know from letters we've acquired from murderabilia sites that Bruder uses veiled messages. He told Nemeth, who drew his tattoos, that he wanted to record his conquests on his body without giving anything away. So, I enhanced these photos. Unless you have some guidance, you wouldn't notice anything. But I spotted some odd shapes that seemed to be camouflaged inside other images. Nemeth even called himself the camouflage king. Natra and I isolated most of them."

I squinted at him. Natra, our dog handler and data miner, hadn't mentioned this. She finds Ayden's manic drive annoying, so she usually assists him only when I ask. She must have thought he had a good idea. I gestured for him to keep going.

"I didn't jump to conclusions, Annie. You're always warning us about seeing what we want to see. Natra and I did separate analyses first. We used that list of places where we'd already documented Bruder living and looked at maps of townships, counties, anything that offered a geographic outline. Natra saw the same thing I saw in his tattoos. I think we have a lead."

He turned the laptop around. The screen showed an image of South Carolina with the counties distinctly outlined. He tapped the tattoo photo again. "Do you see it?"

I looked from the tattoo photo to the map. This was like a puzzle full of busy details that challenges the viewer to say what's missing. I squinted and scanned the areas. Then I saw it. Jasper County. Its perimeter resembled the outline inside the gator tattoo. So did two other counties. I scrutinized them for things that made them different and pointed at Jasper. "If the tattoo is accurate, it looks more like this one, but it's hard to say."

Ayden showed me another photo that focused on the tattoo. "Nemeth was pretty good at his work, and we have other clues I'll explain in a minute. Now look at this. What d'you see?"

I leaned in. "Where it juts out on the western side, I see a number. It's kind of obscured. Is it two?"

"I think so. When I enhanced it, I thought it was a 2 inside a flame. And there's a tiny cross next to it. It's possibly a location marker. Maybe for victim number two. That's speculative, but I think someone could be buried here. If I'm right, we might have a treasure map right here on Captain Kidd's back. This could be our best shot yet at finding Hailey."

Chapter Three

The first time I saw Hailey Harper, she ran past me so fast her current-red braids flew out behind her. Then I spotted a kid we called Hateful Tate chasing her. I kicked his leg and sent him sprawling while Hailey sprinted away. But she'd noticed my move. The next day, she placed a book on my chair at school. I'd seen her reading it. *The Ghost of Dibble Hollow*. Leaving it anonymously would let her pretend she hadn't, in case I tossed it. I picked it up. It didn't take long for us to become friends. For the next four years, until she vanished, we were inseparable. Some people called us Red and Gold, because I was blond.

I was ten, and she was nine, but she was the smart one. Her mother had taught her to read before she'd set foot in school, so she was well ahead of me. Hailey constantly pronounced complex names that enchanted her as if they tasted sweet. The dimples on her round face went in and out as she said, *"Haleakula"* or *"Charlevoix."* I can still hear her giggle. Had she lived, I'm sure her love of sound would've drawn her to poetry. Slender and gangly, she had a distinctively stiff walk from a pin once placed in her right ankle to stabilize a fracture. Although this attracted bullies, she'd declined to have it removed, so I became her protector. To seal our pact, we bought cheap silver bracelets on which our names were inscribed. She called us "Wrist Sisters."

Before I ever heard of the Rorschach inkblot test, Hailey showed me the dramatically different reactions two people can have to the same thing. We'd spotted an abandoned house in the woods covered in dying vines. It had two front doors. I'd heard that the second one once served to remove the

9

dead. The place gave me the creeps, but Hailey said it looked cozy. She hoped it had ghosts. One day, she said, she'd live in a haunted mansion.

Just after I turned fourteen, a series of terrifying incidents invaded our world. We learned about them from a boy at school whose dad was a cop. They dotted southwestern North Carolina, outside Asheville, and southeastern Tennessee. Six kids had vanished in as many months. They found four bodies.

The first to disappear was twelve-year-old Kristin Brown. She was at a friend's house in the county bordering ours when her mother called to tell her to come home for dinner. That was five blocks in one direction and two in another. Easy enough with a bike. Her mother had walked to the corner to watch for her. Somewhere between the friend's house and that corner, Kristin encountered a predator. On a road outside town, cops found her bike. I often thought of the image I'd seen in the newspaper of that abandoned pink bike, lying on its side.

Four months later, a high school student, Carla Davis, went missing from the same town. She was on her bike as well. A fisherman picked up a garbage bag in the river that contained her dismembered remains. Her bike was never found.

In another town, Brenda Nielsen, fourteen like me, walked to the store with her younger sister, Janet. They never returned. Neither did Steve Patterson, ten years old, who went missing the next day. The remains of the sisters were discovered together in the woods under a tarp. Patterson had vanished.

Number six was closer. The body of fourteen-year-old Becca Lynn Young was dumped on a road at our town's limits, missing her white tennis shoes. The police found one shoe two miles away in the foundation of a deteriorated barn. A week later, they found a necklace there as well, which was thought to have belonged to one of the murdered sisters. This discovery confirmed a link... and a serial killer.

Hailey and I sought out the details from newspapers. Becca Lynn was found on her back, her head turned to the right. Her dew-covered porcelain face showed fresh purple bruises, and blood had collected around her nose

10

and mouth. Her scarf was wrapped around her neck, hiding a deep incision that went nearly to the spine. Her stiff legs were splayed out, with her skirt pulled up. Her killer had dumped the contents of her purse, taking small change. He seemed to have ripped off her earrings. Because Becca had been my age, this murder felt personal. It could've been me.

Two weeks later, Hailey and I walked along the roadside where we liked to go look for ponies in the pasture of a small farm.

"Haven't heard anything more," she said. "My mom grabs the papers. Thinks readin' this stuff gives me nightmares."

I'd had nightmares, too, but I didn't admit it. "They don't have any suspects. I heard someone saw a red truck in the area where they found the body."

"Thought it was a black van."

I shrugged. "So, we just avoid both."

Recently we'd been hitchhiking. Looking back, I can't believe how stupid we'd been, but we were kids. We believed we were safe. We wanted to be daring and we wanted to get places. Hitching was the best way. People who'd picked us up were usually nice.

That day, a guy rode past on a Harley. Up the road, he stopped, circled back, and came directly to us.

"Want a ride?" he asked. "It's a nice day for it."

He was cute. He had large dark eyes, and his Harley seemed cool, so we said yes.

He smiled. "I can take one of you first, just down the road, and then come back for the other."

I made a move, figuring I should be first, to make sure it was safe. But he beckoned for Hailey. I felt rejected. Hailey smiled, flung back her braids, and clambered on behind him. He revved the engine. My stomach clenched. This wasn't right. Hailey looked at me. Her eyes changed. She didn't really want to go, not alone. I sensed her begging me to get her out of this.

I reached to pull her off. I touched her arm. Then, I flew backwards and hit the ground. My jaw hurt. I heard the words, "Cherry's mine," before the engine revved and the biker sped off. I jumped up and yelled, but they were too far away. Hailey looked back. I ran down the road and listened for the bike to slow down, like he'd promised. I stopped and waited. They didn't come back. I thought maybe he'd ridden just a bit further than he'd said he would. But time passed. The road remained quiet. They didn't return. I couldn't stop shaking. Finally, I walked back to town alone. I thought of Becca Lynn and felt ashamed. I was the older one. I should have known better. That's what my mother would say. I watched for them all the way back.

I ran to Hailey's house. I hoped she'd directed him there. She'd be home. She'd laugh at my worry. I couldn't wait to hear her make fun of me.

But she wasn't home.

I told Hailey's mother about the guy on the bike. I didn't reveal our complicity. I couldn't. But I knew the situation was bad, and someone had to do something. She phoned the police. When they came, I took them to where the biker had stopped to talk to us. I'd said he'd grabbed her. I didn't want to admit we'd been friendly with him, and that Hailey had willingly gotten aboard.

By then, I was numb. Hailey couldn't be gone. I was her protector. I'd let her down. I couldn't imagine how scared she was. I just wanted her back. If he tried something, I hoped she'd know how to fight. I'd never seen her fight someone, but she'd seen me do it.

The police and townspeople searched day and night. I sensed they blamed me. My mother did. So did I. As the days passed with no sign of Hailey, I realized I'd lost my best friend, and it was my fault. I sobbed every night. When I wasn't in school, I walked that road up and down. I kept twisting my bracelet, hoping I could send vibes through it to Hailey to assure her I'd find her. I was bereft. I hated myself for not insisting on taking the first ride. Better yet, for not telling the guy to get lost. In my mind, I'd see her walking toward me on the road. She'd gotten away. But she was never really there.

Weeks passed. I knew she wasn't coming back. Ever. The police gave up. Hailey's case joined those of other missing kids.

But I kept looking. I went deep into the woods, walked the tracks, and looked in deep holes and farmers' wells. I even entered the abandoned house that had scared me and checked in every room. Sometimes, I believed she could be in there. I wanted her to jump out and scare me. To just be alive. I left notes there every day for a month.

I'd see Hailey's mother out looking for her. I tried to avoid her, but once I ran into her. She looked so sad. I vowed I'd find Hailey. She just hugged me tight and patted my hair as if this reconnected her with her missing daughter.

Bruder was eventually caught in Tennessee when a girl fled from a van he was driving and called the police. Another girl who'd been seen with him was discovered two days later in a shallow grave in the woods. I came across his picture in a news account. I knew he was the same guy who'd taken Hailey. I went to the police to tell them. They added this to Hailey's file. A cop went to Bruder's cell to talk with him. He denied he'd ever been in my town.

I followed the news as Bruder pleaded guilty to assault, abduction, and second-degree murder. He claimed the murder victim had entered his van willingly. He hadn't intended to kill her, but she'd struggled and accidentally got hurt. She did have a head injury, so the autopsy couldn't disprove this scenario, but a finger was missing. They decided that was from animal activity. Bruder got a sentence for negligent manslaughter that came with the potential for parole. Nothing was added for the abduction, for which he'd also offered a credible alternative scenario. That's partly why these salivating groupies fixated on him. They couldn't wait for him to be free.

I memorized three additional cases in which Bruder was a suspect to try to spot his MO—where he'd taken his victims, what he'd done to them, how he'd buried the one and seemingly dumped others. I'd accepted faulty assumptions, like the idea that all of the female teens were linked to the same offender. My investigation had taken me down some time-consuming rabbit holes.

As I trained to be a clinical psychologist, I went to interview Bruder in prison. I made a mess of it. I displayed my loathing, which only amused him. Said he'd picked up kids every day. They wanted to go places, so they willingly accepted rides. Girls, boys, it didn't matter. He always took them wherever they asked, sometimes two at a time. He said he didn't remember

Hailey or me. But he was lying. I believe he'd agreed to see me merely to witness my pain. For him, it was just a game.

Years later, when I discussed Bruder on a podcast, he'd sent me a cease-and-desist letter. It was fake. Some attorney-wannabe inmate had probably coached him. I ignored him. But I'd hit a wall in my search for Hailey. I'd eventually worked out that Bruder had circled back to us because of the red color of her braids. He'd called her Cherry. With that clue, I'd sorted once more through the other abductions, refining my analysis. This narrowed potential search locations.

Now, Ayden had focused us on Jasper County. We made a plan.

Chapter Four

While Ayden and Natra contacted the consultants we'd need for a search, I grabbed a folder from my files labeled "Little Girl Murders." I'd studied these incidents to gain an expert perspective on how offenders snatch kids. Scanning them from time to time gave me an opportunity to let details jump out that I hadn't noted before.

On Valentine's Day in 2017 in Delphi, Indiana, searchers located the bodies of two missing girls. Abby Williams and Libby German had gone for a mid-day hike. When they failed to meet Libby's dad at a rendezvous site, a search had commenced. The mutilated bodies were found in a culvert off a creek on private property near the Monon High Bridge Trail. One cop said there'd been "signature behavior," which suggested sexual rituals that would likely be repeated. These usually involved posing, cutting, biting, or some form of mutilation. Libby had possessed the presence of mind to turn on her phone's recorder, getting the image of a burly man on the dilapidated bridge, along with his gruff voice ordering them "down the hill." Like Hailey and me, they'd been 13 and 14.

It appeared that their killer had noticed kids on the bridge and had scoped out its potential for entrapment. Once a kid crossed to the other side, there'd be no escape route. Offenders like this are patient. They wait and watch for the opportune moment. This killer, in fact, had lived quietly in town, a clerk in a store. He'd been on this bridge with his own daughter.

In another case, a nine-year-old girl was outside a store with two friends when a man rode up on his bicycle and dragged her into a restroom. He then rode off with her on his bike. She'd been so scared she hadn't struggled or yelled. Two weeks later, in the same area, two sisters were taken from their home during a brief period between their mother leaving and their father coming home. Less than two months passed before a man in a red car abducted a twelve-year-old on her way to the store. Her body turned up buried under leaves and debris in the woods.

Then, there was Kimberly Leach, the twelve-year-old in Florida who became Ted Bundy's final victim. In the middle of the day, she'd crossed her schoolyard to retrieve her purse when he leapt from a stolen van to grab her. It had been a bold, risky move, but no one had stopped him.

This was the same MO as the so-called Tool Box Killers, who decided to torture and murder at least one girl from each age group, 13-19. They bought a van, named it "Murder Mack," and drove around until they spotted girls that fit the bill. When they picked one up, they tortured her with tools like hammers and pliers while raping her repeatedly. One of them shoved an ice pick into the ear of a victim, stomping on it to drive it into her brain. When this failed to kill her, he wound a wire coat hanger around her throat. These offenders recorded the screams of their victims on tape as mementos of their grisly deeds.

There were so many more.

Into this file, I'd also placed a list of missing girls who'd likely been murdered. I could barely look at it, especially when I thought about my own daughter, Kamryn. I'd learned what predators look for, how they exploit vulnerabilities, and how they prepare. Bruder was a kid when he'd encountered us, around 17. He'd probably seen us and followed us, watching for us to be isolated. It wouldn't have taken long. We liked back roads. So did he.

I closed the folder, shaken. I knew every detail in these cases, but every time I read them, I thought of what Hailey must have endured. I'd finally accepted I was not at fault, but I still believed I could have done something that would have changed her fate. I could only hope she hadn't been tortured.

Chapter Five

The courthouse for the trial I wanted to observe wasn't far from my lake house in central South Carolina. Media had taken an interest in this case, so a lawyer I worked with had pulled in a favor to get me a good seat. As a suicidologist, I had an advantage. I'd never seen such a scenario—a girl coaxing a boy to kill himself—and it had both legal and psychological implications. But more urgent for me was to speak with Maura Reynolds, a psychologist who knew something about Bruder. Carly Krebs had interviewed Reynolds on her podcast.

I arrived early to get the full picture. Reporters watched one another in the stifling courtroom as if looking for cues in their rivals' posture for the best angle. My seat offered a view of the defendant, Amber Bell, from her right side. If she watched the witnesses, I'd see her profile perfectly.

Allegedly, Amber had formed an online relationship with Trevor Hale, the decedent. He'd been in therapy, but the sessions hadn't lessened his depression. Eventually, Trevor had obsessed over killing himself, and Amber had helped him consider ways to do it. A lengthy record of their texts revealed her involvement. Trevor had backed out several times, which had annoyed Amber. Finally, she'd succeeded in urging him through it. When he didn't come home, his frantic parents drove around to search for him. They discovered his body in his truck near his favorite fishing hole. At age 17, he'd overdosed on sodium nitrate.

Amber had acted devastated. She'd comforted Trevor's family, but Trevor's mother had found notes on his computer that showed Amber's awareness of Trevor's mental state. Police searched her phone. With proof from texts that she'd encouraged Trevor to kill himself, she was arrested and charged with manslaughter.

I wanted to see this girl. Podcasters had commented that she didn't take the charge against her seriously. But I thought the "sneer" they'd described could just be the defensive bravado of a fifteen-year-old.

It's tough to know what goes on in the mind of a kid who'd encourage a friend to end his life. She'd claimed she was doing what Trevor wanted, that he'd needed someone to listen and support his decision. Her attorney, a dynamic Black woman named Janissa Caulfield, said Amber might be guilty of poor judgment, but she'd done nothing illegal. The First Amendment protected her texts. She shouldn't even be on trial. However, Assistant District Attorney Richard Doyle insisted that her actions—or lack of them—had injected momentum into Trevor's decision to die. He'd been ambivalent. He'd aborted his efforts several times. He'd been in therapy. He could have been helped. She'd thwarted his recovery and assisted his suicide.

I watched Amber stride into the courtroom with a guard. She glanced around. Her round face atop a scrawny neck minimized the effect of her pretty green eyes. She looked anorexic in her button-less lavender blazer and tight black jeans. She resembled a scarecrow *sans* stuffing. A matching lavender band held her straight brown hair in a ponytail. I suspected that Caulfield hoped to make her seem younger than she was, with its suggestion of naiveté. On the day of her arrest, Amber's hair had been blond. So, restoring the original color had erased the impression of a seductive Scylla who'd lured a hapless boy to his death.

But the only person to impress was a female judge, Diane Essington, who looked to be in her mid-fifties. I suspected she'd seen her share of manipulative attorneys. The lack of a jury disappointed me, as I like to read their reactions. I sometimes consult for attorneys on jury selection, so the more I observe, the better. Judges are harder to read. The gray-haired Essington seemed stone-faced.

I'd missed the first two days of trial but had read the news coverage. Doyle had questioned the digital examiner who'd extracted the cellphone messages.

Then he'd run through a clique of high school girls who'd known either the decedent or the defendant. Doyle was tall and husky. His confident swagger and expensive brown suit gave the impression he believed he'd already won. His witnesses' mean-girl tales about Amber had supported his portrait of her as a cold-blooded schemer. She'd targeted Trevor on a social media site, Doyle surmised, when the boy's comments about his depression had revealed his vulnerability. She'd lured him into her web.

Today, Doyle looked to continue along the same lines. He pointed to a large photo of Trevor up on a screen. The kid had been athletic, but dark circles under his eyes told of a long struggle with stress and sadness. He wore a team logo baseball cap over his brown hair that showed his love of sports. Someone said he could cite baseball stats like a pro. I'd heard about hints of abuse in the home and hoped to learn more when his therapist, Maura Reynolds, testified. How much she revealed about her client would also tell me about her.

With Trevor's mother, Sandra, on the stand, Doyle read a selection of Trevor's heartbreaking comments. "'I've been thinking about dying since I was six,' Trevor wrote. 'I don't know why, but each day is a struggle to stay alive.' The defendant, this girl here..." —Doyle pointed at Amber—"tells him she understands. She's thought about suicide, too. So, she builds rapport. She seduces him. She *grooms* him. He's the perfect fall guy. She wants him to die. This is a game to her."

Janissa Caulfield rose and objected. Objection sustained.

The slender, hollow-eyed woman who resembled Trevor confirmed that she'd discovered these messages on his phone.

Doyle continued. "As we heard from her acquaintances yesterday, Amber didn't care about him. She only pretended to care to gain his confidence. Is this consistent with what you saw?"

Sandra shot Amber a nasty look. "I heard Trevor say he thought she didn't care. He told her some very personal things, believing she loved him, but she barely listened."

Amber drew in a deep breath. She sat in a stiff position and watched with a frown. Her right foot pointed toward the nearest exit, suggesting she wanted to escape.

Doyle drew out more from the grieving mother, apparently putting her on display for as long as possible. He spent around twenty minutes going over the record of Trevor and Amber's online exchanges, which had quickly moved to texting. During the six months they'd known each other, they'd texted dozens of times a day but had rarely met in person. Sandra confirmed this. Yet Amber had texted phrases that spoke of love and sympathy for his sense of emptiness. She'd often called him her boyfriend.

On cross-examination, Sandra admitted that things could get rough at home for Trevor, their eldest son. Caulfield treated her with kindness but still extracted the fact that Trevor's father demanded a lot and sometimes physically beat their son. Caulfield seemed bent on showing that Amber's assistance was immaterial. Trevor had been depressed enough over his difficult home life to have gone through with his self-annihilation. That was a skillful move. Doyle did not call Trevor's father to the stand. That, too, was smart, but I thought Caulfield would do so.

The judge called for a break. I knew the next witness was the woman I'd come to see.

Chapter Six

I slipped out to call Natra. She kept our case files organized. She told me she and Ayden had pinpointed the potential site more specifically, based on things Krebs had posted. "Can't wait till you see what we've deciphered. It's like he *wants* this site to be found."

"That doesn't sound like Bruder."

"You can be the judge when you see what we've got."

I trusted her judgment. She'd been my assistant and confidante for several years. She even lived in separate quarters on the other side of my Outer Banks house, with her talented Doberdor cadaver dog, Mika. Given Natra's Cherokee roots, she also gave me perspective on spiritual matters, something she'd fully embraced since losing her teenage son to an opioid addiction.

"Did you talk with JoLynn Wilde?" I asked.

Our attorney associate in Georgia, Jackson Raines, had referred us to Dr. Wilde. As a forensic taphonomist, she analyzed factors like weather, bone analysis, and insect activity in the burial of remains. Taphonomy means 'laws of the grave,' and these experts tend to be jacks-of-all-trades regarding the multiple factors involved in outside burials. Often, they've studied at facilities called body farms where the dead are laid out in a variety of conditions to scientifically estimate time since death. Wilde had been to at least two such places. She'd agreed to collect soil samples for us and calculate the impact of weather conditions on buried remains.

"Ayden went to meet her," Natra said. "I'm driving down now with Mika. I want to test her there. See what we get."

"Did you call Wayne?"

That's my ex-husband. He's an investigative special agent with South Carolina Law Enforcement, known as SLED. We share custody of our daughter, who was currently with him. The last time we'd stood together over an open grave, we'd found evidence that exposed a sex trafficking cartel. I continued to work on those cases with him. He knew I'd resumed my search for Hailey and had warned me to include cops if we found something.

"I called him," Natra said. "He thinks we're wasting our time."

"That's because he's heard me talk about this since grad school. He's watched me run down so many false leads. If you talk to Jax, thank him for my seat at this trial. It's perfect."

"He's doing the viewing session with Airic today."

My stomach flipped. Airic, an eccentric medium who claims to see dead people, had helped reignite the spark to find Hailey. He'd envisioned an ethereal redhead with braids near me. I'd seen and sensed nothing. I define these experiences in psychological terms, with Airic reading my behavior. Still, I do accept cases with paranormal angles, and I'd had some eerie experiences. But whatever Airic might attract from some other realm, I'd check it out with every evidence-based tool I had. I needed to not just locate Hailey's remains but also link her to Bruder. For *court*. Neither task would be easy.

I gave Natra directions. "No calls to Jax 'til he's done. I don't want him to have any sense of where we're going. He knows too much already for the session to be completely objective, so let's be careful." I watched people shuffle through the door. "I need to go back in. Reynolds is up next. I'll call you later."

I settled back in my seat and watched Maura Reynolds walk up to the witness stand. After being sworn in as an expert in adolescent psychology, the well-heeled, fiftyish brunette prepared to describe her association with Trevor. She was savvy enough to shift toward the judge, which confirmed her experience as an expert witness. So did her coiffed hair and conservative dark gray skirt and blazer. The only hint of color was a set of small red earrings that matched a muted pattern in her silk print blouse. She knew what she was doing. Impression management was essential in a courtroom.

Hers said poised, confident professional.

Doyle asked Reynolds how she'd met Trevor.

"He attended a presentation I gave for the psychology club at his school," she explained. "The subject was teenage anxiety and depression. I talked about the signals they should be aware of and said they should take seriously any comments they heard about suicide, even in jest."

"And why is this important?" Doyle asked.

"We know from research that about eighty percent of adolescents signal their intent before they attempt or complete suicide. Often, other kids think they're just trying to get attention, and they might be, especially girls. But it's better to take it seriously and be mistaken than to dismiss it and be mistaken about *that*."

I nodded. She was right. The social myth is that few suicidal people give signals. Girls attempt suicide three times more often than boys, but boys succeed four times more often than girls. When they mention it, they mean it.

"Trevor came up to me after the talk and asked about seeing me. I urged him to come with his parents." Reynolds had a maternal manner, the kind of person a troubled kid would seek for comfort and guidance.

"Did he?"

"He came with his mother."

"Can you tell us what happened?"

"Due to privacy concerns on Mrs. Sullivan's behalf, I can only tell you that we discussed Trevor's bouts with depression, and I agreed to see him as a client. He'd apparently seen two other therapists before me. I could tell that his mother was uncomfortable but quite concerned about him. After that, he came on his own, but after three sessions alone, he wanted to stop. And he left."

"Did you learn why?"

"He said he felt better. He had a girlfriend now." She nodded toward the defense table. "I came to learn that he'd been talking with Amber Bell."

Amber shifted in her seat.

"Did Trevor ever return for sessions?"

23

"Once, about a month before he died. He said he was having thoughts about suicide and asked about medication, so I referred him to a psychiatrist who could prescribe something. I later learned he never followed up."

"Did you hear from him again?"

"He made an appointment but didn't show up. He also didn't return my call."

"Would you say he was vulnerable to someone encouraging—?"

Caulfield objected. "Leading the witness."

Doyle rephrased. "How would you describe Trevor's state of mind the last time you saw him?"

Reynolds leaned forward. "I thought he'd improved, but I was also concerned that he was leaving therapy before we'd done the important work. He didn't have a solid foundation for making good life choices that could help him feel better about himself. So, he lacked coping skills for the difficult times."

"What would you ordinarily do in such a case?"

"I'd call and ask him to check in with me. Which I did, twice. He didn't call back."

Doyle cleared his throat. "I'd like to read a few of his texts from the days just before he died, to get your opinion."

Reynolds nodded as if she knew what to expect. I was sure she'd been coached.

Doyle held up a piece of paper and changed his voice to sound like a younger man. "'I have everything ready. I'm going to do this. It will be hard for my mom. My dad won't care.'" Doyle looked at his witness. "Dr. Reynolds, what do you hear in these statements?"

"I hear a boy who's uncertain. He has a connection, a support person, which we call a buffer. This keeps him from feeling completely hopeless."

"So, you think he might have changed his mind, even though he claims to be ready and determined?"

"Yes, certainly. I've heard other young men in therapy say similar things. They're testing out their resolve but also considering reasons not to do it. They really don't want to. They're in pain, and they just don't know where

24

to turn."

"What if Trevor had stayed in therapy?"

Caulfield objected. "She can't know what might have happened."

Doyle held up a hand. "I'll rephrase. Dr. Reynolds, in your experience, when young men seem ambivalent like this, how has therapy helped them?"

"First, it helps them to see more options. Typically, suicidal depression constricts the thinking process, so they perceive few options. A therapist can help someone like Trevor consider his choices, perhaps even give him fresh ideas. This can relieve the pressure."

Smart, I thought. She'd given the judge an image of Trevor gaining hope.

Doyle thanked her. "Now I'd like you to read a few texts to Trevor from the defendant. Then I'd like you to describe the effect these might have on someone who's trying to make up his mind about such a dire decision."

I glanced at Amber. Her cheeks had flushed red. She swallowed but continued to watch from her rigid position, as if she'd been reminded to appear to believe she'd done the right thing.

After showing a page to the judge, Doyle handed it to Reynolds. In a clear voice, she read the contents. "Don't think about it. Just do it. You have to. You can't back out again. You keep saying you're going to do it, and then you don't. You've been so ready. You're just making it harder on yourself when you push it off. It's time, babe. I'm with you. You want this. You're ready. Don't overthink this. Don't be weak."

Reynolds looked up and took a deep breath, as if what she'd just read greatly disturbed her. I could understand that. This case had drawn media attention for these very words. *Just do it. Don't be weak.*

She sat up straight. "These texts would have a strong impact on someone who felt uncertain about his own decision making. Trevor needed guidance. What he found was someone who wanted him to do what he said he was going to do. She twisted his sense of shame against him. No adolescent male wants to be weak. She made his hesitation an act of cowardice."

"So, are you saying these messages pushed him over the edge?"

Caulfield rose to object, but Doyle held up a hand. "I'll rephrase. Might a series of texts like these have influenced Trevor to take his life?"

"Given his isolation and the fact that he had no other support system than this young woman who claimed to be his girlfriend, the likelihood is high that these messages had a significant impact. Not only would he want to seem strong, but he'd be especially vulnerable in front of her."

Amber squirmed. I thought I saw her shake her head, a micro-gesture that showed her true feelings. I wondered what it meant.

"Were you acquainted with the defendant?" Doyle asked. "Had Trevor told you about her?"

"No, I didn't know her, and he hadn't mentioned her during the few times we were in session. But I did learn that she was the one who'd canceled Trevor's appointment with me."

An audible gasp swept through the courtroom. Trials generally offer few surprises, but here was one. Doyle hadn't led her to it. She'd said it spontaneously. I watched Amber. She clenched her jaw and balled her fist around the pen she held for taking notes. I thought she might break it. She turned away to say something to her attorney.

I couldn't wait for the cross-examination.

Chapter Seven

D oyle asked more questions, but he'd already played his best hand with Reynolds. He'd used a witness to show that Trevor himself hadn't decided to forego therapy. Amber had decided for him, erasing a potential route for healing. And she'd encouraged him to kill himself. It didn't look good for her. But something about her responses made me think this strange arrangement was not what it seemed.

When Caulfield took the floor, I made a quick assessment: assertive, righteously offended, and protective of her client. She seemed genuine. I was sure that, as a Black female attorney, she'd endured her share of challenges. I sensed she wouldn't back down. Her muted green blazer over black slacks fortified her serious expression.

I agreed with her that poor judgment is not a crime, but I thought the lines were a little more blurred. Caulfield seemed to think this was all just a media circus and that once the lookie-loos were gone, the law would sweep it away.

"Ms. Reynolds..." she began.

Reynolds lifted her chin. "Dr." Her tone suggested she expected respect. I'd have done the same thing.

"Excuse me, *Dr.* Reynolds. Did you judge Trevor to be in imminent danger of killing himself?"

"If I had, I would have sent him to an evaluation unit at the hospital."

"So, how would you have judged him during the time you saw him in therapy?"

"Troubled. Certainly at risk but not in imminent danger."

"And you have experience with young men like this, is that right? With suicidal boys?"

Reynolds shifted just enough to show discomfort. "I treat adolescents suffering from anxiety and depression. Those conditions can trigger suicidal thoughts. Sometimes, I can't help them."

"Do you remember a boy named Cole Cheney?"

Doyle jumped up. "Objection! Relevance! Dr. Reynolds' clinical work with other kids has nothing to do with this case."

"Your honor," Caulfield responded, "if I could have some—"

"Sustained."

Caulfield looked annoyed. I wondered what she'd hoped to do. The best strategy is to try to discredit a witness. But I agreed with the judge. Reynolds had barely seen Trevor, so her clinical skill wasn't on trial. Her primary function was to show Trevor's lack of effort and Amber's persuasive effect on him. Still, I made a note: *Cole Cheney.*

Caulfield had a Plan B. "Dr. Reynolds, if I show you a message, would you be able to evaluate its potential effect on Trevor?"

"I might."

When the judge granted permission, Caulfield went over to Reynolds and offered her a piece of paper. "This was written by my client. Will you read this out loud, please?"

Reynolds scanned it, then read it to the court. "'I guess you're going to do this. You seem so ready. I'm confused. You're making it harder on yourself when you delay it. That just makes you hate yourself more.'" She looked up.

Caulfield continued. "From your previous testimony, you seem to think this is encouragement to Trevor to end his life."

"Yes, it sounds like she's confronting him."

"Could it also be read as her trying to be caring?"

"I don't see how." Reynolds had shed her nurturing side. Her jaw tensed.

"Well, suppose Amber doesn't want Trevor to die, but he's told her repeatedly—and we have the texts to support him stating his suicidal intent over one hundred times—that he just wants it all to be over with. Couldn't her comment just be echoing what he wanted?"

Reynolds took a breath. "It's possible."

"And wouldn't you say that a young man who makes such statements, who prepares to end his life, who chooses a time and date as Trevor did, is at high risk for suicide, no matter what anyone might say?"

"I believe he might still have been redirected with therapy."

"But what about a non-skilled person? A friend, perhaps. How much effect might someone have who doesn't know how to respond to such a dark state of mind? Isn't it true that people who are determined to end their lives are likely to do so?"

"Trevor seemed uncertain."

"Please answer the question. In your own research on people with very serious suicidal intent who failed due only to some fluke, aren't most uncertain? Isn't that what they say afterward?"

"That appears to be so."

"So, Trevor's uncertainty is not unusual, even among those who believe they really are going to go through with it?"

Reynolds' mouth formed a hard line. "That's correct."

"Hadn't he made prior attempts? Should I show you the record?"

"He had. Twice."

"Serious attempts?"

"Yes. He was injured."

"So, isn't it true that most of those who complete suicide have made a prior serious attempt?"

I thought Reynolds was trying to calculate where Caulfield was going before she responded, but she admitted to the accuracy of the stated statistics.

Caulfield set her feet shoulder-width apart as if to use her body to support her point. "So, isn't it possible, doctor, that Amber's texts had little impact? In the end, even with his uncertainty, the decision was Trevor's, and he was at high risk? Is that right?"

"I couldn't say. Each suicide attempt is different, even for the same person."

I looked at the judge. She probably knew this was a lame response. So did Amber, who seemed to relax. Caulfield had scored a significant point. But I thought Reynolds had retreated. Unnecessarily. I wondered why.

Chapter Eight

During a break near the end of the day, I called Natra again.

"How did Mika do at the target site?" I asked.

"I didn't take her out. The area's large and has more trees than I expected. Good roads, though. Something a biker would love. And we saw two churches. His tattoo had a cross, so that's a possibility. We still have to narrow it down."

"Hopefully, Jax can help. Has he called?"

"Not yet. But JoLynn Wilde came. She took soil samples from the general area and will come back if we need her."

"What's she like?"

"Knows her stuff. Has a master's in meteorology, so Ayden hung on her every word. She's pretty, too. How's the trial?"

"What I expected, mostly, but I think there's more to the story. I haven't had a chance to speak to Dr. Reynolds, but her testimony seems informed. She's professional. That's a good sign."

I saw Caulfield heading my way. She looked directly at me. "Gotta go. They'll wrap up soon. I'll be back by dinner." I ended the call just as Caulfield stopped in front of me.

"Dr. Hunter," she said. "I recognized you." She held out a hand. "I'm Janissa Caulfield. I wonder if I could speak with you."

"Of course."

"You gave a presentation to my attorney's group last year about your work in suicide analysis. I've also heard your podcast. Are you here for material?"

I made a noncommittal gesture. "It's a unique case."

31

"I know your associate, Jackson Raines. That's how you got a seat. I arranged it."

I nodded. "He didn't say who did it but thank you. It's a good seat."

"It wasn't just a colleague favor. When he said your name, I hoped to speak to you."

"Sure. What can I do for you?" I noticed Maura Reynolds at the other end of the hall. She glanced our way. I needed to get her attention.

"I'd like another opinion on my client—"

"I can't—"

"I know. Not mid-trial, unless competency's an issue, which it isn't. But I suspect emotion might trump the law in this case, even with this judge, and I'll need to shore up an appeal. The psychologist who saw Amber for a short time gave me some notes. If you're here on Monday, you'll see his evaluation. If not, I can send you his report. I wonder if you have a few minutes after the proceedings today to just meet Amber. She's not the predatory spider Doyle's presenting."

I couldn't ethically tell Caulfield that Reynolds had been a convincing witness. From what I'd heard today, Amber had been quite callous during the final hours of Trevor's struggle. I thought he could have been saved had she been more encouraging in the other direction. But I also thought her behavior suggested something that defied the prosecutor's superficial accusation.

"I'll meet her," I said, "but I can't commit to anything."

"That's all I'm asking. Jackson said you're fair-minded, and that's what I need."

"Is she suicidal?"

"She has been. But she's hard to read, at least for me. She's had some mood swings, especially yesterday after hearing girls she thought were her friends turn on her so viciously. I think she's been starving herself or purging. If I do end up hiring you down the line, I'd like her to have met you."

I noticed Doyle narrow his eyes at us as I followed Caulfield down the hall.

In a small interview room, Amber Bell sat at a large table, her head down.

She looked up. She'd lined her deep-set green eyes in black, emphasizing them against her pale face, and her arched brows amplified her severe expression. When she saw me with her attorney, she pressed her lips together.

"Amber, this is Dr. Hunter." Caulfield gestured toward me.

A tight shake of her head said she wanted nothing to do with me.

Caulfield leaned toward her. "I think she can help."

Amber's eyes remained suspicious. Up close, her round face looked grey, and her make-up showed uneven patches. She folded her hands in front of her and stared at them. She reminded me of a kicked puppy that's finally learned to stay in a corner. I have plenty of experience with juvenile defendants, so her rejection didn't bother me. I sat down on her side of the table to prevent her from using it as a buffer but not so close that I'd crowd her. She moved away from me.

"Amber, I'm Annie Hunter. I know you're in a difficult position right now. You probably think no one believes you—"

"*You* don't know," she growled. "No one does." She pointed her chin at her attorney. "Not her. Not you. I can't talk to you. I can't say *anything.*" Her jaw clenched, and the muscles around her mouth suggested she desperately wanted to talk but had to shut herself down. She put a hand to her mouth, another buffer move. This girl had something important to say. But not today. It would take some work getting it out of her. But this brief meeting confirmed the opinion I'd already formed: something else was going on.

I folded my hands. "All right. I'm not here to force you to do something you don't want to do. If you change your mind—"

"I won't." Her face flushed, and her stare hardened. "Never. I, I...I won't."

I shrugged toward Caulfield and rose. She walked me into the hallway.

"I'm sorry," she said. "I told her why I wanted to bring you in. I don't understand why she's being so difficult. She really hasn't helped herself at all."

"She wants to talk. I've seen several signals to that effect. For some reason, she thinks she can't. I suspect someone else was involved in this. She's either protecting that person, or she's scared. She's too young to have the kind of stress lines I see on her face."

Caulfield looked surprised. "You got that from two minutes with her?"

"I've been observing her all day. I've watched her responses. They seem inconsistent for the situation. I can recommend my investigator if you want to pursue it. He can dig up things that will help me work with her."

She took down Ayden's number. No matter which way this case went legally, I knew Ayden could get more details. Unless Amber was a psychopath, the idea that even a mixed-up girl would push her boyfriend into killing himself made no sense to me. But her manner didn't resemble the cool narcissism of a psychopath. She was holding something back. I had half a mind to send Ayden on the trail anyway. I was intrigued.

Chapter Nine

My lake house was just over an hour north of Jasper County. We'd been through that area not long ago when we'd investigated a sex trafficking ring. Natra, Ayden, and I gathered that evening in my cramped office to consider our next step. Mika found a place to lie down in a corner. She sighed as if she'd had a long day. I sat in my office chair and placed a glass of *7 Deadly Zin* in front of me. "Let's lay it out. Can't wait to see what you have."

Natra went to the whiteboard, which was already busy with her elegant script. "I'll start." Her long dark hair hung loose today, showing a healthy shine. She loves to chart things, and she'd done a lot of work on this one, using five different marker colors. She made a sweeping gesture over her figures. "After we looked at the target area, we read through the letters we've collected from Bruder to fans who've posted them. I've gathered some from social media groups and true-crime auction sites."

"Did they charge a lot?" I asked.

"No. He hasn't achieved the status of superstar villain yet. We've collected six. He doesn't reveal a lot to any one person, but when we put them together, especially in his letters to Carly Krebs, we identified some tantalizing clues."

I gestured for her to continue. Ayden sat forward and cocked his head, his right foot tapping. I felt his motor running from across the table.

Natra pointed. "The best stuff came from a poem. Not that it's impressive as poetry, but some lines read like codes. We think he puts things out in the open that no one will see for what it is."

"Like he told Pete in that interview," Ayden added.

I looked from him to Natra. "Has anyone else figured that out?"

Natra tapped on the board. "Krebs says she's deciphered some. She claims to be skilled at forensic linguistics, but she's just doing basic graphology. And she lacks the tattoo angle. So far. I think she'll get there, especially with all the suggestions she's getting. She loves bragging about it, which saves us some effort. Before she changed her mind about Bruder, she'd identified a place in Jasper she thinks is meaningful to him."

Ayden nodded. "Near where we went."

Natra showed me a screenshot of the handwritten poem.

Riding the snake by
the Order of Rules
On parallel routes
To the arrowhead
Past a burnt down town,
with a church
where dark things lurk
among its forgotten graves.
106 – 2 – 123
At a campfire seat
I lost to the Devil in a Blackjack bet
that put me in his debt.
Look down for the packet,
near the red tree's knee.
In the hole that swallows a soul.
It's in the sound
Of her fingers and voice
That will prove the choice
Was never mine.

I made a face. "You've made sense of this?"

"Not all of it, but once you get part of it, other stuff's easy. This was posted on the *Killer Hooks* site. It's called 'Mirrors.' That's a clue. We reversed some things, like the numbers. On the surface, they offer nothing, but he mentions parallel routes to an arrowhead where the Devil lurks." She made a gesture to include Ayden. "We thought about his motorcycle rides and looked for roads he might've traveled. If we start him where he lived and bring him to Jasper along the western side where the number was placed in the tattoo, we find parallel roads that meet in a way that looks like the tip of an arrowhead." She showed me.

"One is Route 321," Natra continued. "That's a mirror of 123 in the poem. It runs for over 500 miles from Hardeeville up into North Carolina and Tennessee. It has an unusual north-south-north routing, too, so it intersects other routes like Interstate 40 several times. He mentions riding the snake, which could refer to the curves in that road. It passes through Robertville, a town that was burned during the Civil War, where there's a sign that mentions Robert's Rules of Order."

I nodded. "Impressive."

She continued. "The sequence of numbers, 106, turns around to 601, a route that terminates at 321, where there's another church."

Natra used her finger to draw an invisible line. "601 also runs through North and South Carolina. Both roads run parallel until the point where they intersect in Jasper. I looked up old news items and found a story about Satanic practices in the woods near there. Animal bones were found in a fire pit. Bruder mentions playing blackjack over a campfire with the devil. He also mentions a red tree."

"Did you see one?" I asked.

"No, but I might have found the fire pit. No one's used it lately. I let Mika sniff around, but she didn't alert."

"In several letters," said Ayden, "Bruder hints he was part of a group. He's been inching toward laying the blame for the murder on someone else, like he was just an accomplice, forced into it. I guess that's what he means by 'the choice was never mine.' Krebs says he confessed to the crimes because he was scared of someone."

I tapped my pen. "That girl's like a chigger that dives for your eye and can't be swatted away. I don't care if she spreads conspiracy theories, but getting invested in Bruder's innocence is a problem. It pressures us."

Natra crossed her arms. "The evidence against him is weak. If they succeed in erasing the credibility of his confession, the case falls apart."

Ayden looked at me. "If he gets free, we need security for you."

"Let's not get sidetracked. What about the packet? What's that?"

Natra shrugged. "Maybe something he thinks proves his innocence."

"Then why be so cryptic? Just hand over the packet and let the court decide."

"Maybe he can't," Ayden said. "I mean, he's locked up. He can't get to this packet, so he's sending her."

I took a deep breath. "Great work, both of you. With what we see in the tattoo, it's worth a return to that area. If something's there, we need to get it first. I've studied the cases that seem linked to him, and some are from South Carolina. I'm working on a timeline."

I'd done the psychological profiling, or as my team refers to it, the shrink-wrapping. Technically, I'm not a shrink, but such hair-splitting is lost on them.

"More cases than we know?" Ayden asked.

"I've added some and subtracted some. First, I've noticed flaws in my initial logic. When I was a kid, it made sense to blame one person for all the missing and murdered kids in the area. Even later, when I interviewed

Bruder in prison, I was still an amateur."

Ayden grinned. "You were a slinker?"

"I *was* a slinker. I made assumptions based on bad logic and inexperience. I was just a grad student. Maybe that's why he dismissed me. He knew I didn't have it right. But I've gathered more news reports and police records. I think I have a better handle on it, with focused criteria."

Ayden sat back. "From the original list you gave us, I'd take the boy out of the mix. I thought that right away when you showed us the cases."

"I would as well, except for two things. He's still missing, and he had reddish hair. But he went missing from the same town as the sisters, and around the same time, and I'd eliminate them."

Natra looked surprised. "You would? What about the blouse in the foundation where Becca Lynn's shoe turned up?"

"I looked more deeply into that. It was an ordinary white blouse. Her mother IDed it, but no DNA analysis was done. Nothing about it made it unique, so I'm not convinced it belonged to the girl."

"Why not leave that case in, though?" Ayden asked. "At least as a possibility."

"Because I think the cases in which girls were killed and dumped in the open are different from cases where girls went missing. Bruder's secretive. I don't think he left them for others to find. The victim clearly tied to him, to which he confessed, was buried."

"So, Becca Lynn's out, too," Natra said.

"I think so. I know she was found close to where we lived, but I think, at best, she's in the 'maybe' group, with low probability."

"Well, that reduces our victim count. But it makes our geographical analysis tougher, since we don't know where they're buried."

I leaned forward. "It reduces only our *known* victim count. And we do know where they were when they vanished. I dug a little more, looking at places where Bruder lived or traveled. And some podcasters have identified others, too. So, I think the sisters and the boy are not related to Bruder. But I found a missing girl from a town across the state line from where I lived in Tennessee that fits the pattern: Robin Dahl, age twelve, strawberry blond, riding her bike alone. A young man was seen in that town who resembled Bruder, and Bruder had made a delivery there the day before. And the murder he confessed to involved a redhead walking alone. The kids on my list, including Hailey, had shades of red or reddish tones in their hair." I looked at Natra. "Did Jax tell you anything from his session?"

She shrugged. "Yes…and no. He said they got results, but he wants to show us, not tell us." She held out her hands. "Cryptic, as usual."

Ayden raised an eyebrow. "We're doing spooky stuff for this?"

"I use whatever works. We can see what he's got when we go back down to check the site tomorrow." I looked at the poem again. "I would've never guessed Bruder *read* poetry, let alone wrote it. Let's see if there's any more. But let me first lay out my analysis."

Chapter Ten

I coined the term "remote profiling." It's a mash-up of crime scene behavioral analysis and remote viewing. To devise a suspect profile, one needs a crime scene, a police report, and other forensic data. Add a talented viewer who can mentally "visit" the crime scene—even pinpoint an undiscovered crime scene—without physically going there. Anyone can do this, but those who do it *well* often have other types of mental abilities.

Remote viewing isn't paranormal, not in the spooky sense. It's more of a supra-normal distance perception, a visual gut instinct. The U. S. government developed the Office of Scientific and Weapons Intelligence as a spy program, listing the process variously as remote viewing, nonlocal anomalous phenomena, and extraordinary human body function. The OSWI team, called the "weird desk," involved civilian researchers. I'll admit, this moniker appealed to me. When I explored the history of remote viewing, it only reinforced my sense of its use as a forensic tool. Some of its success stories are astonishing.

From 1970 until 1995, the Department of Defense used this method to probe foreign military secrets, pinpoint overseas targets, and locate fugitives and high-profile hostages. At various times, the NSA, CIA, NSC, and other agencies sought out the OSWI for assistance. Although the program "officially" ended in 1995, the most gifted viewers continued to teach privately.

It all began at the Stanford Research Institute, the SRI, a California-based think tank. Researchers there hoped to send their mental vision through all barriers, no matter how thick, to see distant events or locations, real-time.

Although the military couldn't make this technique reliably replicable, its declassified records show documented feats from several key individuals. I've heard that our government is currently collecting the DNA of these talented viewers.

The test is simple, and I've run it with Natra. Set up a target, such as a specific building with distinct features in a place away from the viewer. Send a person—the *outbounder*—to look at it. Then have the viewer enter a trance state and reproduce the outbounder's perspective as a drawing. It's easy to corroborate.

But RV doesn't always require an outbounder. Viewers have also found kidnap victims and fugitives. It's just better to start the training with an outbounder and a target sight.

I sometimes hear about forensic remote viewing, albeit not the remote *profiling* I've developed. One of the most impressive crime-related stories we'd heard occurred in 2006. Steven B. Williams was missing. A friend of his, photographer Robert Knight, hadn't heard from him in a while, so he was concerned. Williams had moved back to the Los Angeles area when his career as a disc jockey ended. His wealthy father had died, leaving him a substantial fortune. But he'd also suffered from depression.

Knight asked a friend named Angela Thompson Smith for assistance. She'd founded the Nevada Remote Viewing Group, which consisted of a retired airline captain, a civil engineer, a former Air Force nurse, a civilian Air Force contractor, a librarian, and a photographer. Each was asked to focus on a coordinate in the general area where Williams resided. They'd seen his photo but knew nothing else. Collectively, they "saw" a body in the water near an island off the southern California coast. They thought it was caught in a net.

Indeed, a decomposed body with no ID had been pulled in near Catalina Island. The man had been shot. The pathologist estimated the victim had been in the water for two weeks. Knight heard about it and called the morgue to help identify his friend. The chief suspect was Harvey Morrow, a con artist who'd posed as a financial advisor. Morrow had stolen Williams' inheritance. A GPS device, matched against cellphone records, showed that

Morrow and Williams had been together on a boat at Catalina Island on the day Williams was last seen. But Morrow had fled.

The Nevada group gathered again. One viewer sketched a boat with Morrow on board, located in the British Virgin Islands. It turned out that Morrow was in the Caribbean. Eventually, he returned to the U.S. and applied for a job in Montana. His story didn't add up to his new boss, a former cop, who figured out that Morrow was a fugitive. Morrow was arrested and eventually convicted.

Stories like this give me respect for the method. And I've seen similar feats with our medium, Airic, and with Jax's grandfather, Puca, whom he calls a far-seer. So, I'd use RV without hesitation. To combine it with profiling, we'd need a full victimology.

"We start with what we know," I reminded my team. "We look at where our likely victims disappeared and at how close these locations are to Bruder's residences. Then we add his relationship to those places. We've got him growing up in the northern part of South Carolina, but he also lived for a year near Asheville and has relatives in southeastern Tennessee, where he was caught. The geographical features of his preferred travel routes tell us important details about his habits, mobility, and attitude about physical boundaries."

"Where he feels safe," Natra added.

"Yes. His comfort zone. Where he establishes a routine. What does he generally do there? How do others generally use the area? We know he wasn't into sports, aside from riding his Harley, and he was relatively young, so he probably hadn't roamed that widely. He had a menial job making deliveries but didn't have much money for gas."

Ayden sat up. "He's looking for young girls he can lure or grab. So, he travels isolated back roads, hoping for kids on bikes or walking."

I nodded. "Like me and Hailey. And if he's a stranger, it's not much risk to grab a girl in front of a witness like me. He'd be long gone before I could get people searching. No one would know him."

Ayden crossed his arms. "So, based on your new list, what's his crime awareness space?"

"He's not a trapper," Natra said. "He didn't lure victims. He went out hunting."

I nodded. "He roamed around. He seemed to prefer after-school hours or weekends. We can't yet tell how much time passed between abductions, but if I'm right, it was usually a month or two. He took risks, but he seemed prepared, too. He'd know potential escape routes if he needed them. He'd been careful."

"Except for the tattoos," Ayden said.

"Yeah, that's a leak, a surprisingly clumsy one. So's the poem. Let's hope we get more like it. Maybe look for that tattoo guy and see if we can learn more."

"Copy, boss, already on it."

"We just need one victim clearly tied to Bruder to keep him behind bars. I'm going to the trial tomorrow for the morning session to see if I can speak with Maura Reynolds, but you both continue on this case." I handed each of them a folder. "These are the victims I'm considering. Spend time with them. You know victimology. Who they were and where they were will tell us things we need to know about Tommy Ray Bruder." To Natra, I added, "You and I will go see Jax. I want to know what our own weird desk team discovered."

Chapter Eleven

As I drove to the courthouse, I called Wayne, my ex. Ayden had told him our plan, but I wanted to judge his mood for myself. We tended to clash, so I tried to think ahead. If we found something at the site, I'd need him.

Wayne had our daughter, Kamryn, for two weeks, which gave me time to focus on my mission. He scorns my profession, but he's often provided a needed bridge for me. He and Ayden are friends, too, and he recommends Ayden to families for investigation assistance. I want to preserve that association, so I've established an uneasy peace with Wayne. Yet at times, it feels like watching a bank of darkening thunderheads about to hatch a tornado.

"Find something?" Wayne asked. I could almost see his dark eyes, ready to roll upward at anything I might say.

"We're still sorting through data. But we have a target area."

"Annie, it was over two decades ago."

I stifled the urge to remind him I'm not an idiot. "I have new resources."

"I assume you mean Airic."

Wayne had met the quirky medium in a cemetery at night during a raging hurricane. But even in fair weather, Airic was weird, with his long black hair, perceptual challenges, and eye contact mostly with his own feet. But Wayne had witnessed how he'd revealed important clues about the sex trafficking ring. Still, Wayne hated admitting that.

I took a breath. "I'm not asking your opinion. I'm only telling you because we're in your state. And it's a murder case. I'm sure you want to be the first to know."

"Fine. It's your time to waste, Annie. Just don't call me into a wild goose chase."

"Have I ever?" Actually, I had, so I shifted tactics. "I have a pressing reason to do this now. Hailey's killer might get out of prison. Soon! People are working on it. If I could pin another case on him, even just reasonable suspicion, I could gain time to get better evidence."

I heard Wayne pause. He doubts my memory of Hailey's kidnapping. He thinks I've latched onto Bruder as my boogeyman. But, like me, he hates to see child offenders go free, and Bruder did have that conviction. "You find something, you call."

"Of course. I won't mess up a crime scene." I don't know why Wayne thinks he has to man-splain. I'm in the forensic field, too. But he'd been this condescending since we met. I should have seen the signs at the time, but I'd been blindly in love.

I entered the courtroom, intent on speaking with Maura Reynolds. Caulfield would finish with her soon, giving me a chance to catch her before she left. I'd decided against reading the report from Amber's therapist, to avoid skewing my own judgment should I be hired to evaluate her. I knew Amber wouldn't take the stand in her own defense, so I expected the proceeding to wrap up soon. The significant testimony was done. I'd learned about Trevor, and I'd observed Amber's behavior. I knew enough to see beyond the surface facts.

When Amber came in, she looked directly at me. Her mouth retained that same firm line, but her eyes narrowed. I merely nodded toward her. This time, she wore a flowered blouse, but it didn't brighten her scowl.

Maura Reynolds testified for another hour as Caulfield dissected her earlier responses and got her to admit that, despite Amber's shocking texts, she'd sometimes encouraged Trevor to seek help. Reynolds described the research on teenage depression, which Caulfield used to show how mercurial kids could be. When Caulfield tried to edge Reynolds toward discussing suicide pacts, Doyle objected that there was no evidence of a pact. I knew there'd been a rumor of this, but the judge agreed. Caulfield had no place else to go. She was in a corner. And Amber's sour demeanor wasn't helping.

When the therapist finally strode out of the courtroom, I followed her and caught up. "Dr. Reynolds."

She turned around. Her wide mouth formed an inviting smile, but not before I spotted a microsecond of caution. "Dr. Hunter."

I stopped. "You know me?"

"Of course. I've seen you on documentaries and read your papers on suicide. They helped me prepare for this trial. I wasn't surprised to see you here."

"It's a fascinating case."

"And I noticed you with Amber's attorney. Have you had a chance to evaluate the girl?"

The question surprised me. She had to know better. Then she caught herself. "Oh, of course. You can't discuss it. Personally, I'd love to understand her better. But she's so defensive." She drew herself up. "What can I do for you?"

"Actually, Dr. Reynolds, I'd hoped to speak with you about a different case."

"Please call me Maura. We're colleagues."

"All right." I cleared my throat. "Maura. A few months ago, you made some comments on a podcast. I wonder if you have time to discuss them."

"I'm on my way to another appointment, but walk with me. We can talk briefly and perhaps meet another time. Which podcast? I do so many, with all this true crime frenzy lately. Everyone seems to think psychologists have all the answers."

I fell in with her as she made her way to the door. She was several inches taller than my five-foot-four height. "I'm interested in the podcast where you spoke with Carly Krebs. She talks about—"

"Ah, right. Tommy Ray Bruder. She's obsessed with him, I think. So odd, that one. Have you met her?"

"I haven't, although she's flung some barbs at me."

"Right. You have a podcast, too. So you have some interest in Bruder, then."

"Yes. He abducted a girl I knew years ago who's never been found. But as you know, he's been convicted in just one homicide."

Maura stopped and looked directly at me. Up close, she seemed fierce. "Oh, you won't be very happy with me. I can't say much, but I do support the claim that his confession was coerced."

I couldn't hide my surprise. "You do?"

"In fact, I'm acting as an expert on the request for a reevaluation. I think if you read the transcripts, you'll agree." She handed me her business card. "Call me. I can't say much about Bruder, I'm afraid, but let's meet sometime. I'd love to pick your brain about your work. It's fascinating."

A black BMW approached. Maura gestured toward it. "That's for me. Call me. I look forward to seeing you again."

I watched her get in, still stunned. The car pulled away, and Maura waved.

I could hardly absorb this development. Bruder had gained more than just support from some ineffective groupie. Krebs was gathering a professional team on his behalf.

And I'd just shown my hand to one of them.

Chapter Twelve

I tried calling Natra from my car. No answer. I loaded a podcast she'd urged me to listen to, ASAP. I fumed over my stumble with Maura Reynolds. I should have been more careful. At least I hadn't revealed my hope to link Bruder to another victim before he got one foot out the door. But I figured she'd tell Krebs I'd approached her and might warn her to be more discreet. I'd lost an advantage. But I'd gained some intel.

I checked the road conditions and tried to clear my mind so I could focus on the podcast.

True crime podcasters come in all varieties. *Murder Junkie. Forensic Forays. Dead-handed. The Prosecutors' Pod.* The craze began with truth-seekers who sought to bring attention to controversial cases. Some were journalists with a nose for good stories. That was beneficial. Then came chatters—people who just like to yak about crime. They've gained followings, but I found them tedious. Following them were plagiarists, who read aloud the accounts writers had published, thriving with paid ads for thieving someone else's work.

For a while, the cold-case podcasters accomplished things, but competition to solve real crimes, real-time had attracted wannabe sleuths with limited experience. They mean well, but their righteous certainty about poorly considered suspects can damage people's lives. Podcasting conveys status. When their gaggle of fans affirms everything they say, that's hard to ignore.

Of course, among them are psychics who join detectives to give their "spiritual" sleuthing the patina of credibility. Mostly, it just makes the detective look bad. I discuss these issues on my own podcast *Psi Apps*. My debunking has earned me adversaries, but I've also tapped my listeners for tips. Natra carefully sorts through these comments to find the gold.

I turned up the volume. A confident male voice came on.

"Ever wonder how a serial killer thinks? Well, you've come to the right place. Welcome to another episode. This is Monroe, the Murder Mentalist. I penetrate the minds of murderers. I know how they think better than they do themselves. From their brains to your ears, I can tell you exactly why they do what they do."

I rolled my eyes. Another shyster. The name alone confirmed it, along with the measured breathiness of his voice. He explained his business, found at killerbesideyou.com. For $50, he can discern if you need to flee from a risky relationship. For $100, he'll read the mind of a killer in prison. For $250 and up, he'll help detectives with an ongoing case. I could just imagine what Wayne would think. I figured Monroe used basic risk assessment probabilities while he pretended to have special vision. With a moniker like that, no doubt he had a client base, especially groupies who correspond with infamous killers.

Monroe finished his spiel, then introduced his guest. I knew within two words who it was: Carly Krebs. I could envision her stringy blond hair and girlish smirk. It wasn't hard to guess whose mind the murder mentalist had allegedly penetrated. I wondered how he could tolerate how she ran her thoughts together and punctuated nearly every sentence with "literally."

"I'm so glad I contacted you," Krebs remarked. "It was wonderful to find out what Captain Kidd truly thinks, and now I know what to do!"

"Thanks, Carly. For my listeners, Carly hired me to do what I do. I entered the mind of a killer she's investigating. If this is your first time listening, here's the scoop. I got my psychic powers for doing this work after a serial killer strangled me and threw me, bound, into a river. I nearly died. But I mysteriously gained the ability to breach mental barriers, so I use it for good. I turn it to the minds of murderers, and I've discerned many extraordinary things that no cop could find out. Carly's a serious detective. She has a PI license... What's that? Oh, excuse me. She's *applying* for her PI license. But she's spent more time on this guy than anyone else in the world. She's dug up all kinds of information. Right, Carly?"

"That's right, Mr. Monroe. And I've visited him in prison many times, and we've talked about all this, and he's confided in me, but now I need to *do* something."

I bristled. Not only was she a wannabe with no credentials for a license, but she was also making false claims. I breathed in slowly to stay calm while driving. Natra had referred me to this interview for a reason. This was likely the source of Krebs' recent backtracking with Bruder—her so-called proof. I sort of hoped it was, because no court would take it seriously.

My impression of the blond, blue-eyed Carly Krebs was that her face had a subtle asymmetry. Maybe one eyebrow higher than the other, or eyes too close together, or a cheekbone that failed to maintain its balance. I couldn't quite pinpoint it. I thought perhaps she'd had cosmetic surgery that hadn't set right. Anyone who listened to her—if they had the patience—knew she disliked me. And I returned the favor.

Monroe continued. "So, Carly hired me for a mindprinting session—that's what I call my mentalist ability—which turned into several more. And we've discovered something very important about the killer. And by that, I mean I used my power to pull out what really goes on in his mind. Not what he *says*, which could always be a lie, but what he really thinks and feels."

"May I?" Krebs asked.

Apparently, the Murder Mentalist conceded. He probably already knew he'd have to wrestle with her to regain control of his show. She launched into her story. "Just to set the scene for those who might not know or who might know but want to hear it again, I've been investigating Tommy Ray Bruder for almost two years, literally. He killed someone. Or, maybe he did. That's not so clear now."

I gritted my teeth.

"You can check out my own podcast on him if you want to know more. I believe we have the link on Monroe's website, but it's *Killer Hooks*, look for the Captain Kidd episodes, not to be confused with Captain Hook!" She giggled. "At first, I was just discussing serial killers in general, 'specially the obscure ones. You know, we've literally documented over 5,000 around the world, and this guy, Bruder, isn't even on that list. He was convicted of one murder, so no one thought about him, but the more I looked into him, the more I believed he might have killed some missing kids, so I started asking questions, *hard* questions that cops didn't want to hear."

She hardly took a breath. I knew well enough she'd developed this interest based on what she'd heard on *my* podcast. I'd discussed Bruder and his possible other murders there. Krebs often grabbed her ideas from others. She'd pretend she'd learned things from a Deep Throat type of source that she'd really just pirated. But she hadn't learned about Bruder from any shadowy figure. When she'd heard me talk about him, she'd spotted an opportunity to claim her own killer.

I tuned back in.

"...probing, serious questions. I call him Captain Kidd because he didn't have a nickname, like BTK or the Night Stalker, and he went after kids and buried them, like a pirate would bury his treasure. We know about an attempted kidnapping and a manslaughter he admitted but I thought there were more, and I literally linked him to at least ten missing and murdered kids in five different states—"

Monroe broke in. "And then he started writing to you."

"Yes. I'd done three or four episodes on him when suddenly I got this letter from the prison he's in, and I was so nervous about opening it! I mean, I've touched items that belonged to serial killers lots of times, but this felt really personal, like he was right there watching me, literally *breathing* on me."

"So you opened it."

"Yes. It was three pages long. Nice handwriting! He said he didn't like my podcast because he thought I didn't know things I should know, and he claimed he was innocent, that his confession was coerced, which I didn't buy, so, since he was listening, I challenged him on the air. I didn't hear from him so then I went to the prison to confront him myself and it surprised me that he put me on his list and agreed to a meeting. I thought he'd let me come just to tell me to get lost, but when I met with him, he asked for my help and—"

"But you weren't about to just help out a serial killer."

"No way! I know how devious they are. That's when I came to you to find out what he was *really* thinking."

"And together, we learned some intriguing things about Mr. Bruder." I could almost see Monroe grabbing back the mic as he explained his exclusive technique for entering the minds of murderers. "These guys, they play games. They're liars, manipulators. But my process of mindprinting seeps right past their barriers, because they don't know I'm there. I'm a ghost! When their guard is down, I can float in and absorb their thoughts. If you want to see what I've learned from these offenders, please check out my book, *Murder Mental—*"

"That's what I did." Krebs wasn't a second-string kind of gal. "I read your book and knew what I had to do. All killers say they're innocent, so I didn't really believe Bruder, 'specially 'cuz I'd already linked him to other cases. But I also know we've made lots of mistakes, and some people do get railtracked."

"Railroaded?"

"Whatever. I just figured if *you* could penetrate Captain Kidd's mind like you literally did with the others, you could help me know if he's telling the truth, and then I could—"

"And what we got was pretty amazing, wasn't it?"

"It was!"

"And you'll hear it first right here." Monroe described how they'd set up the procedure. He explained that he becomes a channel for killers to speak, like a medium with the dead, only he does it with the living.

"It was chilling," Krebs stated. "One of my best sessions. I could hear *Bruder*, like he was in the room, talking to me."

"He was, he was! Not physically, but psychically. It certainly wasn't me who revealed those things that no one knows about him. I couldn't have."

I paused it and found a place to pull over. *This* was the part Natra wanted me to hear. I backed it up a little and resumed.

"That's true," Krebs responded. "And that's why... I now know... he's *innocent*! He's—"

"You heard it here, folks! It's amazing what I can get."

"Just like in his letters to me, you literally picked up on this murder network. We learned there were others involved, they made him do it. He had to pick up kids, but he didn't know why, but they threatened his family, so he did what they told him. Some were even corrupt cops, which is why he couldn't get a hearing. They blocked him. So, he picked up the girls, but he didn't kill 'em, he didn't kill anyone, and his confession *was* false. He did it to save his family, because this network threatened them. He's a good guy. All the links to kids I'd investigated were correct, 'cept they weren't about him, and—"

"And it's all been confirmed by the girl who got away, right?"

"Right. He picked her up, and she escaped and went to the police."

I knew about that girl. I'd contacted her myself. According to her story, he'd done a lot more than just pick her up. And she'd mentioned no one else being in the van. I wondered if Krebs had even spoken to her.

"And now," said Krebs, "I'm gonna set him free. If you want to help, you can send—"

I stopped the podcast. I couldn't bear to hear her appeal for money. There wouldn't be anything else on this program helpful for us. Except one thing. Motivation. I knew I had to find something on Bruder, *fast*.

Chapter Thirteen

With Mika in tow, Natra and I drove to Georgia. We had gear for exploring our Jasper County site on our way back. I wanted to see this place for myself. As I drove, Natra read me her research notes on Monroe.

"There's a bio on his website, mostly bogus. He's a scammer."

I nodded. "That's my impression. People don't check the facts if they hear a good story."

"He doesn't name the killer who allegedly strangled him and threw him in the river, but he claims he was hospitalized for weeks, on the brink of death. I found no such news reports from where he lives, and there's no river."

"Police records? Surely he reported such a deadly attack."

"Working on it. But he gives no date, so it's hard to find."

"Who saved him? How did he get to the hospital?"

"He doesn't say. But I did find a psychic on an obscure site online with a similar tale about getting her supernatural powers after her mother tossed *her* into a river."

I glanced at Natra. "The mentalist's a plagiarist."

Natra held her phone to show me Monroe's photo. I scanned it. He looked vaguely familiar. Handsome. Nice, broad-mouthed smile. Inviting eyes and a thick mop of wavy russet hair. "A guy like that can persuade anyone of anything. Especially young women."

"Krebs is gathering a formidable team."

I made a dismissive gesture. "A mentalist has no standing in court."

"He has a law degree. Criminal law."

I frowned at her. "That's bad."

"Not from a reputable school, but he passed the bar here and can still work on the case."

I watched the road. So, Krebs had hired a lawyer. And a psychological expert. She was making strides. "So now we know how she shifted her momentum. I'll assume she actually believes Monroe. I suspect she'd hoped for a way to support Bruder's claim. She's got that groupie mentality, and now she has her very own killer focused solely on her. And she can *help* him. That's powerful stuff."

"Being on Monroe's podcast probably added more fans to her base, too."

Something nagged at me. Where had I seen him? "So why's this lawyer a psychic podcaster?"

"Not sure. More followers? Easier to sell a book?"

"He'll need more than a story in court. He'll need real evidence. No judge will accept his supposed ability to penetrate minds and extract thoughts. We have to challenge his credibility, show he's a fraud. Where's Ayden? He can do some gumshoe on this."

"He's checking out that kid, Cole Cheney, that Caulfield mentioned."

"Right." I'd forgotten I'd sent him on this assignment, as well as on a search for the so-called Panty Thief. "I need to keep my narratives separate, although Maura's sort of a bridge between them. I sense we have a gathering storm that might just get Bruder released. That's our current priority." I thought for a moment. "Caulfield hoped to discredit Maura or at least rattle her by mentioning Cole Cheney. That might be useful, so I'll keep Ayden digging. But we need a good lead. Let's hope Jax has one."

Juvenile attorney Jackson "Jax" Raines shares my passion for kids in trouble. *Tenetke*, as his grandfather calls him for the thunder in his soul, is a child welfare activist. Together we'd exposed a dangerous sex ring in a juvenile detention scam, which had rippled into some of my cases. A supposed suicide pact became a double homicide, and Jax had launched civil suits. He's now my attorney of choice when I'm working in states where he's licensed, but I also take advantage of his grandfather, Puca, a shaman with a singular ability I've dubbed "air awareness." He seems to have eyes everywhere. He's shown me more about RV than all my other resources combined.

And Jax knows Airic, the medium who inspired my revived search for Hailey. While I'd been at Amber Bell's trial, they'd conducted sessions, Jax with Airic, and Puca working separately. Jax wanted us to see the result in person. I was eager to get there.

I drove up the long private drive on Jax's ranch. In a pasture to my left, his search-and-rescue border collie, Digger, barked at a dozen summer-shorn sheep. Mika jumped up and whined. She could barely contain herself. These two sniffers had worked together several times. I hoped I could entice Jax to join me again.

I pulled into a parking space. Digger rushed to greet us just as Jax came out on the covered porch of his ranch house. Whenever I see him in jeans and a work shirt, I almost forget he's an attorney. I prefer his country look, but anything he wears looks good on his lean frame. For a second, I wished I'd come alone.

But this was business.

Natra let Mika out. I waved to Jax, then said to Natra, "Seems like every time I come here, something dramatic happens."

"Don't set yourself up," she warned. "He didn't sound excited on the phone."

"I know; you're right. But there were three of them working on this, like Airic insists."

"Annie..."

"Yes, got it. Let it be what it is. Don't impose my expectations." But when I strode over to the house, I remembered that magic had happened here before.

Chapter Fourteen

The first time I'd come, the elderly Puca had invited me into a trance experience in his underground abode that had produced a set of symbols. I'd sensed Hailey nearby, but I'd discounted it because I'd expected it. Even so, the symbols had helped us to find someone more than our GPS had.

Natra took Mika for a quick run with Digger while Jax invited me into the screened porch. I insisted first on a hug. Our attraction was probably obvious to everyone, but we'd agreed to keep it under wraps. A slight breeze with a floral fragrance from honeysuckle vines lessened the heat, and sweet tea and biscuits sat ready on a wooden table.

Jax turned his dark eyes on me. "How's the trial?"

"Worthwhile. Thank you for getting me a seat. Janissa admitted she's your connection."

"She cares about kids. And the law."

"Clearly, although I think she's right about the judge. That woman looked furious at some of the things Amber texted."

"We'll know soon. She makes decisions quickly."

"Speaking of decisions…."

Jax held up his hand. "Patience. You'll need it."

He gestured for me to sit, and poured tea into a glass filled with ice. Natra returned. She had both dogs drink water and lie down outside before she joined us.

I'd avoided giving any clues about what I hoped for. I hadn't even mentioned Hailey, but Jax and Airic knew I felt guilty about her kidnapping.

Jax also realized I wanted to restart my search, and he knew my concerns about Bruder. But our target location was outside Bruder's general territory, and we'd told Jax nothing about Jasper County or Bruder's tattoos. Since RV works best with a target, I'd asked Jax to orient Airic toward a buried murder victim within fifty miles of his house—aside from those in cemeteries. That covered the Lowcountry, the eastern coastal area, some territory to the west, and even part of northern Georgia. During their session, I'd occupied my mind with the trial to prevent Airic from probing me. Natra and Ayden had been similarly engaged. My request had been vague, but I knew Airic had as much talent as those viewers on the "weird desk."

Jax sat down. From his shirt pocket, he withdrew a folded piece of light blue paper. I recognized it. I'd used a sheet from that same stack of blue paper a month ago at Airic's house. Jax smoothed it out and placed it on the table. My heart raced. Natra and I leaned in. I squinted, confused. I saw some rough marks that resembled a tree carving, like kids do with a pocketknife.

I looked at Jax. "What's this?"

"That's what he got."

Natra touched the edge. "It looks like a bulky letter K with some blotches around it."

I picked it up. "He didn't get any terrain markers or physical features, no coordinates that could narrow our search? This is it?" I tried to hide my annoyance.

Jax shrugged. "Airic drew it twice, and he insists it will be useful."

"How?"

"Annie, you know how this works. He gets what he gets. He doesn't know what it's for or how it will help. In fact, after the second time, he said he wanted to stop. He was blocked."

"Blocked?"

"Whatever you're looking for, there's resistance. He didn't like it and refused to push past it. He wouldn't talk about it. And Puca said something similar."

I exchanged glances with Natra before I asked, "Puca didn't get coordinates, either?"

"No. He said there's danger in what you're doing. He thinks you should withdraw. I can't translate well from our language, but it means you're playing with fire."

I sat back. "I can't stop. I have to do this."

Jax held up his hands. "I'm just conveying the messages. And before you ask why I didn't just scan the image and tell you all this on the phone, it's because he'd like you to undergo a cleansing ritual." He gestured toward Natra. "Both of you."

I blinked. "Why?"

"Because he knows you'll ignore the warning and pursue this anyway. He wants to give you some protection."

Natra snorted. I glanced at her. She knew me, too. My strength—and weakness—is to bull my way through barriers, no matter how potentially perilous.

"Okay, fine. It can't hurt." I used my phone to snap a photo of the drawing and text it to Ayden with a question: "Seen this anywhere?" I looked at Natra. "Maybe I should go see Airic myself."

She shook her head. "Won't be double-blind."

Jax tapped the paper. "Give this a chance. If you ignore it, you'll only annoy him. And he's not going to keep looking."

"I need more, Jax. This symbol doesn't help."

"It doesn't help *yet*. Remember when you drew the others? You didn't know what they meant until you saw what they conveyed right in front of you. Until then, it was just meaningless marks on a page. Like this."

That was true. We weren't performing a traditional remote viewing test, where I knew the target's appearance and could compare the drawing against it. We were working in the dark, with a large area that might even be wrong. It was like shooting an arrow into the air and expecting it to land where we needed without knowing where that should be.

I stared at the paper. "The map I drew before at Airic's depicted things that helped us recognize the place when we got there. They were obvious. This is too simple. I'd hoped for something like the map they had for Ted Bundy's victim, Kimberly Leach. That was distinct. *She* was a twelve-year-old. Bundy snatched her in daylight, in front of a witness, like Bruder did with Hailey."

Jax raised an eyebrow. "Hailey?"

I stopped. I'd given it away. But it was time. We had pieces Jax didn't know about.

Chapter Fifteen

Yes, that's what we're doing," I said. "Or hoping to. With Kimberly Leach, they were looking for a kidnap victim who'd likely been murdered. So am I. Bundy dragged the girl to a stolen van and took her to a remote location to rape and kill. The searchers used anything and everything to locate her, and one that helped was a remote-viewed map."

Jax looked from Natra to me. "What happened?"

"Bundy had just been arrested for the Chi Omega murders, but he wasn't talking about the Leach abduction. They did have a specific type of soil in the van he'd stolen, but that still meant hundreds of square miles to search. Planes hovered over this area with infrared cameras to detect a decomposing form. No results. Landfills were searched for potential evidence. Even buzzard experts offered advice. So did psychics. But nothing led them to Kim until a woman used remote viewing."

Jax cocked his head. "And what did she get?"

I grabbed a napkin to draw what I remembered. "She drew two sinkholes connected by a canal. South of them was a railroad track and a highway. North were horses, and west was a picnic area. Along the east was a burnt patch. In the middle, she placed an X for where the body was."

I glanced at Natra. She confirmed my memory, so I continued. "She offered a location, but nothing in that area matched the items on her map. So, the detectives went back to where they'd picked up some cigarette butts that were Bundy's brand. At that location, they spotted a sinkhole filled with water. It had an outlet that led to a second sinkhole—so, two bodies of water connected by a canal. When a dirt road there took them to a burnt field, they remembered the drawing. To the south was a highway that ran parallel to a railroad track, and one of them recalled a state park to the west with some picnic tables. They didn't know it, but they were standing within yards of the body. It was under a collapsed pig shed. Because of the map, they put more effort into the search and found the body. The psychic was wrong about the location. In fact, she was *way* off. But she'd correctly viewed the physical features."

Jax sat back. "Where did you hear this?"

"The prosecutor on the Leach case described it in his book. I've talked about it on *Psi Apps*, and people involved confirmed it. It's one of the stories that support the credibility of remote viewing. So, I hoped I could use this method to find where Hailey was buried. We have a huge area to cover, too."

Jax looked doubtful. "Theirs was more defined. Hailey's remains could be anywhere."

I held up a hand. "I know, but I've heard of a viewing session that located hostages when *they* could have been anywhere. So, you don't absolutely need a defined location. You just need talented viewers."

"As I recall from your own podcast, Annie, the hostage situation had context for making intelligent conjectures."

"So do we." I looked at Natra. "Show him what we have."

She opened a folder that contained the photos of Bruder's tattoo, a copy of the poem, and a map. Jax sat forward. Placing the items in front of him, Natra explained what each was. Jax glanced through the poem before she told him why she and Ayden thought it offered a solid lead. She pointed to the map. "We see an area near where the two roads converge that seems to match what Bruder describes. We found a woodsy area there and looked at some topographical maps from the right time period. I ran Mika, but she didn't indicate. We hoped Airic would get us a more focused location. Mika has found graves much older than this one, but we don't want her just running around with no sense of guidance."

Jax tapped the map. "Where is this?"

"Not far from here," I said. "Bruder drove around that general area. Your taphonomist friend, JoLynn Wilde, collected soil samples. She didn't tell you?"

"I knew what she was doing, but she didn't say where. Double blind, remember?"

"Right. Why don't you come? Bring Digger."

"You mean bring my dog or my shovel?"

I smiled. "Both, if you're offering."

Jax seemed to mentally calculate. "What time will you start?"

"Early, especially with the heat predicted for tomorrow. We'll meet Ayden there this evening, after our cleansing."

Jax gave me a look that said he couldn't believe I'd talked him into it. "Give me directions."

My text chime sounded. I picked up my phone. "It's Ayden. He's seen the symbol before, the one Airic drew. He says it's in Bruder's poem."

I pulled the paper with the handwritten lines toward me and asked Natra, "Is this how he wrote it?"

"I think so. It was posted on the *Killer Hooks* site. Looked like a camera-ready image."

I scanned it but saw nothing that resembled Airic's image. I let the others take a look. Both agreed.

"Then how did Ayden see it?"

Natra shrugged. "Maybe he's misremembering."

"He's an artist. He's got a good eye for detail."

Jax held up a finger. "Maybe we're not viewing it the right way. Bruder's a coder, you said. The poem is called *Mirrors*. Who has a mirror?"

Natra grabbed her purse and pulled out a small compact. She opened it and held it over the poem in a way that let her view the image. Then she pointed. "It's there. It's turned around. See it? And also here."

I looked where she'd tapped. I shook my head, so she traced it for me. Then it jumped right out, like those optical illusions you can't un-see. I pointed to one more place. "It's here, too."

Natra rubbed a finger on the photo of the tattoo. "It's here as well."

I nodded. "It must mean something to him. But this still doesn't give us a location. Maybe Airic just pulled it from Bruder's mind."

Jax was looking at his phone. He placed it on the table to show us a drawing on his screen that resembled the symbol.

I leaned in. "What is it?"

"The Chinese symbol for fire."

"Fire?" I blinked. Puca had said we're playing with fire. Then I gasped. Bruder had also placed the number two inside an image that resembled a flame. To Natra, I said, "That fire pit. We'll start there."

Chapter Sixteen

Preparation for an exhumation can be intense. I'd been on several such teams, as a psychological consultant, a documentarian, and support for Natra and Mika. I'd helped to dig holes, and I'd sifted dirt for bone, tooth, and clothing fragments. I'd watched anthropologists retrieve rotting leather shoes and gently brush away soil to reveal an empty-eyed skull or fleshless femur. As grim as this might sound, there's always a sense of breathless anticipation. Even with all the scientific analysis we have for soil, putrefaction, and weather, unknowns in every case offer the possibility of surprise. I didn't know if we'd undertake a dig, but I wanted to be ready.

We arrived at our pet-friendly rental near the fire pit site just before Ayden, who brought more supplies. I gave him the bottle of cleansing nectar Puca had sent for him and filled him in on our meeting with Jax. I also showed him the K symbol in Bruder's tattoo. He was impressed with Airic's results. "Wish I could do that."

Over dinner, we discussed a plan for the following day before I remembered Ayden's task. I refilled his glass of *Return of the Living Red*, then asked, "Did you learn anything about Cole Cheney?"

"Yeah. He lived near the northern border. Place called Rock Hill. He killed himself. Sixteen. Left a note. Apparently, he had a journal full of depressing stuff."

"No question about suicide?"

"None that I heard, but...."

"But?"

"Maura Reynolds was his therapist, as you thought. I got the impression his parents blame her. I didn't speak to them, but they'd complained in the local paper, and I found their comments. They thought she should have seen it coming and gotten him help. They threatened to sue. I can keep digging if you want, but I got a lead on Pete, so I went in that direction."

I nodded. "Janissa Caulfield obviously thinks the Cheney case is important. Maybe it's just about professional misconduct, but I suspect there's more to it. I'll try to get her to tell me, so let's wait and see. I want you here with us tomorrow. What about Pete?"

"Someone knows someone who knows someone, that kind of thing. I'll get there, boss. Just need time."

Ayden and I dissected Bruder's poem again while Natra scanned news archives for reports about local fires.

"Nothing like that's reported during the time we want," she said, "but about a year before, there was an arson."

"That could still be related. I just hope Bruder's affinity with fire doesn't mean what I think it means."

Ayden raised an eyebrow. "Burning the remains?"

"Yes." My throat tightened, but I continued. "Charred remains decompose in soil more quickly and could force us to make sifting frames."

"I have some in the truck. But I think Jo's bringing her own forensic van." I raised an eyebrow. "Jo?"

"JoLynn. I already warned her about the potential for cremains."

"Why?"

"Because you texted me what the symbol meant. That's pretty important to her calculations. She's on the team for this, right?"

Natra and I exchanged looks before I asked, "Has she done the soil analysis already?"

"Yup. And looked at weather reports for several weeks past when Hailey was abducted. She's good. And she says she has something new. It's just now being tested, so she thought we could try it. She's pretty excited about it."

"She didn't tell you what it is?"

"Only that it involves a drone with a sensor. Which she's bringing. She has everything she needs. We just have to figure out where to start."

I breathed out. "Okay. It's just exploratory for now. I'd like to see this new approach." I turned to Natra. "What's the arson report?"

"This could be good for us. It's in the right area, in the woods. An illegal campfire area was found. I think it's the one I saw. They found scraps of charred clothing. And someone saw two males in the area, in a van."

I perked up. "Any arrests?"

"Not that I could find. Not yet, anyway."

"What color was the van?"

"Doesn't say."

I absorbed this information. Two men in a van. Bruder had been caught in a van with a kidnap victim. Had there been others involved? The idea of a crew disturbed me. The most dangerous killing teams involve male pairings. Of these, the most aggressive are equals—creeps who've met someone as depraved as they are. With no moral boundaries, these partners affirm and expand their deviance. If Bruder had such a partner, there was no telling what they'd done to their victims or how many there might be. I couldn't bear the thought of Hailey at their mercy.

Ayden studied the piece of blue paper that bore Bruder's mark. "Any idea how this will help us?"

"I don't know that it will," I said. "But maybe Bruder marked his spots with it, like leaving a signature. We should keep an eye out for rocks with scratches on them."

"It's been a long time," Natra reminded me. "Rain washes off rocks."

Ayden squinted. "It's still kind of amazing. Airic drew something that we can see in the poem."

"All of us had it in our brain because we've read this poem. Remote viewing shows what someone else is looking at or knows about. It might only mean that Airic tapped into the mental image from one of us."

"Or from Bruder," Natra added.

I nodded. "Right. Or from Bruder. Because Bruder's thinking about it, too."

Chapter Seventeen

As soon as I saw JoLynn Wilde, I understood Ayden's enthusiasm. She had it all. Her navy blouse and pressed khakis gave her a professional polish, but with her auburn hair pulled into a ponytail, she also seemed ready to play. She was thin enough to have been a model, and her pouty upper lip, dainty nose, and blue eyes could have sent her into acting. Instead, she'd opted to tramp around in mucky fields, dig in clandestine graves, and handle moldy bones. I liked her. From Jax, I'd heard that JoLynn viewed herself as a voice for the dead. She'd spend her own money to finish her projects, and her resume showed every important forensic certificate available for taphonomy, or outdoor forensics. Yet, she'd generously told me she'd charge only for work that yielded results.

Ayden and Jax helped her to set up her various kits for collection and preservation on and around a folding table. "I packed some sifting screens, too," she said, "in case we need them. I also have tree-climbing gear and a post-hole digger."

I suspected this was another reason Ayden liked her. He, too, kept his truck packed with "ready for anything" supplies. Between JoLynn's weather expertise and her preparedness, he probably thought he'd found his soul mate. Maybe he had.

"I appreciate that," I told her. "We aren't sure about anything yet. Even if there's a body, there won't be much left."

"Yeah, this soil's hard on soft tissue. Wet and warm, a gourmet meal for bacteria."

We'd returned to the clearing where Natra had spotted the disused fire pit.

We'd run the dogs, but neither had indicated a scent. A few rusting beer cans and broken bottles near some rocks confirmed a teenage hangout, but we'd found nothing that suggested the alleged satanic gathering reported in the news. I toed through a crunchy layer of withered oak leaves and uncovered a few fragments of charred wood. "Not particularly promising, but Bruder mentioned a fire pit in his poem, so we might as well start here."

JoLynn knelt to let the dogs sniff her hand. That was a good sign. She understood this work. Then she pointed to the different items she'd placed on a table. "I've been working on a research project that could benefit you. If our theory is right, this could open up new ways to search for missing people." She looked at me. "You're kind of a test case, if you don't mind."

"I use whatever might work. Where's your research base?"

"I've studied at several body farm facilities, and two of them are testing this method. The teams include all different disciplines, like biologists, botanists, geologists, and spectrographic experts, so it's quite involved. We're lucky they consult for free. But we're expecting some dramatic results. Everyone wants to be part of that."

Jax picked up a piece of her equipment. "This is about leaves, isn't it? I read something about it."

JoLynn nodded. "Right, yes. It's based on the idea that when a corpse decomposes and ruptures, the biological liquids push nitrogen into the soil—a *lot* of it." She glanced at me. "Sorry. Is this too rough? I know this is about your friend."

I waved for her to continue. "If she wasn't cremated, then she decomposed somewhere. If this helps to find her, I want to know how."

JoLynn went over to the table. "I can't be sure, but with your dogs, we might be able to do a real test. No one's even thought of using cadaver dogs yet. I assume they've been trained on different stages of decomp, including cremains?"

Jax and Natra both affirmed this.

"If our potential victim decomposed naturally," JoLynn continued, "and the closest tree roots absorbed nutrients from the decomp, we should see results. When we find the right area, we'll hope the roots retained enough odor to get the dogs' attention. But that's the last part. First, as Jax said, we have to find a tree with differences in its leaves."

Ayden crossed his arms. "That's why you brought a drone."

"Right. Nutrients in the soil affect the leaves' appearance. The nitrogen burst from a body should change the color. From above, those trees will stand out."

Natra looked up from where she squatted with Mika. "Wouldn't other large animals that die in the woods also have that effect?"

"Yes. The breakdown of any large mammal will transform the soil and affect the plant life. When there's no active immune system, the body's necrobiomes—its bacteria—replicate much faster. The soil we have here is particularly absorbent. That's why I tested it earlier. But most mammals that die in the woods decompose on the surface. Buried remains will have a more dramatic impact on tree roots. So, the leaves should show a richer color. That's the theory."

Ayden picked up a hand shovel and looked around. "What about the effect on other plants?"

JoLynn opened her laptop. "We'll record it all, everything we observe. We've already discovered that some plant life dies when a corpse floods the soil with something not natural to the area. But certain plants grow more robustly. So, there could be some change in any of the plant life near a decomposing body, but we haven't fully studied this yet. And if we find a body here, it decomposed a while ago, so we don't have controlled comparisons. But at one research facility, they placed donor bodies in areas around plants to see what happened. After decomposition was complete, they put the soil from under the body around plants in a greenhouse. We're still looking at that. But here's the interesting part. We think the trees that absorb a dead body's necrobiome might not just *look* different. They might also emit wavelengths of light that set them apart."

JoLynn pointed at the drone she'd set on the table. "As Ayden just said, that's where this comes in. Again, let me caution you. We're just learning how this all works, but the theory seems sound."

"Would we see the color difference from a small plane?" Jax asked. "Or a helicopter?"

JoLynn shook her head. "No. It's too subtle. But we do have technology, called hyperspectral sensing, that can detect it."

Jax raised a finger. "That's what I read about. Don't they already use this to find illegal cannabis operations?"

"They do. These devices can pick up signatures across the electromagnetic spectrum. Fluorescence is an indicator of what's in the cell walls of a plant's leaf. In our case here, we think that as the tree absorbs the body's nutrients, its leaves will fluoresce in a unique way. And our sensor will pick it up."

"So it's been tested before," I commented.

"Not like this, not for this purpose. It's been used successfully for soil management in agriculture. That's why I'm relatively confident that if we can locate an area where a body's been buried, we'll pick up signs. And because you have dogs that specialize in human remains, we can see if they pick up the scent. This technology can give them a focused spot." She looked at Natra. "And related to what you asked, they'll indicate only if the remains feeding the trees are human, right?"

"Yes. Animal remains won't distract them."

"So we won't need nuanced detection systems that distinguish between different types of animal decomp. The dogs will do it."

I nodded. "It all sounds good. Almost too good."

Natra crossed her arms. "Let me see if I understand. So, the soft tissue from a corpse dissolves into the soil, the nearby trees absorb it, this unique plant food recolors their leaves, and your drone can sense it."

"That's it, yes."

"I love it!" Ayden's broad smile got a responding grin from JoLynn. I could see from Jax's expression he was glad he'd put aside his work and come. Innovative forensic collaboration like this is rare to witness.

"Thanks," JoLynn said, "but, again, no guarantees." She gestured for me to come over and look at the computer. "I hope to give your dogs a more defined area, maybe a clump of trees they can sniff. I've calculated from the weather and soil during the time period Ayden gave me the probable rate of decomposition. It was efficient, and there's been a long enough period between the body's placement here—*if* it was placed here—that we should certainly see some effect. As long as she wasn't cremated. If she was, the leaves might still change, but it could be too subtle for detection."

"And if wrapped?" I asked.

"If wrapped but not sealed, there'd still be leakage. The decomp would be slower, too."

"It's better than just going out blind," I said. "Let's do it."

JoLynn pointed at the drone. "So we send this up over the trees. Since you think this fire pit area is important, we can focus here first and radiate outward."

Natra removed a tablet from her pack. "I'll keep track of coordinates."

While JoLynn, Ayden, and Jax handled the drone and its sensing equipment, I texted Wayne with our location, adding, *If you can, you should join us. We have new tech. Intriguing.*

If we did find something today, I wanted him close by. Even if we found nothing, he'd appreciate the technology. He loves being the first to know. It would earn me some credits.

Over several hours, we had many starts and stops to replenish liquids, eat lunch, and check the data. A white oak tree showed distinct wavelengths that confirmed coloration differences, but the dogs failed to alert on anything on the ground near it. Jax and Natra worked them, but they showed no indication of buried human remains. That was disappointing. The same thing happened with another tree.

"I really thought this would work," JoLynn said. She seemed embarrassed.

I put a hand on her shoulder. "It's a good idea. There's still time."

"This heat can't be good for the dogs."

"They'll be fine," Jax assured her. "We're giving them water and shade."

After our second meal break, when it seemed we might have to call it quits, another oak tree drew the dogs' attention. It had a root that arched up away from the ground. They both sniffed at it. Digger sat.

"That tree might've absorbed something through its roots," JoLynn said.

Jax had Digger move back. "They couldn't have buried a body here. There's not enough room." Then he leaned in. He gestured to me to come, and

73

pointed at the tree's trunk. Digger barked. Mika went into her alert position. Jax scraped away moss from where a six-inch wide scar had altered the black bark's fissured growth pattern. I gasped and put my hand to my mouth. I didn't need to refer to Airic's drawing to know what I was looking at: carved deep into the softer flesh of the trunk, in primitive strokes, was the Chinese symbol for fire.

Chapter Eighteen

JoLynn joined us. Her eyes widened. "That's manmade damage. Does that mean something to you?"

Ayden took out his phone and showed her the photo I'd sent him of the symbol. "This is what we're looking for."

I knew he wouldn't have told her we'd used remote viewing to get it. He'd wait for my approval, and I wasn't ready to bring a die-hard scientist into our mixed-method approach. We needed her. So I said, "It's from a piece of writing linked to the killer."

JoLynn stepped close and touched the bark, which had the rough quality of alligator skin. "It's a *Quercus marilandica*. This tree is fairly young, as trees go." She pointed. "If he buried someone here two decades ago, he cut it lower, down here." She pointed. "Blackjack oaks take—"

I froze. "What?"

"Blackjack oak. It's a relatively slow-growing tree."

I looked at Natra. In the poem, Bruder had mentioned playing blackjack with the Devil at the fire pit.

"Well, it's not red, like he described," I observed, "but this has to be the tree."

JoLynn picked up some acorns and dropped them into a small pouch on her belt. "It's in the red oak family, if that helps. The leaves do turn red, sometimes a very bright red."

"And that root resembles a tree's knee," Natra said. "The poem refers to that, too."

I felt a chill. "It's all falling into place. Let's get some shovels."

75

Ayden fetched his battery-powered auger to break up the hardened topsoil. We dug several holes in different spots near the tree before we got confirmation from both dogs that *something* related to human remains was buried here. JoLynn prepared her hand tools for the careful digging we'd have to do to avoid damaging bone. Ayden and Natra set up some sifting frames. We had no idea how far down we'd need to go. I sensed the sun beginning to set.

I thought of Hailey. Whatever we found here, it would look nothing like my former friend. But I knew what she'd been wearing when Bruder grabbed her. He might have burned her clothing, but I thought that clumps, or even just strands, of her red hair might still be intact. JoLynn had said this was unlikely unless she'd been wrapped in something. But she'd worn a bracelet. She'd had it on that day—the one with her name etched on it.

I sensed the solemn mood that had settled around us, seemingly confirmed as trees overhead blocked the light. We all knew we might soon see the remains of a girl buried in this dirt. Wayne hadn't come, but he'd texted that he'd check in at the end of the day. I asked Ayden to keep in touch with him so I could help JoLynn prepare to work inside a grave. Natra took both dogs to a separate area to give them water and tie them up. She then went to fetch flashlights from Ayden's truck. He also had a battery-powered floodlight.

The digging commenced. About three feet down, Jax stopped, held up his hand, and stepped out of the hole. He got on his knees at the edge and reached down. I went over and stood nearby as he brushed dirt from something. It was medium blue. And plastic. He looked at me. I breathed in the faint musty odor.

"She's wrapped," I said.

JoLynn stood at the edge. "Obviously not fully sealed, since the dogs alerted."

We heard a motor near where we'd parked.

"It's Wayne," Ayden said. "I'll go get him."

JoLynn looked at me. "Should we wait?"

"No. For all we know, it's someone's bag of garbage. But let's all put on gloves."

JoLynn grabbed a two-inch soft brush. Jax and I used trowels to move more dirt away while JoLynn brushed soil off the object and Natra took pictures. The lumpiness indicated that some part of this victim was still intact. Using just my thumb and forefinger, I gingerly lifted one edge of the blue plastic. It appeared to be a tarp like a painter might use to cover a floor. The top end, at least, was open, so her liquefying parts with the necrobiomes had drained out.

"Stop, Annie! Everyone stop!"

Wayne strode toward us, followed by his partner, JD Riley. JD, taller and heftier than Wayne, was sweating, like he'd had a rough day. They went to the edge of the hole we'd dug and looked down. We'd uncovered enough for them to see a plastic-wrapped form large enough to be a body.

"I'll be damned," Wayne said. He stroked his dark mustache. "You found something."

I introduced them to JoLynn. "I couldn't have done it without her research."

"I've worked with law enforcement," she offered. "I'm on an approved list for your agency. My papers are in the van, if you need to see them."

"Good enough for me." Wayne held out his hand for a trowel, and Jax stepped back to give him room. With JoLynn's guidance, Wayne moved enough dirt off the wrapped object to pull back the plastic. Natra backed away so JD could lean in to take photos with his phone. Wayne held up his hand for me to stay back, but Jax nodded to let me know we had a body. I felt a lump in my throat as my eyes moistened. Wayne made a call for a CSU team.

Over the next hour, as it grew dark, Wayne and JD worked at uncovering and moving the wrapped object from the hole. My team knew we had to stay outside the perimeter Wayne had taped off, but Ayden hovered with a bright flashlight. Ordinarily, we'd have been told to clear out, but Wayne understood what this meant to me.

Natra and Jax took the dogs to the fire pit area. JoLynn handed me a clean tissue.

"How did you find this?" Wayne asked.

JoLynn gave him a brief description of the drone and its sensors. Wayne looked baffled, but JD said, "Ah've heard a tha'yat. Didn't know they could use it."

"And we paired it with the dogs," I added. "Dr. Wilde found the tree, and the dogs alerted us on where to dig." I didn't tell him about the mark on the tree. We had photos, should we have to provide more details. Until then, our journey to this grave would remain in my own files.

JoLynn glanced at me but said nothing. Wayne gave me a look, one eyebrow raised, that said he knew there was more to the story.

Jax picked up a flashlight to provide light from a different angle, but darkness crept in. Wayne gestured for JD to position the floodlight over the remains. He waved me closer. "You're not to touch anything. Understand?"

"Of course."

"There probably won't be much left."

"She had a metal pin in her leg. She refused to have it removed. That would still be here."

Wayne bent down. Ayden came around to the other side to offer light. JoLynn stepped closer and peered down. I heard another motor. Digger barked. Other cops would be here soon—or media. I wanted to see the remains.

I held my breath. The trees seemed to bow over us as if they wanted to see, too. Wayne lifted the edge of the tarp. It tore. He pulled on it, but it was stuck. Ayden handed him a pocketknife. He carefully separated the deteriorated plastic from whatever it was stuck to. I blinked hard. JoLynn touched my shoulder. JD took more pictures.

I felt as if I were the only one there, standing over the wrapped remains of a girl who'd once been my best friend. She'd launched adventures, laughed at everything, and helped me through hard times. I'd protected her, until I'd failed her. I half-expected her to sit up, open her eyes, and ask, "What took you so long?" I swallowed hard.

Wayne beckoned for Ayden to angle his light beam.

Chapter Nineteen

I stepped close to look for myself as Wayne pulled back the wrapper. The odor of decomp was weak. I saw only a few clumps of bone. The skull had collapsed, and only the large joints seemed to retain their form. If clothing fragments remained, it would take an expert team to sift through all this to find them. No strands of hair were visible.

"Can I see where the legs would've been?" I asked.

JD uncovered that part. Ayden handed me his flashlight. I explored the decomposed bones with the light beam but saw nothing to indicate that this individual had ever had a surgical implant. I shook my head.

"They'll probably have to use elemental analysis," JoLynn offered. "If we find teeth, we can extract DNA."

"Even if it's not her," I said in a thick voice, "it's linked to Bruder. We found it from clues he wrote."

"And we'll process everything," Wayne assured me. "But right now, we need you all, except Dr. Wilde, to go back to your vehicles, go on home, and let our team do its work. We'll be here for several more hours."

Jax put an arm around my shoulders. A CSU team passed us as we returned to the fire pit. There, I pulled myself together.

"This has to be a Bruder victim," I said. "All the clues connect to him. If Wayne needs a full accounting of our work, we'll provide it, but let's first see if they find some DNA on the wrapping. If we can show at least a reasonable link to Bruder, we can counter his legal team and keep him in prison. That buys us time to keep looking." To Jax, I said, "Please let Airic know he helped. I realize he doesn't want to work on it anymore, but let's see what plays out."

"Whatever you need," he said. "I'll admit, I didn't expect much, but this was impressive."

I turned toward Ayden and Natra. "Tomorrow morning, we start looking for any Bruder documents we don't yet have, especially any photos of tattoos or drawings. Now that he's supposedly innocent, those items will lose value. Buy everything. Ayden, let's get on Pete the Panty Thief. Maybe he has more to say."

"Sure thing, boss."

"And don't pressure JoLynn. She won't be able to discuss this case." I gestured back toward where we'd just been. "Not while she's officially engaged. But I'll try to get her back with us."

As we entered our separate cars, another van pulled in. I spotted the TV station logo. "Wayne won't be happy," I told Natra. "Text him to send an officer out here. And make a note to check the local stations and papers tomorrow. We'll get more from them than from Wayne. If this victim isn't Hailey, we have other missing kids in our Bruder file."

"Wayne will ask for all our notes," Natra said.

"I know. I think he'll accept the combination of JoLynn's technology and the dogs. We can say we saw the carving on the tree and thought it was a marker without telling him what Airic drew. We also have the poetry—the blackjack oak and the fire pit."

"How soon do you think Bruder will get the news? I assume he won't be pleased that someone figured it out."

"Or, the *wrong* person figured it out. I'll make sure he hears about it. I'm already thinking about a podcast. I plan to challenge Krebs and her murder mentalist."

Chapter Twenty

As expected, we learned details from the news before we heard from Wayne. The remains of a decomposed individual had been found in a shallow grave in the woods, buried some time ago. Police had found no ID, but an item of jewelry indicated a female. An investigation was underway to identify her and determine more precisely what had happened.

"In other words," I commented, "they don't know much."

Wayne had texted while we were en route to say he'd meet us at the lake house. And he was there when I pulled in. Natra took Mika inside while I went over to him.

"You hear the news?" he asked.

"I did. What's the jewelry?"

"An earring."

"Were you there all night? You look tired."

"Once we moved the remains and taped off the area, I left it with JD. I wanted to be home before Kamryn got up."

I knew he was bending over backwards to attend to our daughter. Under his watch, she'd been abducted just a month before. But she seemed to have recovered. "So she's with a sitter?" I asked.

"Yes, Annie, the one you approved. And I'll be home early today. But now I need to know how you found these remains and what you know about this victim."

"I can give you some leads from my files. I've made some calculations based on missing persons reports and what I've learned about Bruder's routes and whereabouts."

I invited him in for coffee. He hesitated. It's not easy for Wayne to enter the lake house. We'd bought it together, with high hopes for fun times and a nice retirement getaway. A few years later, I got the place in our divorce. He's never quite gotten over that. But he came in.

"Can you tell us anything?" I asked. "You know we won't talk to anyone."

He breathed in and crossed his arms as if considering. He knew he couldn't deny me a *quid pro quo*. "There's a ligature," he said, "mostly rotted. The victim's been there a while, in changing soil conditions. As you saw, we found mostly just bone remains. No clothes. Some intact teeth. Some wire that suggests braces."

"Braces?" I considered this. It would eliminate Hailey but could link the remains to a missing girl in my files.

"We'll get confirmation on that. Your friend, Dr. Wilde, was very useful. She estimated the age from the remaining skull fragment and gave us ideas about the burial site."

"JoLynn? She certainly knows a lot. It's the first time I've worked with her."

Wayne accepted a mug of coffee. "You won't be happy, but we're hiring her to consult. So, she's off your team for now."

I shrugged. "I figured. At least for this case."

"Annie…"

"There are others, Wayne. In fact, her sensor device picked up stuff from other trees in that area. The dogs didn't alert, but maybe we didn't search enough. I have no doubt these remains are tied to Bruder, and I think you'll agree once you see what we have. And if we get more leads that might benefit from using JoLynn's drone, I want her free to help us. That technology is amazing."

Wayne gestured. "No promises. Show me what you have."

We entered my office, where Natra had set out the results of our analysis. I told her about the braces. She nodded and walked Wayne through the reports of missing kids that bore physical and geographical similarities.

"There are two in particular that you'll want to check out," she said. "I've made copies of our files on them, but they were both 12. And one had braces.

Robin Dahl. She was grabbed off her bike in Tennessee, in Bruder's territory. The other is Kristin Brown, but she seems less likely, mostly because this burial happened when the leaves of that tree near the grave were red. That narrows the timeframe." Natra gave Wayne a folder.

"But how did you know where to even start?" he asked. "Because it looks pretty strange that you'd walk into the woods and, within the space of a few hours, locate a grave."

I gritted my teeth to stop my retort. "We didn't just walk into the woods. We had a good idea about general location, and JoLynn helped to narrow it down. We were there all day, over twelve hours. We had two experienced sniffer dogs on the ground and clues from things Bruder had written or done. I don't think anyone would put us on a suspect list. It was a solid investigation."

I heard a text tone and saw a message. It was from Janissa Caulfield.

"I need to take this. Natra can tell you how we pieced together the clues from Bruder's messages. Then you'll have what we know. And I hope you'll keep us in the loop if we're right about the victim."

I left them to call Janissa. Whenever Wayne gets on my nerves, I usually let Natra handle it. She keeps her cool better than me, and she knows what *not* to say.

"The decision just came in," Janissa told me. She sounded out of breath. "We lost. The judge is sending Amber to prison for eighteen months."

"Janissa, I'm sorry. That's disappointing. I expect you plan to appeal."

"Yes, I do, on principle. And I'd like to hire you to talk with her, even though we can't get it into court. You saw things the other psychologist didn't notice. I think you can get it out of her. I've told her about your podcast. I think she listened to one or two while we were waiting. She's intrigued but still resisting. It's almost like she *wants* to be in prison."

I couldn't turn it down. My primary work is in suicide and staging, and this was a unique case—especially since Amber had done little to help herself. Plus, I did think she was hiding something, so she was a challenge. And I still hoped to ask Janissa about Cole Cheney and Maura Reynolds. The latter could advance my work on Bruder.

"I'll look at my schedule," I told her. "I'm in the middle of a case today, but I'll get back to you soon."

As I ended the call, an image from the courtroom flashed into my mind. *Monroe.* That's where I'd seen him before. At the trial.

Chapter Twenty-One

Within half an hour after my latest *Psi Apps* episode aired, Maura called. She wanted to meet, ostensibly to discuss my research. I knew better. And I was ready for her. I made a date and then called my team together.

It had been two days since the public had learned about the victim discovery and just a day since I'd posted a podcast in response to Monroe's interview with Carly Krebs. I'd challenged their claims about Bruder's innocence. I didn't mention the body. Not yet. Although no one had yet identified the girl we'd found in the woods, Wayne had told me my lead seemed to be paying off. It was his way of thanking me for the shortcut.

I figured the discovery had stirred up things with Bruder's team. He would certainly have understood the implications for his case. I suspected he'd urged them to move things along. He wanted to get out before anyone tied this victim to him.

In the podcast, I called out Monroe's claim to have paranormal abilities and challenged any listener to send me proof that the offender who'd allegedly tried to kill him was in that area at the time. I compared the murder mentalist to a collector I'd once investigated who'd charged huge fees to see his display of sham murderabilia. He'd shown a plastic bag removed from Ted Bundy's car, dirt from John Wayne Gacy's crawlspace, a lock of hair from Charles Manson, murder twine from Dennis Rader's shed, Jeffrey Dahmer's stand-alone freezer, and numerous handwritten letters and artworks from killers. He'd claimed he'd acquired them through police auctions. Any of these items was easily faked. Who, exactly, had "authenticated" them? No one.

In fact, not one item had any provable provenance. When the actual items turned up elsewhere, the cagey collector had been exposed.

Monroe, I said, made claims that were just as difficult to corroborate. "Who'd know if Joseph DeAngelo is secretly pleased with his publicity?" I'd asked. "And how could we get Bittaker, now deceased, to tell us if Monroe managed to read his thoughts?" I'd gone on to claim he was taking advantage of gullible people. The statements he'd made in his book and on the air about how this or that murderer thinks could have been lifted from their interrogations. Or he'd just made them up. He hadn't said one thing that was provably paranormal nor given any insight into a killer's mind that we didn't already know.

"Where's the thoughtprint that leads us to an undiscovered victim?" I'd asked. "If he's so good at this, why doesn't he close some cases or help us find missing victims? Why doesn't he sit with cops during interrogations to help them sort through truth and lies? Why doesn't he locate killers we haven't yet caught?"

I took apart the gushing comments Krebs had made, asking why she'd misrepresented the assault report of Bruder's rescued victim. I'd asked why she'd enlisted Monroe to help her figure out Bruder's mind rather than urge him to locate the supposed network of killers who'd allegedly made him pick up girls.

"Mentalism in the hands of amateurs," I added, "is nothing but pseudo-psychology with a sexy label. It's all an act. And it's not paranormal. To use this fraud to support lies like those Tommy Ray Bruder is telling is both naïve and dangerous."

I felt satisfied that I'd called him out. The responding comments arrived in a flood, some in support, some against, and others just wondering what mentalism really is. I asked Natra to sort through them to see if any comments suggested that Krebs or Monroe had listened. I'd hoped to mobilize them. They'd been talking as if Bruder's claim of a false confession would get him sprung. I wanted them to know they had a significant hurdle—me. I expected I'd get support once the girl from the woods was identified. I prayed for a DNA match on some item that would lead back to

Bruder.

When Ayden arrived, he was effusive about the episode. "Love your boldness, boss! Hit 'em where it hurts. So does Jo, by the way."

I raised an eyebrow. "You've seen her?"

"Sure. Wayne didn't mind. She says her research team is pretty excited about the search results. I think they're going back."

"Back?"

"She couldn't talk about it, but there's *something* that interests them."

"Well, for now, we've lost her, so be careful. Wayne says they hired her for a more pressing case. But she can work with us if we identify another possible spot for a burial."

"Then let's get another."

"Any luck finding the Panty Thief?"

"Soon, I think. And we'll probably have to grease his wheels. Ready for that?"

"In this case, yes."

Ayden slapped a folder onto the table in front of me. "I've circled back to the tattoo photos to look for other suggestive shapes or symbols."

Natra watched the screen. Without looking our way, she offered her opinion. "We can't just go find another grave. We have to be careful now. Your podcast made you a target."

I nodded. "That's my intention. I want to kneecap Bruder's team before they gather steam, and Monroe's the weakest point. He'll either come at me or decide that Krebs risks his own media following. In the process, we're making friends of the cops who interrogated Bruder, if they're still around. 3-M's making them look bad."

Natra looked over. "3-M?"

"Monroe the Murder Mentalist. 3-M."

"What if Wayne's team can't prove Bruder's link to our victim?" Ayden asked. "We don't wanna reveal to Bruder how we know, right? He'll stop the leakage. But he's gotta know someone figured out the location from his messages. You don't just find a buried body randomly."

I considered this. "He's already sent drawings and letters, and we've gathered copies. We've got the leaks. If we go over everything carefully, I'll bet we'll find one or two more. Even one more would help. I just hope it's about Hailey."

Natra chimed in. "We have items to sort through. And I think he'll come at Annie with something. He can't help himself. And Monroe won't stay passive. In fact, look at this."

I came up behind her to read the screen.

Monroe is aware of you, the anonymous writer said. *He's in your head. He knows your thoughts. Beware.*

I snorted. "That's probably him… or Krebs. I hope so. I want them to alert Bruder that I'm not buying his claim. He'll be hit from two sides—the grave discovery and my assault on his team. He'll start scrambling, maybe make a mistake. Keep looking. I figure there'll be more. And, Ayden, you stay on Pete. He's the tattooist. I'm certain he'll have more to say. But don't give away what we learned from his work. Not yet. Only if we need to. And when you find him, I want to go with you to see him."

"Copy that."

I rose from my chair. "As for me, I'm going to see Amber Bell. There's something about her response to Reynolds that tugs at me. I want to know what it is before I meet with my sister psychologist."

Chapter Twenty-Two

I arranged to see Amber before I spoke with Janissa, because I didn't want Janissa's bias to influence me. To some extent, it already had. Both of them knew things about Maura, so I'd deal with them one at a time. Amber would be the most challenging. But according to Janissa, she'd listened to some of my podcasts. She'd seemed intrigued. This gave me a way in.

Janissa had arranged for a small room that was a step up from what I normally experienced in a correctional setting when I worked for the defense. A guard brought Amber in. I don't know exactly what color to call her faded uniform—sort of greenish—but it didn't look so good against her skin. It did, however, fit her scowl. Her dark eyes were like two hands raised in a protective stance, lest I come too close. I invited her to sit down.

I never let a table come between an interviewee and me unless I have to use it for assessments. I don't like the buffer it affords them. With open space between us, I can watch their hands and feet. But I have a talent for facial micro-expressions, too. Amber wasn't good about shielding those. No one is, really, except those who don't feel. The research on lie detection is inconsistent, so I just watch for gestures of discomfort. They don't necessarily signal lies, but they show me places in the interview where I should apply more pressure.

Amber dropped into a chair as far from me as she could get in that eight-by-ten-foot room. I'd expected that. But I didn't expect her first question. She squinted a little and raised her chin before she asked, "Do you really believe in ghosts?"

It's a common misconception that accepting the potential for paranormal phenomena is the same as believing in ghosts. It's not, but I get the question a lot. And I have an answer, which I offered to her. "I believe we should stay open to the possibility of the existence of things that don't fit our cultural frames. We tend to think that for things to be considered real, they have to be visible and measurable. I don't see why we have to live by such restrictions. So, I'm open. Why do you ask?"

Instead of answering, Amber glanced at the door as if she thought someone outside was listening. Then she gave me that strange little sneer. "Ever seen one?" She had an odd nasal quality to her voice, almost as if she had a cold. Her accent suggested she hadn't grown up in the area but had acquired it by moving here.

I shook my head. "No, I haven't, not that I can definitively say was a ghost."

"So you *might've* seen one."

"Maybe." I sensed that being dismissive might close a door. She was going somewhere with this.

She looked at the door again before she scanned the room. Then she cupped her hand over the top of her mouth as if to block the view from a ceiling camera. "I've seen Trevor. He's been here."

No matter what a client says, it's best to flow with their perspective, to learn what they think. No judgments, no corrections. For the moment, she'd seen a ghost.

"In your cell?" I asked.

She dropped her hand. "Outside, usually. Just standin' there, watchin' me. I go away and come back, and he's still there."

"Is he angry?"

She nodded.

"At you?"

She shook her head.

"At who, then?"

She squinted. "You couldn't see it? Right in front of you?"

"Does he want something?"

She sneered. "'Course he does! He knows I don't belong here. He's upset."

90

I had to be careful. "But not with you?"

She withdrew. Her left hand clenched. I had to get her relaxed. "Do you miss him?"

She shook her head. "Not really."

"I thought he was your boyfriend, a guy you loved."

"Nope. That's what—" She caught herself.

"Why didn't you say this in court? Or have your therapist say it? That could have made a difference."

The shake of her head was as tight as her lips.

"Did you cancel Trevor's appointment?"

Amber's eyes moved before she said, "Sometimes she does what she's told. She doesn't have a choice."

I sensed from the change to third person that I'd gotten too close. I'd seen other clients adopt the same defense tactic.

"Amber, who are you afraid of?"

Her eyes blazed. "No one." But a quick crimp of facial muscles suggested otherwise. This girl was scared. Deeply scared. She *wanted* to be here. For some reason, she felt safe here. Then something occurred to me. "Did someone else have your phone?"

She stared at me. Several minutes ticked by. Then she said, "Contact Trevor. You can ask him. He knows. *Now* he knows. Don't let this happen again."

I leaned toward her. "Do you want me to do something? Is that why you agreed to see me? Do you want me to get you out?"

Her eyes widened. "No!"

I cocked my head. "You don't belong here, but you want to stay."

Abruptly, Amber stood up. "That's all. Don't come back. Ask Trevor. You know how." She went to the door and knocked. A guard opened it. With a sneering glance at me, she shambled off.

I hadn't expected a meeting like this. The girl intrigued me more now than before. I had to know more. I hadn't yet read accurately between the lines. *Something* was there. She seemed to think I should already know. *You couldn't see it? Right in front of you?*

91

No. I hadn't.

I told Janissa that Amber hadn't offered much, but I thought she'd been trying to send me a message. I'd need another meeting. I asked for the full transcript of the incriminating texts sent between Amber and Trevor. Then I formed a plan.

"Trevor" was either a delusion or a veiled message, most likely the latter. I doubted Amber had really seen a ghost. I now believed the girl in prison had barely known Trevor at all. So, why had she let herself be convicted for aiding his suicide?

Chapter Twenty-Three

Meeting with Pete Nemeth proved challenging, but my PI knows how to schmooze. Ayden had tracked the Panty Thief through several more prison stints for burglary since sharing a cell with Bruder. Now on parole, he'd settled on a remote piece of property. Ayden had pushed through several barriers to get the guy on a phone. Nemeth had initially resisted meeting but then had changed his mind. He'd seemed to like Ayden's appreciation for his art. He'd given directions to "one of" his hideouts. His behavior suggested paranoia, so I was sure he'd ignored his parole prohibitions and had a few guns.

Ayden drove us onto the dirt lane that would take us to the hideout. We passed several hand-painted warning signs. I spotted a surveillance perch in a tree. Ayden had already caught a glimpse of a rusting blue-and-white mobile home in the midst of what looked like a community dump. Junk cars, trucks, and a few forty-foot shipping containers formed a barrier around the abode. Nemeth liked muscle cars. I saw a Mustang, two Camaros, and a Cougar. Ayden pointed out a black Pontiac Firebird he liked. He'd taken no photos, since Nemeth might have a surveillance system.

I looked around. "If someone this spooked is willing to see us, there has to be more to the story. This isn't about helping *us.*"

Ayden nodded. "He got beat up in prison a few times. My intel suggests there was a vendetta. Maybe he's just a snitch."

"Was he beat up before or after he gave the interview about Bruder?"

"Don't know."

"Maybe Bruder directed someone to send him a message. I doubt Bruder was pleased about being quoted on his tattoo strategy. So much for being a camouflage king."

We'd gone over Pete's published interview. It had taken up less than a page of a tatty newsletter devoted to "life inside." After complaining about food and dental care, Nemeth had bragged about the hardened criminals he'd met and how his inking skills had won him favors. The passage about Bruder's tattoo request had been vague: "He drew what he wanted me to burn on him. He could wear his notches with no one knowing, is how he put it."

Nemeth had refused to meet us publicly. He'd told Ayden, who quoted him in his own vernacular, "Gotta keep mah peraime'tah, if ya know what ah mean. It's mah sanc'shary." I guessed he thought we might lure him outside his border so someone could go rustle through his stuff. *Something* was here.

Ayden stopped near the corroded shell of a blue Dodge Challenger with broken windows. It blocked the lane. "We'll walk from here. Maybe I should go in first. Just feel him out."

I gave him a look. "Don't protect me. You know better." I patted my side where I kept my .380 under a loose shirt. "Just keep your Glock ready. I'm sure he doesn't care about violating parole. Assume he's armed. When one of us talks, the other watches."

I heard a dog bark. Then another. They sounded vicious. And big. "I'd guess Rotties or Dobes. Hope they're tied up."

A short, bony man came up on the other side of the Challenger. I thought he had a gun. He peered at us, reached behind himself as if stowing a weapon, and beckoned. My heart raced, but I got out and approached him. I was glad we'd put a temporary tracker on Ayden's truck. If we didn't get back, Natra could find us. Within four feet of the man, I caught a nasty whiff of cigarette smoke, dirty shirt, and crusty sweat.

Pete "the Panty Thief" Nemeth was no taller than five-foot-two. He had to have been tough to be that small and survive prison. The knife sheath on his belt confirmed this impression. His thinning gray-streaked hair, along with an unkempt beard the color of old cement, placed him in his fifties. His khaki T-shirt surprised me; it bore the faded image of Picasso. I hadn't expected any level of sophistication. Then again, maybe he'd just rummaged through someone else's discards. Stress had etched deep lines around his mouth, and his arms were covered in colorful tattoos, mostly of provocative female nudes. I noticed a purple thistle tattoo—the Scottish national flower—on the back of his left hand that suggested a proud affiliation. Not surprising in this area, or on him. The legend about this resilient weed was that it had helped to warn the Scots of an approaching enemy. Stained jeans completed Pete's outfit. Despite dog crap and broken glass in the yard, his dirty feet were bare.

He gestured with a wide sweep of his arm. "C'mon. Ah don' bite... lessen yous's off'rin.'" His yellow grin showed two missing teeth.

I fought the urge to glance at Ayden. Nemeth seemed friendly, but his squinting brown eyes shifted between us. Vigilant. I introduced myself and looked around for the dogs.

"They's in the back, ma'am," the recluse assured me. "I give 'em some bones. They sweet thangs, when ya knows 'em."

He hadn't exactly said they were tied up.

Nemeth gestured for us to follow him across a clearing to a rickety lean-to that seemed more to have fallen against his corroding trailer than been planfully constructed. I picked my way along an overgrown path and took a quick look around. I sensed someone else here, but I saw no movement in the trees. A glint of light high in a pine tree suggested a camera.

Inside the lean-to were several metal folding chairs, and against the walls, I saw piles of magazines and newspapers—seemingly decades' worth, like in a hoarder's home. The place reeked of mildew. I figured some of these piles had fused together.

"We kin meet out he'yah." With a jerk of his thumb toward the trailer, Nemeth added, "I ain't much fer visitin'. Didn't clean."

Through a window I saw more stacks and knew I could never have gone inside. At least a lean-to with no door offered air...and an escape.

"Kin I git ya sumpthin' ta drink?" Nemeth asked. I swallowed and fought the urge to grimace. There was no chance I'd drink something *he'd* made, let alone from a glass he'd cleaned—if he ever did. The sound of rustling drew my attention to a pile of magazines. I nearly gagged when I saw a two-inch black roach emerge and skittle down to another hidey-hole. I realized the whole place could be full of bugs. Maybe a few brown recluse spiders. Ayden touched my shoulder, and I jumped. I assumed he was as eager as me to get this done and clear out.

"We're fine," Ayden said. "And we have a long drive back, so we won't take up much of your time."

"Shore thang, suits me." Nemeth sat on a wooden folding chair and invited us to follow suit. I didn't want to sit anywhere in that place. I imagined roaches climbing up the chair legs to get into my shirt. Or the chair collapsing. But I sat.

I kept my breathing shallow to shut out the stink of dog feces as Ayden offered compliments about Nemeth's artistic ability. I knew the subject of money would soon come up. I made myself focus. Sitting on the edge of the seat in case I had to launch off it, I ignored other noises and leaned toward our host. "Mr. Nemeth—"

"Pete. Just Pete."

"All right. Pete. Thank you for letting us meet with you."

"You ain't frum 'round he'yah," he said. "I kin he'yah some no'ath in ya."

"North Carolina," I said. "Not very far north."

"Ah. So frum whe-yah Tommy like ta rahd."

I wasn't quite sure I understood, but I said, "Yes, that's right."

Ayden removed a folded copy of the article that featured Nemeth's interview and held it up. The tattooist leaned forward and blinked several times. I wondered if he could read.

"We're interested in a comment you made in this article," Ayden said.

"Yah, ah know. S'what ya said." He held up his right hand.

I removed two twenties from my purse and handed them over. He looked at them and back at me.

"There's more," I said, "if it's worth it."

I knew we were taking a chance. If he wanted more, he could just call his dogs. I arched a little to show the outline of my gun. A noise behind me sounded like something in the stacks. Maybe a mouse... or a snake. I drew my shoulders together and hoped nothing would drop from the ceiling.

Ayden folded up the article. "You tattooed Tommy Bruder. As I mentioned, I've seen pictures. You said he told you he wanted to display his notches on his body without giving anything away. Did he tell you what he meant?"

Nemeth glanced over his shoulder toward his trailer before he nodded. "Shu-ah, shu-ah. Tha's wut 'e sa'yad. Ah dun 'em lack ah wuz tol' an' I shudna said nut'in.'"

I went alert. "Did he do something to you?"

Nemeth rolled his tongue around in his mouth, poked it inside one cheek, and spit something into a can at his feet. I shielded my nose as subtly as I could from the reek.

"Wadn' him." Nemeth closed one eye and lifted his chin toward me. "You ain't ta only ones t'want his 'ridg'nals.'"

I froze. "His originals. You have his actual drawings?"

He eyed me. "Meybe yes, meybe no. How'd ah know *they* didn' send ya?"

"They?"

He gave us a look, as if we knew what he meant.

"The ones who made Bruder pick up the girls?" Ayden asked.

His eyes blazed. "No wun made him do nut'in'! He gits out, they'll kill me, lak they awready trah'ed." Nemeth looked straight at me. "Ah hep you an' you hep me."

"Yes," I said. "If you have his drawings, I can use them to raise suspicion about other murders. We'll prove he's a killer, a *child* killer." People like Nemeth despise offenders who harm children. I knew Ayden was looking at me to curb my making false promises, but I had to get those drawings. "How did you manage to keep them? That had to be clever."

Nemeth squinted as if deciding what to say. Then he opened his mouth into a tobacco-stained grin. "Ah dun sent 'em out ta mah gal. When he wanted 'em back, I said the guahds tossed mah cell and took evruh'thang. But Tommy, he don' buy it. Then when Ah said those thangs—" he gestured toward the folded article in Ayden's hands, "they come an' wallop me gud. They bin through this place, oh, they shu'ah tossed it, but they don' know whe'ah ah hid 'em. And they ain't no one wants ta go through these he'ah stacks." He gestured around. I was sure he was right about that.

"So, they're here," I said.

"Meybe yes, meybe no."

"Pete, if you want us to find something that will keep Bruder in prison, we need them. You help us, and we help you."

He waited for a moment, watching us. "Got me a frien' who listens t'all them radio shows. She tole me Bruder's gittin' out. An t'others bin hrassin' me agin. I jus' wanna be rid ah awl this and move on, git away frum he'yah." He shook his head. "You won' find me he'yah agin. Got me a good place tah hide."

I pulled out three more twenties. "Here's the rest."

Nemeth snatched the bills and gestured over his shoulder. "They's up the'ah."

I looked up. Nemeth tossed his head to indicate I should go ahead and search. That is, I should prod a stack or pull out a magazine and risk disturbing some rodent nest or insect hive. I glanced at Ayden. *Now* was the time to protect me. I regretted warning him not to.

Ayden made a move, but Nemeth smirked and got up. He went over to a stack. He counted until he hit eight. At the eighth stack, he climbed his spidery fingers up over his head. With a quick gesture, he pulled on a magazine. It seemed stuck. He yanked it. The stack toppled. Roaches raced out and dropped to the ground. I jumped up, knocking over my chair. Something hit the back of my neck. I swatted it and found a squished centipede in my hand. I flung it away and stepped outside.

Nemeth just laughed. "They ain' gunna hurt ya. They's mah gahdians. Ain't no one comin' close ta these he'ah crittahs."

I'd have rather tackled the dogs than a swarm of creepy crawlies. I ran my fingers through my hair. Ayden emerged with some grubby-looking papers. He waved them and winked. "Let's go."

I didn't have to be told twice.

"Nice ta meet ya!" Nemeth called out. "Come on back if'n ya wanna look 'round some mo'ah. Maybe you'd like ta meet my pappy!" His cackle told me he didn't expect to ever see us again.

Before I got in the truck, I wiped off everywhere I could reach and tried not to think of bugs that might have hitched a ride. Inside, we pulled on latex gloves and carefully peeled apart the three pieces of stained paper—the "'ridg'nals." Bruder's handiwork. A dead spider was stuck to one.

Under these conditions, I knew, the DNA from Bruder's handling could be degraded, but we'd take no chance on contamination. Ayden had gripped only the outer edges of the bottom corners. The paper had aged, and the ink was barely visible. Two pages were ripped, but the fire symbols and the numbers inside each of three irregular shapes were distinct. We already knew the Jasper County shape, with its number '2' marking the spot where we'd dug up a body. This map provided the needed link between Bruder's knowledge of the grave location and the tattoo that had led us to it.

I pointed at another number, barely visible. We looked at each other before I voiced it: "He's killed four."

Chapter Twenty-Four

Wayne ushered us into a cramped, humid conference room where JD and two young detectives sat around a scratched oval table. I smelled burnt coffee and sweat-infused cologne. JD introduced us to Tim Wheeler and Debra Goldsberry and said he'd told them about the suspect. Wheeler seemed untested, with his close-cut brown hair and wrinkle-free blue shirt. He munched on a bagel while dark-eyed Goldsberry squinted at me. Both dressed as if they were new to the job, in pressed khakis that pegged them as cops. Wayne would train that out of them.

Natra had captured high-resolution photos of both sides of each of Bruder's three pages for our records, but I needed Wayne's CSUs to analyze the paper. I could have gone to a private lab, but these items were relevant to his investigation. I'd already told him I thought the drawings were outlines of counties, maybe in this state, maybe in others. He needed to see them.

I transferred each drawing from my folder onto a sterile piece of butcher paper in the middle of the table. Ayden described how we'd obtained them. There was only a small chance of a problem with provenance, I explained. The "artist" had given them to Nemeth, who'd had them in his possession since he'd been out of prison. Perhaps his "gal" had handled them, but I had no reason to believe she'd swapped in a set of fakes. Perhaps a defense attorney would try that argument, but commonsense would cancel it. The real issue would be Nemeth's decision to keep them, which suggested he'd known or suspected something more about Bruder's crimes.

The detectives leaned close to examine them. Goldsberry shrugged. "Just

100

blobs."

I took a breath to keep my cool. "We know from our prior work that each drawing outlines a county, and the numbers might indicate victims. One drawing contains two numbers, for a total of four. We've looked at counties in Tennessee and the Carolinas, along Tommy Bruder's known travel routes. In some places, the ink has faded, or there's a grease spot obscuring a line, so we have a margin of error. But at this point, we've identified a dozen potential counties that resemble the outlines."

JD looked at me. "How'd ya do that?"

"We traced the outlines and used a computer superimposition, as well as my team members separately eyeballing them. Of course, we're assuming some things about Bruder, but it's a place to start."

"Whah didn't y'all come tah us, Annie? That's a nasty risk goin' up they-ah in the woods ta see this he'yah cha'ractah."

I shook my head. "He's so paranoid there's no chance he'd've let a cop near his place. There could be others there, too. I sensed someone watching, and he mentioned his father."

JD grabbed a muffin, which resembled his own muffin-top belly. "Xactly mah point."

"Anyway, he might be gone now. He said he had several hideouts and was heading to another."

"Whey'ah?"

"Didn't say. It sounded like you'd never find him. And he doesn't have a phone, so you can't trace him that way. Ayden located him through a friend of a friend. From what I could tell, Nemeth just wanted to dump these drawings on someone who could do something with them that would also benefit him."

"You pay 'im?" Wayne asked.

"I did. And I know you think maybe he just duped us with fake papers to get the money, but three of these outlines resemble shapes in Bruder's tattoos, including the one we used to locate the remains you're investigating. That's pretty good confirmation. And you can see the paper's old and the ink's faded. Nemeth didn't just draw this when he heard I was interested in

101

his comments about Bruder. They smell like they've been stored for a while in his stack of old magazines. There's even a mildew spot on one. That supports their authenticity, but please feel free to test them."

"He drew these maps on Bruder," Ayden added. "He camouflaged each number in the tattoos with a fire design, according to Bruder's instructions."

I tapped the edge of the butcher paper. "The important thing is this: he designated these locations with numbers and also with his special mark. I'm certain Nemeth didn't know we're aware of Bruder's symbol, so he didn't draw it to fool us. And you can't just figure out a location from Bruder's tattooed map, even if you have the right county. We needed the clues from his poem. And we did get results, as you saw for yourself."

"We'll work with y'all on the rest," JD said. "Got any mo'ah—?"

I held up a hand. "I'm not yet sure these counties are all in your state, and without more clues, you could search for months and never find a burial site. We're working on getting some. What we need from you is an analysis that ties Bruder to these papers, even just one of them. That would strengthen the circumstantial evidence. And we need the Jasper victim's identity and anything that ties Bruder to her."

"*We* need those things," Wayne said. "This is now in our hands."

"And we're here, giving you what we've got."

"And there's another thing," Ayden added. "This guy, Pete, said there are others who want these drawings. He didn't say how many, but he said they'd harassed him before, and recently they've started up again. Maybe Bruder heard about the body discovery, and he's sweatin'. Maybe he wants to recover his drawings or threaten Nemeth into silence. He has friends on the outside."

Wheeler took another bite and nodded. Goldsberry glowered at me from beneath brunette bangs. I suddenly realized why she was eyeing me: she'd either been with my ex or was flirting with the idea. She didn't like me. I narrowed my eyes to assure her I knew, then tapped the edge of the paper. "And Bruder's spreading that story, too, about a criminal gang. He's sent such messages to podcasters. He wants to use the idea of being a compliant accomplice to minimize his involvement and get a new hearing. I initially thought he was lying. Now I think he had at least one partner. We're looking into that."

Wayne cleared his throat. That was his signal for me to step back. "*We* can look into that, but as you said, he was arrested in another state. Not our jurisdiction. We're close to an ID on our victim. Then we'll look into potential links to Bruder. But if he's true to pattern, he picked up girls he didn't know. Without something to link him from the tarp he used, we'll be back to square one."

I looked around. "Just FYI, I didn't pay Nemeth to snitch; I paid for a piece of the puzzle. An important piece, it turns out, regardless of whether you get DNA off it. He did not manufacture these maps the day before we came, but please do whatever you need to do to authenticate it." To Wayne, I added, "I think he gave them to us for his own safety. The money was just a bonus."

Wayne glanced at Ayden, who nodded, so he said, "Noted."

"I'll give you everything I get that's germane to your investigation, but until you have a case, you're limited by state lines." I gestured toward Ayden. "We're not. Ayden and I both have PI licenses in other states." That was for Goldsberry's benefit. I wanted to say more, but I noticed the detectives shifting in their seats, as if uncomfortable with the tension in Wayne's face. I'd said enough.

Wheeler took the lead on filling us in. I figured Wayne had suggested this. The young cop cleared his throat. As soon as he spoke, I knew he was from the Midwest. The flat A in his accent suggested Ohio or Michigan. He began by acknowledging me. "We appreciate the help you've given us." A subtle twist of Goldberry's lip told me they'd discussed me, likely mocking me. I'm used to that. And my direct gaze told Wheeler to think twice before he tried this to my face. As long as he did his job competently, I could ignore a fatuous attitude.

"We sent the remains for analysis," he said. "We're waiting for DNA results from the teeth. There was no rod in her leg, but two fingers from one hand were missing."

I cocked my head. "Cut?"

IN THE DAMAGE PATH

"Seems so."

"That might be a signature. A finger was missing on Bruder's known victim."

"We're looking at it. Preliminary findings support the ID of the person you named, and we're sifting through dirt from the scene to locate other potential evidence." He glanced at Wayne, who gestured for him to continue. "So far, nothing's turned up in the area near the primary grave that might have been dropped. It's pretty old, with lots of seasonal changes. It'll take time."

I nodded. "Please include the fire pit."

Wheeler looked at Wayne. So, they weren't aware of it.

I took over. "Around the time of the burial, someone called in a fire in the woods in that area. JoLynn Wilde knows where it is. I don't know if it's related to the murder, but it could be. Some fabric fragments were collected, although I doubt they were saved. But do check. No one was charged for setting the fire, and our boy Bruder's a fire freak. I think it's worth sifting."

Wayne gestured with his head for Goldsberry to leave the room. I guessed she'd be making a call to the on-site team.

Wayne focused on me. "Anything else?"

"Find out if they still have Bruder's van."

"Actually, Annie, I did think of that. And they don't, but they have the items they removed from it. And, yes, before you ask, they vacuumed the van. I've got someone there looking through what they have. I'll get an inventory."

"Can we get a copy?"

"No."

I knew he'd say that. "Look, I'm bringing you what I have. And I'll continue to do that. But please watch how Bruder's case proceeds. You might need to argue in a Tennessee court to keep him locked up until your investigation's complete."

A vein in Wayne's forehead bulged. "We know what's at stake, Annie. Just don't be paying snitches. That doesn't help."

"Okay, well, we think another spot of interest is in northern Oconee

CHAPTER TWENTY-FOUR

County." I pointed to the drawing with the number 4.

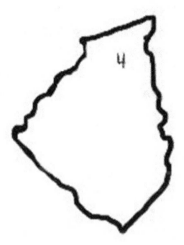

Wayne raised an eyebrow. "Can you be more specific?"

"Nope. This is what he drew. The shape matches the county boundaries. It does resemble some counties in neighboring states, but the computer tells us it's closest in shape to Oconee."

"Got anything else?"

"We're looking through what we've collected. But see if there were any suspicious fires in the woods during the time period of interest. Start from Bruder's arrest date and work backwards two years."

Wayne's brown eyes looked dangerous. I was right at the line.

"Thank you," he said, his mouth tight. "If you think of anything else, please pass it along."

Wayne glanced at Ayden, who nodded. Their bro-bond irked me, but it helped to keep communication with Wayne open for me. I thanked the team for their time and we left. I'd given them breadcrumbs. They knew about the podcasters, Bruder's letters, and the poem that had led to victim number two. They knew about the tattoos, and they could request a closer look at Bruder's body art. They also had his original drawings. Wayne knew the date of Hailey's abduction, so if he IDed the Jasper victim as the girl I'd named, we'd have a sense of the timeline. Robin Dahl, potentially number two, had been abducted a year before Hailey. These cops could do everything I was doing. They had the same info. But I was still a step ahead.

I hadn't exactly been dishonest. But we did have something. We just didn't yet know how it related. On the day after we'd exhumed the body in Jasper County, Krebs had posted more of Bruder's items. Most repeated his innocence claims and his fawning appreciation for assistance. But one item stood out. Another poem.

Chapter Twenty-Five

Back at the lake house, I saw that Natra had printed Bruder's new poem on our whiteboard so we could dissect it together line by line. I turned on the *Mozart in the Morning* music collection to feed our creative brain function.

From the drawings, we'd identified eleven counties with the potential to be Bruder's burial areas. Oconee in South Carolina was one, but the shape also resembled Green and Anderson in eastern Tennessee and Madison in North Carolina, near where I'd lived as a kid. But we'd jointly agreed, and the computer had confirmed, that Oconee most resembled the drawing. It gave us a place to start. One step at a time. One map at a time.

Natra had linked items in the poem from the *Killer Hooks* site to Oconee.

"I think I have it figured out," she said. "I did look at the geographical aspects of those similar counties, but several words link to Oconee. Once you get a few, others fall into place."

I leaned on my desk. "Does Ayden agree?"

"He ran off to follow a lead." Natra raised an eyebrow. "Did he tell you he's seeing JoLynn?"

"No. He knows what I'd say about that."

"He insists he hasn't asked her anything about the dig. I think he'll observe protocol, if only to avoid Wayne's wrath. But I don't see an accomplished woman like her sticking with a gig worker."

I shrugged. "Ayden has his charm. He's got that blue-eyed blond thing going. He's athletic, skilled, smart, caring, and he likes smart women. That has appeal. I figured their mutual passion for weather would draw them together, so I'm not surprised. Maybe we'll get some benefit, but I'll remind him to behave."

Mika got up and cocked her head. She whined.

Natra went to her. "What is it, girl?"

She trotted out of the room, then returned to sit on her pad. She remained in a vigilant pose, ears alert.

Natra shrugged. "She's been out, so it's not that. She did the same thing earlier this morning."

"Let's get to work. She'll let us know if she needs something." In front of the board, I cocked my head. "I wonder why he sent this to Krebs now."

Natra pointed toward the top left of the board, where she'd posted a screenshot of the poem she'd lifted. "Look at the date. She seems to have received it around when the news reports came out about the body discovery. So, maybe he was still playing the game and now regrets sending it. I'll watch to see if she takes it down."

"Yeah, that would suggest he's instructing her. He must realize by now we used clues from his Jasper County poem to make that discovery. It's too random otherwise. You don't just stumble over a body buried in the woods two decades ago. He'll know he needs to be more careful. And so do we. If someone harassed Nemeth for the drawings, that same person might have figured out who brought the SLED team to the burial site. Bruder knows that much. So, Ayden's looking into Bruder associates. Still… Bruder *likes* this game." I pointed. "This poem, 'The Devil's Fire,' looks rich with references. We already know his fire symbol, and he's referred to the Devil before, too. I think it relates to his murder activities."

Natra pulled up a map on her computer screen. "There's no flame on this one, but based on the number's position in Oconee, I have an idea that—"

I held up a hand. "Love your thoroughness, as always, but let me read the whole thing first, without distractions."

I crossed my arms, took a breath, and scanned each line. One word jumped out. So did some names.

Some boys like to run away
Some boys like to stay and play

Joseph 3 and Robert B looked for opportunity
To feed the fire for heart's desire
That makes the devil's salad,
With cherries, plums and red berries
For dinner and dessert.
ST liked a riper fruit
Wanted it to be cooked
All were forked for same pursuit.
As toothless men dance
to a fiddle, and riddle the piggies who float
over lost ones submerged,
mourned by white water ghosts.
The devil's at the end of the double ones
where witches may ring the bells.
Now berry's the spirit
but no one can hear it.
pass the bloodstained flower
to step to her bower

I snorted. "Not much of a poet, but I'd say it's a murder tribute." I stepped over to tap on each of the three names. "I can figure out some of this. He's naming child killers he admires. We already know about them. Joseph Duncan the third, that's probably 'Joseph three.' 'Robert B' could be Robert Black. And ST, I'm not sure, but it sounds like a cannibal. Maybe Serhiy Tkach. I'll look up their cases. We might find clues there."

Natra nodded. "I got that, too. But they weren't around here."

"No, but Duncan had a website for ranting. He beat three people to death so he could kidnap two kids. So, we've got similarities. Robert Black drove a van, like Bruder, and looked for girls...."

I couldn't say it. He'd looked for girls alone, walking or riding their bikes. That's how Bruder had seen Hailey and me—as he prowled on an isolated stretch of a back road where we were walking.

"And Tkach," I added, "claimed to have suffocated and raped over a hundred young girls. Or at least, their corpses." I cleared my throat. "I'd guess that's the 'riper fruit' in that line. The fruits and berries refer to Bruder's victims, I'm sure. They're all red." The word, 'cherries,' made me cringe. That's what he'd called Hailey, and I've noticed the reddish color in the hair of victims I'd linked to him. I wondered if he'd given each girl he'd snatch such a nickname. "He's mentioned 'berry' in this poem twice, and the second time it appears to indicate she's dead."

Its covert meaning was hideous but didn't really help. We needed clues like the red tree and blackjack reference from the other poem. With those, we'd been able to direct the dogs.

I continued. "This victim is number four, so if we can get her identity, as well as the one from Jasper, I'll know where to add Hailey."

Natra handed me a page. "I've made a list of the missing girls you researched, with the dates."

I glanced through it. I'd tentatively placed Hailey at the number five position. Either my calculations were off, or the maps offered only a partial picture. Twelve-year-old Kristin Brown had gone missing two months before Hailey. "Let's copy the file on Kristin Brown for Wayne, just in case. She vanished from that area. He already has Hailey's file."

"Done."

"Good. Now, in this poem, we have a red flower, which is pretty common, and white water, so we're looking for a river, maybe." I glanced at Natra. "Am I close?"

She went to the board and picked up a blue marker. "Oconee County is former Cherokee territory, so it was easy for me. With his reference to water, I looked for a river or lake. He says white water, and there's a Whitewater River—it's named that—and it flows into Lake Jocassee. That's a Cherokee word for 'place of the lost one.'"

I gasped. "That's quite a coincidence. I wonder if he realized."

"He had to. It's too perfect."

"No kidding!" I went over to my wall map of South Carolina to see Oconee County for myself. I pointed. "Devil's Fork State Park! It's right here. That's where he'd set the devil's fire. And, look! The closest town is Salem." I looked at the poem and read the line, "'Where witches may ring the bells.'

CHAPTER TWENTY-FIVE

So we've got lots of words and phrases here that support your idea."

Natra brought my attention back to the poem. "There's more. He mentions a ghost. There's a legend about a young woman who fell in love with a member of another tribe. Long story short, he was killed and beheaded. She walked on the surface of the river to meet his ghost. But this area was dammed in 1973 to make the lake. It covered an old Cherokee village. Of course the people had been removed, but his poem does refer to a submerged group and to lost ones."

"Right, and he says, 'now berry's the spirit,' as if his victim's ghost has displaced the one in the legend." I peered at lines that seemed unrelated. "But what's the piggy? And the dancing man? Did you figure that out?"

Natra raised a finger. "Not quite sure. That one stumped me, so I researched the area. The flooding of the Jocassee Gorge was featured at the end of the movie *Deliverance*, which also included a scene at the Mount Carmel Baptist Church Cemetery, now submerged there. Maybe I'm stretching it, but those images fit. There's a piggy scene and a toothless dancing man. I don't doubt Bruder's seen the film."

I read those lines again.

As toothless men dance
to a fiddle, and riddle the piggies who float
over lost ones submerged,

"Okay, I see the possible movie references. This poem seems more sophisticated than the Jasper one. It's harder. In the film, the man treated like a pig was on a raft, floating down the river. The 'lost ones submerged' could be the village or the cemetery. We'll keep that in mind. But what about the double ones?"

Natra pointed at the map. "Route 11, the only road that goes in through the Devil's Fork. It passes through Salem. You have to take it to get to Lake Jocassee. And I think the 'bell' he mentions is the Oconee Bell, a rare flower that grows there. A walking trail lets people see it." She sorted through her stack of papers and pulled out a color photo of the flower.

I peered at it. "But it's white, not bloodstained. I figured he meant a red flower."

"Look closer."

I did. "Ah! Reddish stems and leaves. That does look bloodstained." I tapped it. "The clues certainly seem to fit that area. We need to tell this to Wayne. It'll help him narrow down the search. They can use their sniffer dogs."

"This poem suggests the victim is buried near where people walk to see the Oconee Bell. That trail's just over a mile long. Maybe we should take Mika up there to make a preliminary sweep. We could cover it in an hour or so."

The dog jumped to her feet and trotted over to us. She's always ready to work. I fussed over her and gave her a treat before I asked, "How far is it?"

"Three hours. We could get in and out before sundown. Or we could camp there, if a site's available, in case we need more time."

"We should wait for Ayden. *Someone* is out there who knows Bruder. He—or they—might know the burial locations. They might know about us. So, we take extra care."

I scanned the poem again. "There's gotta be something in here that will lead us. JoLynn could send her drone over the trees again, but let's see if we can pinpoint it more specifically, or just confirm your hunch. Bruder used those three child killers. Let me do some research. Maybe I can see something in their cases. Why *these* three?" To Natra, I said, "You focus on the terrain, see if you can do anything more with this poem."

"Just don't make me watch that movie again."

"Hmmm. Maybe I'll watch it. I'll think about it like Bruder did. He wouldn't throw it in unless it meant something. It's certainly about creepy predators. But let's see what we find in other sources first. Or maybe we should just ask the murder mentalist."

Natra held up a finger. "I nearly forgot. He's responded, and you should listen to his podcast about you."

I'd expected 3-M to meet my charge with something equally aggressive. If there was one thing he wanted, it was credibility. But he'd met his match. With me, people *earn* their credibility. "Is it bad?"

"Sounds just like a sleazy attorney. But he's got a following. They think he's got a special connection with Bruder. You can see how he's building Bruder's case. He wants to neutralize you before you have a chance to be heard."

Mika growled. She ran from the room. Natra and I followed. At the front door, she barked and jumped at it, scratching the wood. Natra pulled her away. We looked at each other. We'd both heard it. A car engine, fading away. My property is isolated, with plenty of warning signs not to enter. No one accidentally drives up my road.

I grabbed my Glock from a table drawer and signaled for Natra to open the door.

Mika ran out. She sniffed around the yard. I looked for car tracks in the dirt, but it was too packed to show anything. I saw no car down the lane, either.

"Let's look at the video," I said.

Natra called Mika back. Inside, she reviewed my security cam recording while I watched, weapon ready, from the window.

"Look!"

I went over. All I saw was a blank screen. I should have seen trees. "Back it up and keep looking."

I strode outside to examine the security cam on my porch. Some type of putty covered the lens. Someone had been here. I didn't touch it, in case we could get forensic evidence off it. I took a photo and called for Natra.

She inspected the gummy substance. "Maybe done this morning. The cam was fine yesterday, and Mika would've barked if someone got this close just now."

"She *was* restless. And we had music on, so maybe she couldn't hear. But you were here this morning. She'd have barked if someone came on the porch."

"We went for a walk."

"And no one's on the video before this stuff was put on it?"

"Nothing clear. I could see only a blurred image. I sent it to Joe to see if he can get something more."

I breathed out. "We have to be more cautious. Now I'm convinced Bruder had a partner. And he—or she—was just here."

Mika yipped. Nose to the ground, she moved quickly along a trail that only she could detect. We followed. She went around the side of the house and stopped under the window to my office. Barking twice, she went down into her alert position. I stared at the grubby burlap bag in front of her. My heart raced. Something the size of a bowling ball was in it.

Natra beckoned Mika away and gave her a treat. We backed away. Whatever was in that bag stank...of death.

Chapter Twenty-Six

Wayne's team removed the bag and putty for analysis. On preliminary inspection, the bag appeared to contain only dirt, but I knew they'd have to sift through it and do an elemental analysis before they could confirm this. I doubted the putty would yield much. Inside, we showed Wayne Bruder's recent poem. He stared at it as Natra told him what we thought.

"We have to go to this park," I said. "If Bruder's heard the news of our discovery, he might have an accomplice dig up whatever's here."

Wayne shook his head. "No."

"Whoever dumped that bag might've seen the poem on our board and knows we know. Why would he dump the bag right there if he weren't standing there? Why not toss it on the porch?" It disturbed me to envision someone with ill intent outside my window, watching us.

"Wouldn't Mika have barked if someone got that close?"

"Not necessarily. We had music on. I think the person parked on the road and walked in. Or crept in. We heard a car engine back here."

Wayne crossed his arms and slowly breathed out as he studied the poem. He asked Natra to walk him through it again. I wanted to get moving, but I forced myself to be patient. Wayne took photos with his phone.

Finally, he seemed to grasp the stakes. "Okay, I'll get someone to watch the entrance. This guy's savvy. But don't even *think* about a midnight requisition crew." That was a private joke from our financially strapped grad student days, when we'd fake-plan supply "acquisitions."

"We'll be there first thing in the morning to go in."

Wayne shook his head. "The way I see it, worst case scenario, they've only just now seen what you've discovered. So, if they're planning to dig up remains, they'll hit that dumpsite tomorrow at the earliest. Right?"

I couldn't hide my annoyance. "So you think a killer's accomplices will observe the park rules? No walk-ins after hours? And by the way, you can camp there and stay in cabins, so they could pose as someone with the right to be there."

"I said I'd get someone in place."

"He could already be there. It's three hours away, and it's been that long since someone left that bag."

"Annie, it's a public park. What do you think he's going to do there?"

"Dig up evidence."

"He's not digging holes where people can see him."

"He can wait till dark, when no one's on the trails. That's what I'd do. And that's soon!"

The expression on Wayne's face told me I'd finally made a mark. He left the room and went outside to use his phone.

I looked at Natra. "We need to get up there. Find a place for us to stay as close as possible, so we can be there when the park opens tomorrow. Locate Ayden. He can work his AirB&B connections for dog-friendly places."

Wayne came in to say he was leaving. "Keep your gun close tonight. And Kamryn's not coming here till this place is safe."

I raised my hands. "Of course."

"I'll post someone here."

"No need. We're heading up there."

"Don't go in ahead of us. We'll be there by sunrise."

"You should use Mika. I know you have handlers—"

"Fine, Annie. Just don't interfere."

I stood my ground and lifted my chin. "You believe me now, don't you?"

His jaw tightened. "Let's see what we find. If you're two for two, we'll develop a task force. Got any more poems?"

"We're looking through our file."

"Well, don't hold out."

When he left, I walked around, stopping at the crime scene tape that barred us from the area where Mika alerted on the bag. No usable footprints had been found. I rubbed my arms and wondered what the creepster had seen through my window. I wished I'd opened the bag when we discovered it and taken some samples, but I knew better. And Wayne knew I knew better.

I went in, locked the door, and took my laptop into the kitchen to look up Bruder's murder mentors. I heard Natra on the phone. We'd have to leave soon. My go-bag is always packed for two nights, which seemed sufficient. I was ready.

I searched my files until I found the three child killers I thought were referenced in the poem. Tkach had been a cop in the Ukraine during the 1980s. He'd used his training to deflect other cops from figuring out his murders. He'd go to recently retarred railroad lines because the odor would thwart dogs from detecting his scent. Also, he wanted his colleagues to think the killer had followed the victims from a distant town on the rail line. But when he'd gone to the funeral for a victim—the daughter of a friend—someone recognized him as a man seen with the girl. Under arrest, he admitted that over twenty-five years, he'd killed more than one hundred women and girls. But I saw nothing, aside from his clever deflection, that helped us with Bruder.

Joseph Duncan III seemed more relevant. He'd killed a family in Idaho to kidnap a girl, 8, and a boy, 9. He'd kept them captive, repeatedly assaulting both. He'd taken videos of himself naked, raping the restrained boy and claiming, "The devil is here, boy, the devil himself! The devil likes to watch children suffer and cry!" Duncan got his start at age 15 by raping a boy at gunpoint. After he went to prison for murder, he maintained his blog through a groupie, who posted his letters. Bruder had begun in his teens, too, and he was likewise using people to keep his notoriety alive.

The third killer, Robert Black, had murdered four girls he'd picked up in his delivery van. The youngest had been five. He'd assaulted several others and remains a suspect in more. He developed a thorough knowledge of back roads, which he used as hunting grounds and disposal sites. He changed his appearance several times, using beards, mustaches, a shaved head, and different types of glasses. He tended to keep the girls for hours to repeatedly assault them before killing them. He was finally apprehended in the act of an abduction. In his van were restraining devices, a sleeping bag, girls' clothing, assorted ropes, sticking plaster, a Polaroid camera, a mattress, and sexual aids. He said he liked to dress in the clothing of little girls.

I wondered if Bruder had similar paraphilias. How long had he kept Hailey? When had she realized he meant her harm? Had he tortured her? Yelled out the devil's name? I shut out the thought of her sweet, round little face, eyes wide in terror, knowing that no one was coming to rescue her.

Natra interrupted. "Ayden got us a place."

"Great. Where's he?"

"Believe it or not, he's an hour from our destination. Near Greenville. And he says he's found something important. He'll meet us there."

Chapter Twenty-Seven

On the way, we listened to Monroe's latest podcast. He held nothing back. Just after he provided the intimate thoughts of a spree killer I'd once evaluated, Monroe said, "This psychologist thinks she understands him, but his thoughtprints say otherwise. None of her tests even came close to the truth. I'd call that professional incompetence. She should return whatever outrageous fee she received, because she was w-a-ay off. And I dug around for more about her, cuz she's pretty visible. She calls *me* out as a fraud, but she claims to seek proof of ghosts so she can be invited to haunted places to get stuff to mock. She uses people for her gain."

I'll admit, I find hokey tales far more often than genuine incidents worth a second look, and I could be snarky. But I sensed Monroe just warming up. I glanced at Natra.

She pointed at the phone. "Keep listening. That's just the appetizer."

Monroe sounded sneery. I could just imagine his expression when he said, "She's got a word for those of us who put our sweat and tears into solving cold cases. Slinkers, she calls us. But Hunter's a slinker, too. She sees what she wants to see. What does she call that? Confirmation bias."

Natra turned up the volume. "Here it comes."

"For those of you listening, you know I'm trying to help an innocent man, Tommy Ray Bruder, get out of prison. You heard Carly Krebs describe her own change of heart about him. And I emphasize *heart*. We have an entire team investigating this, and we've all come to the same conclusion. He was set up, first by the real killers and then by the police. Can five of us, all from different parts of the justice system, be wrong? I ask you."

"Happens more than you think," I muttered.

"And if we're right, then some people are in danger. Because the real killers are out there. Not to mention the damage done for the past two decades to a completely innocent man, locked up unfairly. Now think about Dr. Hunter. She's determined to stop us, because she claims Bruder abducted a friend of hers. She says she witnessed it. You can check out her podcast, listen to her for yourself. But she's been stupid. She contradicts herself. On another podcast, she demonstrates how trauma affects memory. She said a witness to a crime can't offer reliable eyewitness evidence because she's been exposed to a horrific event. So, wouldn't that also apply to a fourteen-year-old girl named Annie who supposedly saw her friend get on a motorcycle with a stranger and watched them ride off? Wouldn't that trauma *affect* her, even compromise her identification of the kidnapper? You bet it would! And did! Ergo, by her own reasoning, her account is unreliable."

"A-hole!" Even as I steamed, I had to admit he'd been clever. "He got me. And now he can rally his fans while also preparing to undermine me at a hearing. He'll make me a flawed witness. And probably use my past testimony about similar situations against me." I glanced at Natra. "I've coached other attorneys on the same strategy." I made a sharp turn that made Mika jump up in her seat and pushed Natra to the door. "That does hurt us. We need solid evidence. I hope Wayne makes that identification."

"*And* links it to Bruder," Natra added.

"Right. Do I need to listen to any more?"

"It's just more of the same. Nothing of substance. But anyone who might be waffling on Bruder could now lean more toward him. He really did you in."

"Shut it off. 3-M might be a fraud, but he's a savvy opponent. We need to keep in mind his pose as a murder mentalist. That's *his* weak spot."

"Better not say 3-M on the air. He'll have a nickname for you. Addled Annie or some such thing."

I nodded. "Yeah, you're right. Maybe I should stop the frontal assaults.

He just annoys me."

"Did you notice that car following us?"

I looked in the rearview mirror. "Hmm. Sedan or van?"

Natra glanced at the side mirror. "Gray sedan. It joined us just before we got on the highway."

"Got any alternative routes?"

"Take the next exit. Let's see what happens."

In a few minutes, I was off the highway. The sedan didn't follow. But something else occurred to me. "When you went for a walk this morning, did you lock the door?"

Natra shook her head. "Not sure. I wasn't going far."

We looked at each other. "I think someone went in. That's why Mika was restless. She smelled someone who doesn't belong." I swallowed. "Maybe someone planted a bug, heard everything we said about the poem." I drove in silence as I absorbed this. "I'm glad he wasn't still there when you came back. He might have killed you both."

"He must be more interested in information than elimination." She tensed. "Stop the car!"

"Why?"

"Because it was there when he was there."

"It was locked."

"It could have a tracker."

I pulled over and opened my door.

Natra grabbed my arm. She whispered, "Wait. Let's think. They don't know we know. They believe they're using us. So, can we exploit this? Turn it around?"

I stayed in my seat, though I really wanted to just find the thing and rip it off. I breathed in. "You're right. They already know we've pinpointed Jocassee and have ideas about the poem. And I told Wayne we're headed there tonight. So they might already know where we're going. Did you talk with Ayden about where we're staying? Mention the name?"

"No. He texted me the information. I put it into the GPS."

"And you had your phone this morning when you went for a walk?"

"Yes."

"So, I think we can safely rendezvous there. We'll park away from the place and have Ayden pick us up. Text him to stay alert."

I drove back onto the highway. I considered the situation. If we were right about who'd done this, I had an open line to Bruder. And he might have sent a message, whatever that bag was supposed to be. I hated that his associates could have entered my house, but I also appreciated the opportunity to set a trap. I just had to figure out how.

Chapter Twenty-Eight

Ayden had that look of discovery that lifts my heart. I had him running in several directions, but I knew he could keep them straight. Not only had he gotten us a comfortable dog-friendly rental home near our destination, he had a pizza and a bottle of *Ghost Pines* red wine breathing.

I accepted a glass. "There's no ghost in this case."

He shrugged. "Not yet."

Natra held up a finger. "Actually, there's a ghost legend."

"Maybe you should call Airic," Ayden said. "See if he's got anything new. We're running dry on that score. Right, Mika?"

She yipped and came to him for a vigorous ear rub. Natra raised an eyebrow to warn him not to feed her from the table. Ayden saluted.

I opened the pizza box and grabbed a piece. "He's not keen to work this case, but I plan on getting back to him." I lifted my glass in a toast.

We gathered around the dining table while Natra related to Ayden our suspicions about a bug in the house. He listened, wide-eyed. "No word yet about the burlap bag?"

I shook my head. "No. So, they haven't found anything obvious. But Mika's reaction to it was strong."

Ayden looked from Natra to me. "He was *that* close."

I narrowed my eyes. "Who?"

Ayden slid a brown 8x11 envelope toward me. "This guy, maybe. I found a likely associate."

It was my turn for surprise. "Of Bruder?"

123

"Of Bruder. Turns out, he had a cousin a few years older who was involved in a bizarre crime situation. Really bizarre! There was a nasty murder, and basically everyone got away with it."

"Why?"

"Distribution of responsibility, I guess, and just plain cuckoo. You're gonna wanna hear this before you make a plan about keeping that bug in your house. I think this guy's dangerous, and he's still in the area. You don't wanna be close to him."

I removed a stack of papers from the envelope. "Keep going."

Ayden gestured at the papers. "That's copies of news clippings, with some records. I think there's more, but I got what I could before the place closed for the day. This happened nearly three decades ago, so it was hard to find stuff on short notice."

"Give me names," Natra said. "I'll find it."

Ayden wiped his mouth. "Take notes. It's complicated. It starts with this 35-year-old woman, Cassandra LaRue. She owned a large house just outside Greenville and had a daughter, Teresa—or, what passed as her daughter. Turns out the girl was kidnapped as a three-year-old, but no one knew that 'til later. Anyway, LaRue made her house a hangout for neglected tweenies. I think one kid was homeless. And one was Bruder's cousin, Keaton Keller."

"Not Bruder?"

"No. But there's a link. I'll get to that. So, the kids who hung out called this woman Ma. She took them to parks, the mountains, and beaches. She gave 'em all kinds of goodies, including drugs and alcohol. She bought 'em clothes. She even let some stay with her when they didn't wanna go home. Basically, she was grooming them and watching for vulnerable ones."

I grabbed a tablet for my own notes. "I think I saw this movie. Sounds familiar."

Ayden nodded. "The plot probably came from this case."

"Where'd you find this information?"

"From an appeal. Ma was initially convicted of murder, but she challenged, and the conviction was overturned. The legal document named all the kids involved, which surprised me. And Keaton and a girl named Reese Wendham were charged with Cassandra as co-participants."

Natra copied down the names.

I leaned forward. "Who was killed?"

"Teresa, the alleged daughter. She was eleven. For reasons not made clear, Ma kept her chained to a claw-foot bathtub for weeks and made the others beat her every day with a plastic bat."

I gasped. "What? Why would they do it?"

Ayden finished chewing and wiped his mouth. "I told you, this is weird. Here's how she operated. Apparently, she had a sexual fetish for harming kids. She liked to see their bruises and broken bones, and hear them scream for help. But she didn't want to do it herself, so she used a coupla creepy maneuvers to get these kids to do it so she could watch."

"My god!" I closed my eyes to take it in. I'd heard of males with such fetishes, but not females. But I did know of mothers who'd made some of their kids harm their siblings. I urged Ayden to continue.

"The really whacky part is how she persuaded them. She said an ex-con—a killer—was watching them through cameras in the house, and he'd directed her to make the kids become enforcers. He'd designate a kid, usually Keaton, to beat the others. If the enforcers resisted, the ex-con threatened to torture them and kill their families. So, they did what they were told, and also kept it quiet. Eventually, Ma started speaking as if this guy inhabited her, like he was another personality. She'd inject herself with something and start speaking in a low voice."

I looked at Natra before I asked Ayden. "How old were these kids?"

"Around ten to twelve."

"Impressionable, but who'd believe such a story? And why didn't they just go home to their parents?"

"When the beatings started, Reese and Keaton had already moved in. They had no place to go. And maybe they weren't that bright. Maybe that's how she picked them. And Ma got them to cut off all ties."

"Isolation, ignorance, and dependency," Natra commented. "Powerful tools."

I held up a hand. "I don't understand. Why did their families allow it?

125

They were too young to be on their own."

"Like I said, she identified kids whose families didn't care. Substance use, overcrowding, neglect. Keaton's dad was in prison. The court report said his mother did come to Ma's house once to get him, but when he refused to leave, she gave up. She was an addict and had her own problems, I guess."

"So, Ma would inject herself to make it seem like she was putting the killer's personality inside her?"

Ayden nodded. "Yeah. She called him Pa. So, he was Pa to her Ma. She'd switch back and forth, like a good cop, bad cop in the same body."

I rubbed my face. "And her second maneuver?"

"Hypnosis and guided imagery. Basically, brainwashing."

"So, she used fear and cognitive retraining."

"Right. Apparently, she'd train them on key words that triggered them into action."

"That's remarkable! And so predatory. She had a sexual fantasy that involved beating kids—"

"We saw that before," Natra said. "That guy who grabbed kids to break their legs so he could keep them in his room."

I nodded. "I remember."

"This was just girls, apparently," Ayden continued. "Keaton was her primary enforcer, although I think she'd initially beat him too."

I sipped my wine to consider this information. "Okay, that tells us her developmental pathology. Maybe she was beaten as a child. Victim becomes victimizer. She looked for kids she could force into doing things that aroused her."

Ayden sat up. "And there's one other thing. I think this is important. Ma had sex with Keaton."

I stared. "How old was he?"

"Twelve, going on thirteen."

"Good lord! A powerful incentive for a boy. And how long did all this go on?"

"Almost a year. Reese and Teresa had healed bones from earlier breaks and a lot of bruises."

"Was Reese chained up, too?"

"She said she was. And she was starved and made to wear diapers until she agreed to help beat Teresa. She was kinda treated like a neglected dog. But it came to an end. After one beating, Teresa went unconscious. The kids just kept hitting her to get her on her feet, maybe scared they'd have to take her place. But she didn't move."

Ayden took a bite of pizza while we waited. He gestured for patience. "I've been at this all day. I'm hungry. Sorry. So, anyway, Ma thought Teresa was dead. She knew they had to do something with the body, so she bought duct tape and some large plastic bags. She made Keaton wrap Teresa from head to toe."

Natra stared at him. "Alive?"

"According to the records, Keaton kept saying she was still breathing, but Ma turned into Pa and ordered him to continue. He put the bags over her and taped them closed. They broke open a wall to stuff her inside and sealed it with wallpaper. That's what one article said."

I hugged myself against a sudden chill. I could only hope the poor girl hadn't regained consciousness to find herself helplessly bound and suffocating inside an inescapable black tomb. What a horror.

Ayden continued. "It all unraveled a week later when Ma ordered Keaton to beat Reese. She was thirteen. She decided enough was enough and ran to the police. They didn't believe her. The tale was too fantastic. She was taken back to her family and they said she was a habitual liar who made things up to impress people. So, after a few days, Reese snuck back into Ma's house to find proof."

"That was bold."

"By this time, Ma was packing up to abandon the house and flee with Keaton. He saw Reese and came at her with the bat. But he had a black eye and other bruises, so Reese figured he was Ma's new target. Reese urged him to go to the police with her and get Ma some help. He'd just have to inject Pa into her, so the cops could arrest them both at the same time. Then they'd see how Pa had forced her to do these things."

Natra made a face. "Reese thought Pa was real? Crazy."

"I know. But they'd been brainwashed. Give me a sec." Ayden checked his notes. "Right. At first, Keaton didn't respond. He just helped Ma pack things up. The next day, Ma took a bat to him and broke his hand. He went to the police to bring them to the house."

I shoved my plate away, having lost my appetite. "So they found the body."

"The place still smelled of decomp. It was probably easy to find her. And the autopsy showed she'd lived for several hours after being taped up."

I cringed. "I hoped you wouldn't say that."

"The police went back to Reese, and she confirmed everything. She also showed them where Ma kept a stash of pictures she'd taken of Teresa chained to the tub. The DA figured this was a slam-dunk first-degree against Cassandra LaRue. But Cassandra blamed Keaton. Said he'd taken advantage of her severe mental illness to force her to do things to the kids. He'd beat her, too, and he'd killed Teresa, the daughter she loved."

I shook my head. "Did that work?"

"It might have until they discovered Cassandra had kidnapped Teresa. The other kids weren't even there at the time. But then she found a new scapegoat. Pa! She said Pa had made her abduct Teresa and bring in Keaton to enforce the captivity."

"She played the mental illness card. Multiple personalities."

"She tried. The DA did get a conviction, but the kids had described the whole Ma and Pa scenario in enough detail, with enough consistency between them, that a psychiatrist convinced the appeals court that due process had been denied. An evaluation showed that Cassandra had dissociative identity disorder and was therefore too psychotic to be deemed responsible. She got a get-out-of-jail-free card."

Natra leaned back and looked at me. We'd seen this hired-gun scenario with mental health experts too often.

"And where's Ma now?" I asked.

"Dead. An accident."

I raised an eyebrow. "And the kids?"

Ayden tapped the papers. "I found some op-ed pieces about them, and an article that covered the crime on an anniversary. For some, they were heroes, bringing a female sadist to justice. For others, they were bad seeds who should have acted much earlier. Reese, in particular, was thought to have been a cold-hearted psychopath destined for a life of crime. Both went to juvenile for brief stints. Their names were changed before they were released, but Keaton took his back. He said he hadn't done anything wrong, and he wasn't giving up his name."

"I beg to differ. Can we find this Reese?"

Ayden gestured toward Natra. "Maybe she can get through the red tape of juvenile records."

"Okay, Jax might help with that. He knows people. We might need her. And you think Keaton's an accomplice for Bruder. He'd be in his forties now, right? Did you find a photo?"

Ayden sorted through the papers and pulled out a copy of a news clip. "Best I could do."

I examined the blurry photo. Not as striking as Bruder, and thinner, but still handsome. He had short dark hair and the kind of arched eyebrows that make me think of calculating predators. I did see the family resemblance in his long neck and strong jaw. I passed it over to Natra.

"You said his father's in prison?" I asked.

Ayden nodded. "Was. He's dead now."

"Any brothers or other relatives who might be helping him?"

"Not that I saw. He and another kid were arrested together for a car theft. He had some arrests for petty stuff, like drugs. He got some jail time, but not prison."

"He had to've been damaged by the sexual abuse and being forced to beat the others, not to mention by Cassandra's accusations. And wrapping up a girl with duct tape. Any suspicion of his involvement in Cassandra's death?"

"That happened years later, just after she was released. A psychologist had determined she was no longer a danger. But she was obese and barely able to care for herself. Within a few months, she apparently fell down the stairs and hit her head."

I narrowed my eyes and looked at Natra. "Let's get that autopsy report. Or talk with the coroner. A lethal crack to the head, maybe with a baseball bat, could've been inflicted and then disguised as the result of a fall."

Natra wrote it down.

"I don't believe it, either," Ayden said. "And one more thing you should know. Keaton was at Bruder's trial. A crime reporter spotted him and mentioned his notorious background. That's proof they're acquainted. And the next day, someone set a fire at the newspaper office."

"You think it was him?"

"It was arson. And I'd guess he's an angry guy."

I sat back. "Great work, Ayden. We've got a potential murder partner for Bruder who's been abused and who'd abused others, specifically kids. He was sexually conditioned toward it. And he probably learned he'd buried a girl alive that he thought was dead."

Ayden checked through his notes. "Oh, and also, Cassandra made him chop off Teresa's fingers. Forgot that part. She wanted to keep them."

I stared at him. My heart pounded. "Oh, god! We need to learn more about him."

Natra followed my track. "He's not a partner."

I shook my head. "He's Bruder's *mentor*. And he's out there!"

Chapter Twenty-Nine

J D and Tim Wheeler parked next to us in the Devil's Fork State Park lot, near the sign for the Oconee Bell Trail. The brief bloom season for these flowers was long over. We'd already seen part of the trail without Mika, in the dim pre-dawn light. The sticky air, even then, had predicted a muggy day.

I operated on the assumption that Bruder had been here, perhaps with Keaton. I'd watched the curving path from their point of view. Some of it was dirt, but we'd also walked on wooden planks and bridges. Trails of white ribbon that caught the breeze marked the way, but the path was always visible despite the abundance of dead leaves. I watched for fire symbols carved into the thick red maples or white oaks, especially near water. A pond and some streams offered soft dirt for potential burial spots, but uphill areas seemed more covert. I wondered if they'd set any fires. I figured Keaton had influenced not just his cousin's murder ambitions but also his attraction to fire. If they'd worked together, either could have carved the mark we'd found before. Ayden's story about Keaton had filled in some holes. Maybe *he'd* harassed Nemeth to get the "'ridg'nals." Maybe he had other associates. If Keaton had been outside my window or in my house, he likely knew we'd come here.

"I see a few spots off the trail that could be a dump site," I said to JD.

"We crossed a bridge," Ayden added. "Could be underneath. Or on the high ground. And with all the excavation in the park years ago, there'd have been fresh loads of dirt available."

Like Tkach, I thought, scouting for recent work on railroad lines.

131

JD raised an eyebrow at Ayden's comment. "That's a grim thought." He went over to a cop he'd posted at the parking lot entrance to direct unauthorized people toward the other side while we worked. I went to help Natra get a travel bag ready in case we were out for a while. When JD returned, I asked, "Did the cop on watch last night see anyone coming or going, maybe a slender guy, fortyish?"

JD gave me a look. "Now, Annie, you got some info'mation, jus' let us know." He opened a terrain map. Mika looked up expectantly. She knew we were about to work.

Tim squinted at her. "What is he?"

"She," Natra corrected him. "A Doberdor, a cross between a lab and a Doberman."

He crouched to pet her. "Wayne says she's pretty good at this."

"She's excellent. Best dog I ever trained."

JD nodded. "She's a good 'un. We got anothah dawg handlah awn his way. Plus that young lady with the drone. Couple hours."

"By then, we should have results," I said. "The trail's only a mile and a half. If there's nothing here, the park is too large to just search blindly. It's over 600 acres. So, yes, you'll need JoLynn or a very large pack of dog handlers. Did you find anything in the bag you collected at my house?"

"It's at the lab, Annie. Ah cain't discuss it."

I knew him well enough to know if they'd found something, he'd give me a signal. He didn't. But *something* was in it. Mika didn't give many false positives.

Ayden stood away from the group, watching the woods. I went over to him.

"Did you hear that JoLynn's coming?"

He nodded.

"I know you're seeing her, Ayden. You don't have to hide it."

"Not hiding it. But I don't want to mess up anything. She has her work; I have mine."

"So, what's up? What are you watching?"

He shrugged. "Just a feeling. I sensed it on the trail, like someone's watching."

I scanned the trees. Most were too thin to hide someone, but here and there, an older oak or hickory could provide a shield. If Bruder's accomplice were here, he had the advantage.

Ayden crossed his arms. "I really hate these guys who target little girls."

"Me, too. I worry every day about Kamryn." We'd recently had a close call with my daughter.

Ayden cocked his head. "Didn't you say you contacted Bruder once?"

"I interviewed him. I was in grad school, thought I was a hotshot closer-type. Didn't work."

"What's he like?"

"He was around thirty, then. I think he only agreed to see me so he could relive what he'd done and see my anguish. These guys get off on the impact they have on others. I'll never forget the weird light in his eyes and the smirk under his mustache when he denied he'd been near my town."

"Think you're still on his visitation list?"

"I doubt it. Why?"

"Just wondering what you'd stir up if you went to see him now."

I squinted at him, about to press for more when Natra called to us. She gestured to come. They were ready to head out.

"Just think about it," Ayden said as we walked over. "He knows you're being vocal about his guilt. He just sent you a message, right?"

"Only if we're right about who was at my house."

"You know lots more than you did before, boss, especially with the tattoos. You have weapons, and you have skill. I think you make him nervous."

"I'll consider it, pending how this search turns out."

JD turned toward us. "Y'all stay behind. You know the drill."

Ayden and I waited until after Natra and Mika got a start, followed by the detectives. Tim carried a small notebook. I touched Ayden's arm. "Watch for marks on the trees. It's lighter now. We can see better."

Mika ran into the woods and returned, as Natra directed. A squirrel darted across her path, but she paid no attention. In full work mode, she sniffed at tree roots, plants, and the soil. Tim seemed fascinated. JD's posture suggested he disliked this assignment, outside in the heat. Sweat had already soaked through the back of his light gray shirt. He stumbled on a tree root that crossed over the path. I preferred him to Wayne. We got along okay. He even liked the ghost stuff. He'd confided things he'd seen, insisting I never tell Wayne. And unlike Wayne, JD was patient.

We passed signs that described the flora and fauna we'd see along the trail. After ten minutes, Ayden stopped. I turned to him. He watched something I couldn't see. Then he left the path and strode over to a small tree, some twenty yards away. When I caught up, he was examining the leaves. Red berries were just beginning to ripen in a cluster. Ayden looked at me. "This is a flowering dogwood."

I stared at it.

"And the leaves will turn red. Had one in our yard growing up."

I glanced up the path. The others were well past us. I texted Natra to turn back. Mika reached us first, so I had her circle the tree. She sniffed along the ground. Natra ran up. "What's up?"

"Red berries."

Her eyes widened. Tim came next. I explained about the reference in the poem. He nodded. "Worth a shot."

JD lumbered up to watch. Natra worked the dog, making her sniff at areas that formed increasingly wider circles. But Mika didn't alert. Finally, she sat, panting, and waited for her treat. She was done. Natra tossed a baseball cap for her to play with.

"There might be other trees like this in the area," I said. "Let's keep watch for them. And cherry trees, while we're at it. But they have to be mature, more than twenty years old." I pulled up images of a cherry tree on my phone and showed it around.

"Seen some on the other side," Tim said with a gesture.

We found two more dogwoods and a cherry tree. None yielded results. By now, the bugs were getting to me. My repellant was wearing off. We'd covered more than half of the trail.

Tim went back to check for the other dog handler while Ayden forged ahead to locate the target trees. I sat on a wooden bench. Mika came up to lick me. I gave her some of my water and praised her. She was doing her best, I knew, but she picked up on disappointment. We'd need to take a break soon.

Ayden appeared up the path. He stopped and beckoned. Then he turned and disappeared. We found him some ways off the trail, up on a ridge. I climbed up to see another dogwood. Mika sped past me. Natra and I both ran after her.

At the top of the ridge, she sniffed at a spot, circling it before she yipped twice and gave her signal. JD caught up. I stared at the ground as Natra took Mika away.

"I can't believe it," I said.

JD nodded and looked at me with a grim expression. Ayden stood with his hands on his hips. He pointed. "I guess we know where the dirt in the burlap bag came from."

There was no doubt from Mika's reaction. This was a body dumpsite. Or, had been. Now it was just a three-by-five-foot hole. But the dig had been recent. At the bottom of the hole was a cluster of fresh red berries.

Chapter Thirty

We didn't wait around for the crime scene unit. They'd have to take samples, sift through dirt, and record video. I'd looked for a symbol carved into a tree, but JD had insisted we leave. He wanted only cops there now. Tim had made a fuss over Mika before he went out to purchase food and water for a long day. He seemed to have a new respect for our team.

I had to distract myself. Had Hailey been buried there, only to be moved to where we'd never find her? It was beginning to feel like a nasty game I might never win. But I believed I was getting closer. We'd been just hours from this discovery.

Ayden called JoLynn. She was close, so he told her what had transpired and rerouted her to our rental place for lunch. She arrived just as I set out a platter of crab salad on croissants.

"Jax sends greetings," she told me. "We had quite an interesting session with his grandfather yesterday."

Ayden winked at me. *That's* why he'd gotten the *Ghost Pines* wine. He'd known about it.

I poured her a glass of lemonade and invited her to sit. "I meant to call him last night, but we had to be up early today."

"He knew I'd see you. And it's kind of my story to tell. That's what he said."

"Aren't you still working for Wayne?"

"No. I mean, they'll pay me for going out of my way today, but my work is freelance. After Ayden called, SLED confirmed they didn't need me. They've brought in a state anthropologist to work on the recovered remains, and the digging at the Jasper County site is done. I think they've cleared it and put boards over the hole. Wayne said I could send my sensor results to our research team, so they're excited. They all want to meet Digger and Mika."

The dog raised her head. Too tired to get off her pad, she waited for a command.

"It's okay, girl." Natra made a hand gesture to reassure Mika her job was done for the day. The Doberdor snorted and put her head down.

I took a seat. "Too bad you came all this way."

"It's fine. It's on the way to Chattanooga, where I'm heading after lunch."

Ayden pointed at her. "Meteorology meets murder."

JoLynn smiled. "It's an intriguing forensic case. During a storm over there a few months back, a guy was killed. Determined as weather-related, but now they're not so sure. They want me to give an opinion."

"So you're done with our Jasper County case?" I asked.

JoLynn made a hand gesture that suggested otherwise. "I thought so, till last night."

Ayden leaned toward her. "So, tell us."

"Well, I hadn't expected to get pulled into a séance. Or, I guess it wasn't quite that. Jax had another word for it. I was at his farm to set up a training area. My drone inspired him, so he's bringing in some dog handlers. My research team will also be there."

Natra perked up. "When?"

"Not sure yet, but he'll tell you. There's a lot to set up in advance."

Ayden cleared his throat. "And the séance?"

"Okay, right." JoLynn took a quick sip of her lemonade. "So, I don't ordinarily think much about all this paranormal stuff. I didn't even know that side of Jax. We mostly deal with legal things. But his grandfather—Puca?—was in some kind of trance, and Jax asked me to help anchor him. That's the way he put it. I guess they generally work in threes?"

"Right," I said. "But he has Dylan."

"Dylan was away. And actually, the message was for me. Or for us." She gestured around the table.

Natra smiled and nodded. Ayden pulled his chair closer.

"Us?" I asked.

"Well, I guess you know how it all works, down there in his cave."

I nodded. I'd been there, underground, where Puca did his spirit work. I'd once envisioned Hailey there during a trance session. The experience had upset me. But it had also encouraged my current effort to find her.

"I didn't really know what to do, but Jax said just to sit quietly. I had to dress in white cotton and go in barefoot."

I'd done the same thing. "No tea?"

"Yes, there was tea. I'd even thought maybe it had made me hallucinate except for how specific the result was."

Natra leaned in. "What did you see?"

JoLynn turned toward me. "Do you know what the girl looked like? The one you think was put in that grave?"

"Yes. I have her description from the missing-persons report."

"Okay. So, I didn't know much about her. Ayden didn't tell me. You didn't. But it's possible I overheard something from one of you. I didn't, but I know you like to cover all bases. And you're right to be careful. I admire that."

I looked at Ayden. He held up his hands and shook his head. "Nothing from me, boss." I turned my attention back to JoLynn. "What did you see?"

She hugged herself. "I still get shivers. I'm the least likely person to be a channel. I've never even considered doing something like this. I've always kind of laughed it off. And I didn't *see* anything, at least not distinctly. It was more an impression. It felt female, like she was behind me. I wanted to look, but Jax had told me to sit still. It wasn't cold, like you always hear, but just... very... *physical*. I knew I had to go back, like I was *directed*."

I leaned in. "Directed?"

"To the grave site."

JoLynn drew a piece of paper from her pocket to show me.

It was similar to the drawing Puca had presented to me from my own session. Just primitive lines that formed an irregular shape.

JoLynn laid it on the table. "Puca drew this. I didn't understand it. Neither did Jax, but he said I'd know what it meant eventually. I'd know when I saw it."

Ayden could barely keep his seat. "That's what happened to us!" He looked at me. "Remember, Annie! When we saw those planters on the highway and knew they matched your drawing?"

I nodded. He was referring to an earlier case.

She held up a hand to indicate there was more to the story. "Jax and I went back to the site. Police tape was up, but no one was posted, so it wasn't still protected. Not fully. Jax wanted to see if we could link the drawing to anything. He'd gotten something, too. Maybe that's why they work in threes. You merge what everyone received, right?"

Mika jumped up and came over to Natra. The dog had sensed the rising excitement. Natra let her stay near the table.

"What happened?" I asked.

"Jax wouldn't tell me what he'd received. He wrote it down, folded it, and gave it to me to open when the time was right. I'm so curious! How do you know when the time is right?"

Ayden pulled Puca's drawing toward him. "This could be anything."

"Right, but in context, it made sense."

"So you saw it," I said. "You know what it is."

"The area around the grave had been trampled. When I was there that night, there were a dozen people. You saw them. I told Jax that any processing now would be contaminated, but he said that didn't matter.

We got there late in the afternoon and walked around. He wondered if there might be another dumpsite there, so he looked for that symbol on other trees."

"Did he find any?" Ayden asked.

"No. We were there for a while, but I didn't see anything that resembled the drawing. Jax told me not to look *for* it but to just stay open."

I nodded.

"He told me to let my impression lead me. I didn't want to believe I'd actually received a message from the dead, but Jax said it's more often thoughts or impressions from the living." JoLynn looked at me with wide eyes. "So, I relaxed and tried to let it guide me. I went over to the dumpsite and let my mind wander. Then I saw it." She tapped the lines on the drawing. "The crime scene tape. This is the shape it made. I think something's here."

I breathed out.

"We have to go back," Ayden said.

I shook my head. "We'd have to go through Wayne. We tell him what? That we got intel from the air that something's still there?" I looked at JoLynn. "Did Jax have any advice?"

"Well, there's one more part. It's on his piece of paper. After we figured out what Puca's drawing meant, Jax said what *he* received is for you. I haven't looked at it."

She extracted another folded piece of paper from her pocket and gave it to me. I felt all eyes on me as I opened it. I desperately hoped it was about Hailey. But it was just more enigma: a triangle with a symbol at one point.

I shrugged and passed it around.

"What does it mean?" JoLynn asked.

"I don't know. But the symbol looks familiar."

Natra studied it. With her level of immersion in our data, I thought she'd surely recognize it from something. But she handed it back. "I agree. There's something familiar about it, but nothing comes to mind."

I stared at it for a moment before I asked JoLynn, "Did Jax give you any other ideas about it?"

"No. I thought you'd know what it means."

I shook my head. "Let me find out what's happening with the evidence." I grabbed my phone and texted Wayne to call me before I said, "Bruder's got a dangerous partner out here. We need to find the other graves before they're dug up."

"His damage path," JoLynn commented. "That's what you need to figure out."

I cocked my head. "Damage path?"

"Like a tornado, what it leaves behind. That's how we figure out their characteristics. We look at the devastation between their point of origin to where they finally lose steam."

"Exactly!" Ayden slapped the table. "We need to remap Bruder. Maybe he's just a spin-off tornado from his cousin's damage path."

My phone rang. It was Wayne. I grabbed it and excused myself. I went outside for privacy. When the call was done, I sat on the porch and stared at the road. Ayden came out and sat next to me.

"You okay, boss?"

"Not really. They're releasing the identity of the remains from Jasper. It's Robin Dahl. But there's no physical link to Bruder. Despite the tattoos and poem that led us to the grave, he could always say he had info from the real killer."

"What about at the park? Anything there?"

"JD found nothing on the trees. What we saw is all there is, unless elemental analysis offers something. So, I can't tell if it has anything to do with Hailey. Another dead-end."

Ayden frowned and touched my shoulder. "Any *good* news?"

"No one's come back to the lake house. It's safe to return."

"About that."

I looked at Ayden. "What?"

"I was thinking of going with Jo to Chattanooga. It's less than four hours. She's on a case, but she's also giving a demo. I want to see it. I can be back tomorrow night."

I considered it. I had to go see Janissa, and Ayden had done plenty of work on our case. "Okay. That's fine. We're stalled right now. Go ahead." Then I remembered. "There's one more thing. Wayne found someone in law enforcement who's dealt with Pete Nemeth. There's an old warrant out for him, so they put some effort into tracking him down. They found his place. The trailer was torched."

Chapter Thirty-One

The red Jeep Wrangler parked at my lake house made me smile. Jax! He'd accepted my invitation to a 'wine, dine and mine'—a brainstorming session with food and spirits. I'd adopted the practice of working in threes, but Ayden had gone with JoLynn. Jax said he'd been thinking about the case, so he agreed to come. Secretly, I hoped he also liked an excuse to see me.

As I parked, Mika raised her head. Once Natra opened the door, she shot out of the car and sped down the path. I heard Digger bark. I followed Mika down the path to the lakeshore. Jax waved and came toward me. I felt revived. And safe. He always seemed clear-headed, even when we'd endured a hurricane as we chased down his brother's killer. I welcomed him with a hug.

"Any more developments?" he asked.

"They have an ID on the remains we found but no link to Bruder. Or to the Devil's Fork site. JD took soil samples, but I don't need a lab to prove it was a grave."

"Mika told you."

"Yes." I watched her bark and circle Digger. "Wish we'd had Digger, too. JD trusts Mika's nose, but two sniffer dogs are always better. Maybe their dog handler confirmed." I gestured for us to go back, and Jax called for the dogs. We headed up the path.

"Did you go inside and read the poem?" I asked.

Jax nodded. "I did. And I checked the *Killer Hooks* website, but there's nothing else."

"Sounds like JoLynn had quite the experience in your remote session." I hoped I didn't sound as jealous as I felt.

Jax gave me a sidelong look, as if he'd sensed I was fishing for something else. "Puca received something related to the grave site. JoLynn was there, and Wayne's responsive to her, so I thought it was better that she get it than you."

I nodded. "You made the right call. But I'm not sure she'll persuade Wayne to go back in. Certainly not with spook signals."

Jax shook his head. "Love your pithy tags, Annie. She only needs him to release the site or authorize her to keep looking. She won't tell him about the session. And by the way, she surprised me. She felt something. I didn't expect that. Maybe I should have, with her affinity for unsettled weather."

We entered the house and went into my office, where I grabbed bottles of iced tea from my mini-fridge—raspberry for me, green for him. "Any ideas on what that triangle drawing means?"

Jax sat down. "It's from Airic."

I stopped in my tracks. "I thought he was quits with this case."

Jax shrugged. "Puca invited him into a session. He never refuses his mentor."

"And...?"

"There's a context. That's why I came. Wine and mine, as you said. Maybe we can mine some gold."

I sat down and gave him a suspicious look. "So Puca and Airic received these things *before* the session with JoLynn. Sounds contrived."

"You're new to how we work. Our sessions are like picking a harvest. You could fill your bag with all the fruit you see, but it keeps growing. Since I'm staying involved, Puca will keep watching. By extension, he watches others linked to me. He thought JoLynn might attract something, and she did want to return to the site. That was all her. And she could be right." He shrugged. "Too soon to say."

Natra came in with a plate of cheese and apple slices and sat down with her notepad. I thanked her and leaned toward Jax. "Did *you* get anything?"

He looked up at the poem on the whiteboard before he said, "I think there's another person involved."

"So do we. That Keaton guy."

"I mean a *third* one."

I frowned. "Why?"

His dark eyes showed concern. He pointed at the board. "When did you write this poem here?"

"After we found it on the website," Natra told him. "I wrote it the next morning while Annie went to Wayne's office. Around 9:30."

Jax nodded as if he'd expected this response. "I think someone moved the remains at Devil's Fork before your trespasser showed up here. He didn't see it on the board, drive three hours to the park and then return to leave the bag. There wasn't enough time. But the digger must have known you'd seen the poem, or that you'd eventually see it. When did you put the map of Oconee County up there?"

"Same time."

"So, someone knew you had Bruder's map before you drew it here." He looked at me. "That means someone on your team, or Pete Nemeth, and whoever Pete might have told, is aware of it. Maybe JoLynn knew?" Jax raised an eyebrow.

I shook my head. "She knows now, but she didn't know before she was invited into the investigation there. I'm sure Ayden didn't tell her."

"Someone knew you had the maps, and someone knew a poem existed that could lead you to the Devil's Fork grave. The question is, are these two working together or against each other? One seemed to want to lead you there, but the other didn't."

Natra nodded. "Makes sense. The digger wouldn't have exhumed remains in the middle of the day, not there. It's an active recreational spot, still in season."

I rubbed my face. "The poem alone could lead someone like me to the grave. Krebs posted that, so a lone person could have figured I'd see it, emptied the grave, and then come here and left the bag."

Jax leaned back. "The poem doesn't isolate a location without the map."

I looked at Natra. She shrugged and said, "Not this fast, probably."

"I'm still not convinced."

Jax looked at me as if he thought I were being deliberately stubborn. "Didn't Nemeth tell you several people came to him?"

"He did, yes. And now someone's burned down his place."

"Or *he* did," Natra said. "He told you he was leaving."

"Hoarders don't burn their own stuff. I hope he got out, but I don't think he set the fire. I think someone came after he left, couldn't find the maps in all those stacks, and just burned everything to destroy them."

Jax tapped the table. "This poem and map signal to *your* watcher your awareness of Devil's Fork in Oconee County. You also got it right in Jasper. He knows you have some kind of guide. You were at Nemeth's. And soon, you were looking at the right spot. *Someone* is aware of you. Be prepared. Be *over*-prepared."

I felt a chill. "Why didn't they burn down *my* house, then?"

"You've got cops patrolling. Whoever's aware of you likely knows your connections with SLED. No one will investigate an arson at Nemeth's, but your place is a different story."

I sat up. "So, who'd know I have the maps?"

"Someone who knows Nemeth, I'd guess. Maybe that person told him to give the maps to you."

"Why?"

"You're pretty vocal about Bruder, Annie. Your listeners know you want to link more victims to him. And now one's been discovered."

"No one's mentioned Bruder yet in the media."

"Which limits our interested parties. Maybe his cousin, Keaton Keller."

I gasped. My heart raced. "You looked him up!"

"Didn't have to. I saw a presentation a few years ago on the Cassandra LaRue case. Keaton was a suspect in her death. The situation was unique, so I asked to see his juvenile file. I still have my copy, so I read it again. He's dangerous."

Natra held up a hand. "Slowly. I'm taking notes."

When she was ready, Jax continued. "One person or another has abused him since childhood. You won't like this, Annie, but Bruder might be telling the truth. Maybe he *was* forced, just the pick-up guy. Keaton Keller's damaged. He's one of those victims who turn the violence they endured on others. He's got a serious mean streak. When he wrapped up that little girl, cut off her fingers, and stashed her in the wall, he didn't think he'd done anything wrong. That was his testimony. He seemed confused that anyone thought he'd committed a crime. He called himself an enforcer. If he failed, there'd be dire consequences. But he was scared of losing LaRue. That's what mattered to him. That's *all* that mattered."

Natra looked up. "But he went to the police."

"Because he thought he could save LaRue from the man who supposedly coerced her, this 'Pa' character. Only there wasn't any such man. And Keller was shocked when LaRue was arrested. He blamed himself."

I leaned in. "Was the girl, Reese Wendham, a suspect in LaRue's death? Or just Keaton?"

"I read only his file."

I stared at Jax. I felt Natra watching me. She knew I'd resist this new hypothesis. I breathed in and expelled it before I spoke. "Okay. What am I missing?"

Jax leaned toward me and put his hand on mine. "The bigger picture, Annie. You're focused on Bruder. For you, *he's* the bad guy. But if he's a pawn in a larger game, you're fishing for a tiger shark while the Great White swallows you."

I felt a flush creep up my neck. "And who's the Great White?"

Jax studied me. "Are you really listening?"

I got up, saved the image of the poem on the board, wiped it, and picked up a black pen. "So we don't lose sight of this, here's what's in *my* mind."

I placed the numbers one through four along the left. I drew a B to the right and circled it, then drew lines from the circle to each number. "B is Bruder. From info on his maps and tattoos, we believe he's linked to four murders." I pointed to each number. "One victim's been identified, and one has an eyewitness—me. Maybe Hailey was in the empty grave, but if not, we could have a third one there." I gestured toward Jax. "We now think his cousin, Keaton Keller, could be involved." I drew a K below the B and circled it. Then I stared and blinked.

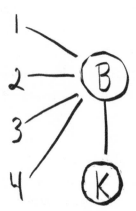

I turned to the others. "Keaton. *He's* the burner. We thought the K image was a symbol for fire. But it's also his initials."

Jax stood and came over. He picked up the green marker and drew another circle on the right. Then he drew lines from his mark to the circled initials B and K to form a triangle.

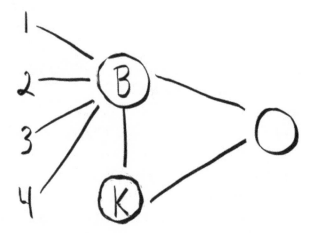

He tapped the edge of the board. "This is Airic's contribution, or how I see it. First, he got the 'K' confirmed at the Jasper site. Then he got this." He pointed to the empty circle at his triangle's apex. "It suggests a third person, currently unknown. Whoever it is might be the game master. If you figure that out, you won't need poems or maps. This person knows the whole board."

I stood back. "The symbol Airic drew isn't exactly a circle. It resembles a flower."

Natra looked up at me. "You should talk with Bruder. He might be ready to tell you more. He's trying to gather allies."

I felt a hot flush. "I'll *never* be that man's ally!"

"Still, he might think it's worth a shot to get you on his side. Then you can pick through what he says. He might reveal a name."

Jax set down the pen and crossed his arms. "I agree. But you need an open mind. He knows who's involved. I suggest you play it like there's more at stake than keeping him locked up. He wouldn't be revealing things, even cryptically, if this were just about him. In fact, maybe his recent visibility has put him in danger."

I frowned. "Why would *he* be in danger? He's sending the messages."

"I'm just offering ideas."

"Well, you haven't yet told us the impression *you* got in the session. What *aren't* you saying?"

He nodded. "You won't like this."

"Jax!"

"Annie, you're so strongly invested. I don't know if you can appreciate this. But my impression was of the poet. The one who wrote the Oconee poem."

"And?"

"And…it's not Bruder."

I waited a beat. I didn't like tension between us, but Jax didn't budge. I took a breath. "What about the maps and tattoos? The poems coordinate with them."

"Someone else knows about them. I think Carly Krebs is being used. Her fascination with Bruder has made her an unwitting channel."

I sat on the arm of the couch. "So, who's the poet, then?"

"Maybe Keller. We saw the K on the tree. And in the other poem, *Mirrors*. What I have on file for him is consistent with the predatory energy I felt around this poem. I still feel it."

I couldn't deny I'd sensed that too. "How would he know—? Ahhh... you think *he's* the killer."

"I think he could be."

"And the first poem?"

Jax shook his head. "I have no impression from that one, even with the embedded K. But the styles are different. The second one is easier to figure out, but in Jasper, we'd never have found that girl if not for JoLynn's drone, not from the clues we had. It wasn't a set of directions like this one is, not unless he provided a way to decipher it."

"A way? To...Krebs? He sent the directions to *her*?"

"Maybe."

"But if she'd followed it and found the grave, that would've undermined Bruder's whole case."

Jax shrugged. "Depends on what he said. Remember, he's claiming he was framed."

I pointed to the circle without the initial. "Maybe this is just the lesser accomplice. Could be Pete, who had the maps. Maybe *Keaton's* the game master."

"Whoever it is, Annie, he's playing a very treacherous game. With *you*."

Chapter Thirty-Two

In the morning, I prepared to meet Janissa. I still burned from the evening before. Jax had rattled me. Again. He had a way of exposing the stone foundations of my notions as nothing more than sand. He trusted the spirit messages, 'though he conceded their ambiguity. Like the K symbol. Did it stand for fire or for Keaton? Or both? We'd hashed it out over dinner and late into the evening, trying out different theories. Each had holes. I'd argued for my own, which made me feel safer, but I couldn't ignore what Jax believed. And his logic was solid. There was definitely *one* other person involved, probably Keaton. And he might have gotten very close to me. Given what we'd seen at the Oconee grave, it hadn't been hastily emptied. Someone had drawn us there, and that person—or a third one—had used the location to send a message. The berries hadn't dragged themselves to that hole.

Before he left, Jax had urged me to be careful. "Cold cases with living killers are perilous."

Even now, I glanced out the window and sniffed for smoke before I checked the surveillance cam video. I doubted our intruder would return this soon. But he could also be unpredictable, maybe bordering on psychotic.

Keaton had to be damaged by the bizarre situation with "Ma." Turning that same domination on his younger cousin wouldn't be a stretch. I needed to know what had happened with Reese. She'd been part of this, but she'd kept her new identity, which would pose a hurdle. Jax had promised to look into it. Once we had more info, I'd get Ayden or Natra on it. I had no doubt Reese could tell us things...if she were willing to. She wouldn't be the first victim to turn me away.

Like Amber Bell. I sensed she had a secret about someone with a significant role in her situation but didn't want to expose them. I had to get my mind back on this. Janissa had sent over a file of the available text messages from Amber's case. I opened it. When Natra came in from Mika's walk, I invited her to join me.

"I'm putting Bruder aside until I can make a new roadmap," I told her. "I hate when Jax erases the one I had."

She hung up Mika's leash. "Like you do with Wayne?"

I snorted. "Touché. I admit it. But we need more info. I appreciate Puca's spirit sessions, but I'd trade them for some cold hard facts."

"No, you wouldn't."

"Okay, no, but I wish we had more corroboration. It's like a cop's gut instinct. Who cares unless it leads to something solid?" Mika pushed at my hand for a treat. I gave her a head rub. "If Jax is right and Keaton's trying to direct this, we should see another poem. Probably soon."

"Nothing new on *Killer Hooks* this morning."

"But what did this guy accomplish by directing us to an empty hole?"

"Duping delight?"

"He's in his late forties, if not older. He's not having a juvenile lark. And he's playing on several fronts, with multiple games that probably converge in some way we can't yet see."

Natra winked. "Call 3-M."

I snorted. "Yeah. Monroe would know." I sat back. "I gotta stop obsessing. I could do this all day, but I need to work on the case I'm getting *paid* for. I'm not ready, and I'm meeting Janissa today."

I spread out the papers. Natra showed me how she'd organized them.

I looked them over. "I should visit Amber again. Maybe I can get her to draw some pictures, like in an assessment. Maybe she'll slip me some clues."

Natra cocked her head. "She likes ghosts."

"Meaning?"

"Automatic writing. She's hiding behind a ghost already. Channeling it—or letting her *think* she's channeling it—might encourage her to show what she really wants to say."

I gave this some thought. "Intriguing idea. First, let's look at the texts. I think there's something there. Or something *not* there that should be."

Doyle had introduced the most damning of Amber's texts in court, and Janissa had responded with the most mitigating. Any juror might believe they had the whole picture. But that's not what I saw when I looked at the digital download in order, especially framed with Trevor's comments. There were many more texts than the jury had heard.

The transcript was wrenching. Trevor showed significant fear and uncertainty as he prepared to end his life. But I needed a sense of their actual relationship.

"It's just weird," I commented. "Amber supposedly told people Trevor was her boyfriend, but she hardly ever spent time with him."

"Kids today run their relationships on their phones. Not much depth to that."

"Yes, but he was a physically healthy teenage boy, and they'd lived within an hour's drive. He had a vehicle, but they didn't hang out. So, what's in it for him? What's this about? Janissa thinks Trevor was depressed and wanted to die. Amber, his girlfriend, had encouraged him to go through with it, supposedly expressing her support. He'd been to see Maura Reynolds, but then Amber canceled his next appointment. More support? I don't know. Seems more like erasing support."

Natra set down her coffee mug and leaned over me. "Look at the progression of the texts."

"First, let's think about her behavior. She does all this texting with him. She hears him die. But then, when his body's found, she acts devastated. She comforts Trevor's family. Then Trevor's mother finds notes on his computer that show Amber knows more than she let on. When police pick her up, her cell phone records show she'd told Trevor what to do. So, all of this looks bad for her, but clearly Trevor did want to die."

"Seems like she wanted it too. But why?"

"Let's start here." I pointed at a longer text. "Trevor writes that he has everything ready. He's determined. He says, 'I'm going to do this. I just don't know how to do this to my mom.' Then Amber writes, 'Don't think about it. You keep saying you're going to do it, and then you don't. You're ready. Just be strong. It won't take long.'

Several more texts from Amber echoed these sentiments, growing almost insulting. I shook my head. "It's hard to believe she cared about him. I don't see compassion here, despite her claim."

Natra flipped a page. "That's what Doyle said, right?"

"Yeah. Her acquaintances said she didn't care about him, so in court, she came off as duplicitous. And that's the impression I had. He'd pledged his love to her, but she'd offered wooden replies. She'd never really connected. Her responses to Trevor's anguish and confusion follow a pattern: 'man up,' 'it'll be quick,' 'don't overthink,' 'why is it taking so long?' Like she was reading from a menu."

"Maybe she was."

I looked at Natra. "Meaning?"

"Maybe someone else wanted Trevor dead."

"I thought of that. But who? And why? None of the investigators found evidence of someone else involved. There aren't any texts to her phone that direct her."

"Maybe they weren't looking for that."

I read through the transcript again with this in mind. The phrasing repetition jumped out. I stopped and leaned in to reread one part. Then I placed the transcript in front of Natra. "Do you see anything unusual here?"

She read for a few minutes, then shook her head.

I pointed. "During the hours before Trevor finally ended his life, there was an interruption in the flow of texts. Right here. Amber took a call. She mentions a friend checking in. Doesn't it seem odd she'd accept a call when she's talking to her boyfriend about the most desperate moment of his life? When she might actually hear him die? Why not just let the other call go?"

"A kid might do that. Especially if she wants an alibi. Could've set it up that way."

I breathed in. "Maybe. I'll ask Janissa about Amber's phone records. I want to know who called her. But here's what I noticed. Just after the call, she urges Trevor to delete his messages. By then, he's slurring his words and telling her how tired he feels. He's probably having difficulty breathing. And then..."

Natra pulled the transcript close. "You're right. She repeats a phrase. 'You need to rest.' She says it three times."

I went back through the transcript and saw variations of this theme. "There's a change during their final conversation. She said it different ways earlier, but here, right here, she says it exactly the same all three times." I looked up. "You're right. I think someone gave her instructions."

Chapter Thirty-Three

I checked with Ayden on my way to Janissa's office. He was in the field with JoLynn. The phone reception was spotty, so I kept it brief. "Did you call Wayne?"

"Did ya one better, boss. JoLynn has a friend at the police lab, so she's got the inside track."

"That dirt has to be from the empty grave."

"Don't hold your breath. Somethin's up. We should know soon."

"Text when you know. Just FYI, stay vigilant. Keaton's out there, and Jax has info that matches yours. We could have a problem."

"Copy."

I ended the call with an uneasy feeling. Ayden had just added another unanswered question to my growing stash. What could the lab have found in that sack of dirt? I felt as if I were pushing against a stuck door that had a secret latch. I couldn't force it. I had to find the latch. I thought if I could just get one significant mystery solved, others would yield as well.

Janissa had her files ready when I arrived. She already knew I thought Amber was hiding something. She'd had the same impression, so she was eager to give me access to her records. She'd put her investigator on the mystery caller.

I think it's always better to show than tell, so I used my copy of Amber's texts to explain my concern.

Janissa scanned the strange pattern. "She seems to be repeating several different things, like 'don't overthink' and 'just do it.'"

"I agree. Ordinarily, repetition could just show her cognitive limitations.

She can't think of any other way to say it. But that phone interruption signals a change in behavior, like it's urgent she get with the program and do it right. Like she's being coached. Honestly, Janissa, it reminds me of a hypnotic instruction."

She made a face. "As in, after I say this phrase you'll act like a chicken?"

"Not quite. More like the caller would've prepared Trevor to be nudged by a phrase past a tipping point."

"The caller *wanted* him to die?"

"I'd say so. I sense that Amber's not really close to him. He thought she was, maybe because he was so vulnerable. Maybe she's helping someone else. Now that I reconsider this, it's like she's doing something she doesn't want to do because someone's making her. I hear foot-dragging and irritation. She'd been working Trevor for a while."

Janissa put her hands on her hips. "If that's true, then she belongs in prison."

"Maybe. It depends on why she did it. And right now, it's just a guess. I'm trying to make these pieces fit."

"Should you see her again? Tell her what you think?"

I shook my head. "I'd rather not tip my hand just yet. If she gets nervous, she might alert the caller. I need her to just think I'm working on her case. But do try to find out if anyone's contacted her since her conviction."

Janissa's phone buzzed. She lifted an eyebrow and picked up. She listened before a look of disappointment crossed her face. When she ended the call, she said, "Sorry, Annie. The number's from a burner phone, activated with fake info."

I held up a hand. "My digital guy once told me to try to locate the store where it was purchased. You might be able to focus on the area with location traces and look up possible points of purchase. Cops can help, if you have a connection. There might be surveillance video."

"Worth a try." Janissa made a call. While she was talking, I looked through her file on Amber. Beneath transcripts of Amber's interrogation was a set of photos of Trevor's body, with blotchy red and blue patches from cyanosis. I spread them out.

He'd used a method, once rare, but increasingly more common with the spread of suicide chats on social media. You can get sodium nitrate, a powdered meat preservative, in a suicide kit, pre-measured into a lethal dose. He'd purchased one and ingested the substance with swigs of beer. Amber had assured him it would be painless. I doubt it was, but I wondered how she knew. Sodium nitrate deprives the body of oxygen, causing hypotension. He'd likely experienced altered states of consciousness. The anguished expression on his frozen face seemed bathed in surprise and regret. He'd died alone in the woods. He'd been there nearly two days before they'd discovered him. By then, he'd been bloated and discolored. It had to have been heartbreaking for his family.

I've seen many death photos, but they always bother me, especially with kids. This death, I thought, had been preventable. In that moment, I hated the girl I was supposed to be helping. I barely heard Janissa say, "Surprisingly, we've located three stores where the phone could have been purchased. The buyer wasn't sophisticated or possibly wasn't trying to hide the purchase. And they all have a surveillance camera."

I nodded. "That's good. It'll take a while to go through the film. I could have my investigator do it." Ayden, I knew, would hate me for dragging him away from his weather lessons.

"I have my own, Dr. Hunter. I'll get on it."

"My digital guy, Joe, could be helpful. Here's his number." I wrote it down. "I'll let him know you might call. He's quite innovative." I didn't mention Joe's various inventions from his Dark Web explorations. He's a cyber security expert who does some work for me in exchange for using my private digital lab. I'd already filled him in on this case, since it leaned so heavily on cellphone communications.

When Janissa told me the store locations, I realized I could stop there myself on my way home. Once we'd finished our business and made a plan for me to see Amber again, I got back in the car. As I was about to call Ayden, my phone rang. To my surprise, it was Maura Reynolds.

"Hello, Dr. Hunter. I'm sorry I didn't get back to you right away. I'm in Tennessee. I'm doing an assessment here on Tom Bruder. He's been depressed…well, a bit more than that."

Just the sound of his name flushed me with red-hot wrath. But I controlled my voice. "More?"

"I really shouldn't say. Some kind of news coverage that's disturbing him. He's pretty despondent. I'm concerned he's suicidal."

I waited. I sensed she wanted me to say something. "Do you want another opinion?"

She pulled in her breath. "Well, I'm not sure. I mean, you're certainly the expert, but that might be a conflict of interests."

I knew bait when I saw it. And I had my own. "Or an opportunity to change my mind about him. Your attorney thinks I don't really know what I saw." I despised giving 3-M any ground, but it seemed the best way to play this game. I was sure Maura's concern was an act, but it would help me bypass some visitation formalities.

"I'd really value your opinion. I've learned so much from your research. I'd love the chance to collaborate *and* change your mind. Let me ask my team. I'll call you back."

"I'll be waiting."

I wasn't going to wait. She'd ignored professional protocol for a reason. I could just hear my team's response. Ayden would light up. "That's your way in!" Natra would warn me it could be a trap. I suspected it was. No doubt Bruder had learned about my resistance to his legal maneuvers. I was sure he'd told Maura I'd instigated the discovery of the remains, and they had to neutralize the damage. But I thought I could tread the treacherous waters.

The idea of seeing Bruder again, armed with what I now knew, flooded me with energy. I could be one step closer to finding Hailey. A very *big* step. I had Natra book me on the next available flight and drove straight to the airport.

Chapter Thirty-Four

I saw the weather warnings as I got off the commuter plane in Chattanooga late that afternoon. My gamble had paid off. Maura had called just before takeoff to invite me to the prison.

Ayden picked me up. He said JoLynn would try to meet us later. "We need to watch this storm front, boss. It's almost suffocating! Can't believe your flight wasn't delayed."

I snorted. "Don't pretend you're not hoping for nasty weather. You thrive in it. I should be in and out before it gets bad. I just need to make my connection with Bruder so I can follow up on my own. I'm sure this invitation is his idea."

"What's he got in mind?"

"To see what I'm up to or to stop me."

Ayden shook his head. "He doesn't know you. There's no stopping Annie Hunter when she's on a track. He's in for a nasty surprise. So, I got something from Wayne. Coupla things. He said there's no remains at Nemeth's place, so Nemeth got out before the fire."

I nodded. I knew Ayden felt badly that our visit might have caused the loss of the Panty Thief's property. "Anything else?"

"The soil from the bag at your place." Ayden looked over. "It's not consistent with the Devil's Fork hole."

I frowned. "There were traces of decomp, which we know from Mika. In both places."

"Yes, the lab confirmed that. But the bag contained a lot more red clay. So maybe it's from another one."

"Red clay! That's up and down the entire Piedmont range. That doesn't narrow it down. I need to tell Jax."

"Already done. He's checking the Jasper County grave, but Jo said she doesn't think it's from there. Remember, she already took samples. But she can't eliminate other locations in that area. Natra went to help look for holes. Wayne said JoLynn can go back with her drone."

"Good work. You've been busy. And we know there must be other graves. They could be there. Let's hope for some clues."

"Our cold case is heating up. What's next for me?"

"Not sure. You might be back on the Amber Bell case."

Ayden glanced at me. "Not suicide?"

I shrugged. "It's suicide, but maybe not as simple as it seems. I'll tell you on the way."

With Ayden driving, we made good time. He absorbed the new data about Amber without saying much, but I knew his brain was alive with ideas for leads. He sped too fast around a couple of turns, and I had to remind him to be careful. As we arrived at the prison, I noticed darkly ominous skies to the south. Ayden called JoLynn at the weather center, and she urged us to be vigilant. The humid conditions were ripe for a major storm.

"If it gets worse," I told Ayden, "make reservations for us to stay put. I don't know how long I'll be, but keep watch. I'll trust your judgment. Meaning your *protective* instinct, not your compulsion to indulge in extreme conditions."

He grinned. "Copy, boss."

Maura called and told me she'd made emergency medical arrangements for me to get through the prison protocols. Soon after Ayden dropped me off, I found myself face to face with 3-M himself, Monroe the Murder Mentalist. I hadn't expected this.

He was a foot taller than me, with a bit of middle-age pudge straining at his belt. His navy tie and white shirt clashed with his snug jeans and leather bomber jacket. He took a stance in the middle of the hallway, thumb-in-belt, to make it clear I wasn't getting past him. But I got close enough to show he wouldn't easily stop me. Close enough to smell cinnamon on his breath.

Close enough to see that the folded lower lids of his hazel eyes were like a chameleon's, especially when he blinked. Despite wrinkles settling in and some gray threading through his russet hair, his face displayed a boyish quality. A vagrant curl begged for someone to smooth it back in place. It wouldn't be me.

Monroe looked down his nose. "I don't approve of you being here, but Dr. Reynolds insists we accept your help." He spoke so softly it almost made me lean in.

I knew this ploy: low-key dominance. I raised my chin. No one had a better right to be here than me. "Maura said there's a suicide note. I created the field guide for note authenticity. It makes sense for her to consult me."

"You're biased."

"So are you."

He smirked. "I'm sure you'll dismiss whatever I say, but he's agitated enough to harm himself. That's what I read from him. His thoughts are all scrambled."

I peered at him. I'd considered Bruder's legal team to be a sham, a way for 3-M to surf on the success of Carly Krebs' "Captain Kidd" podcast. He had the funds to hire Maura, but he had to know this team had little chance in court. I couldn't calculate what was in it for them. And then there was Bruder. Of course, he was desperate to get out before more charges were added, but faking suicidal depression made no sense. I figured it was bait. He'd learned of my specialty in suicidology. He wanted me here. I had no doubt that Maura or Monroe had filled him in on the content of my podcast, including my memories of Hailey—"Cherry" to him.

"We'll be in the room, too," Monroe said. "Dr. Reynolds and I."

"I prefer to see him alone."

His jaw tightened. "Then turn around and leave. Because that's not happening."

"Fine. Just don't interpret him to me. Let him speak for himself."

"I know you don't believe—"

"It's easy to guess how a killer thinks and exploit a gullible audience. I'm not a gullible audience."

162

Monroe sneered. "You should drop the attitude. I could do things for your career."

I bit back my sardonic retort. I just needed to see Bruder. "I'm here for a consult, and we're wasting time."

"First, there's this." Monroe handed me a piece of paper. "What's your take?"

On the paper, I saw a drawing with a few brief handwritten lines. A stick figure with a sad face stood near a burning house. Looped around its neck were two ropes, one on each side, which led at angles away from the figure to form a 'V.' Each rope terminated at a tiny circle with something scribbled inside. Another line above the figure linked the circles to complete a triangle, like Airic's. My impression was of someone caught between two forces that were working together.

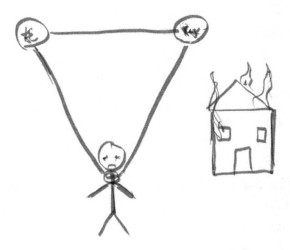

Monroe interrupted my thoughts. "We think he might be planning to contrive this in his cell." He air-drew a triangle.

I cocked my head, thinking, *If you're so psychic, why are you guessing?* His eyes narrowed, as if he'd realized his mistake. "That's what he's thinking. That's his plan."

I wouldn't give him the benefit of *my* doubt. Or tell him what I really thought. I felt sure Bruder did not have the means in his cell to pull this off. But the drawing told me Jax had been right. There was a third party. One of them was the primary choreographer. Whatever was scribbled in the circles might reveal what I needed to know. I had to see how Bruder managed the game. Because it was *his* game, not Monroe's or Maura's.

I leaned in to read the three phrases.

fire buries Everything

in Pieces, they Laugh

Half asleep, th-ree se only the red bloom of doom.

It made no sense. I noted the odd spacing and spellings, as well as the misplaced capitalizations. This guy liked his codes, yet the style differed from the dumpsite poems. I read it again and opened my hand to request the drawing. "I'll need to ask him about it. I assume he knows you have it."

Monroe pulled it away. "Dr. Reynolds has already asked him. He's not talking."

"Have you requested a suicide watch?"

He hesitated. So, no.

"Okay, how did you get this note? Suicide plans are generally secret. Why would he give you this?"

"A guard found it in his cell."

"That means there's now a suicide watch on him. As his attorney, you should know that."

Monroe's face flushed before his mouth formed a thin line. "Of course there is. That's why they let you in."

He turned and escorted me to a cinderblock room with a bare table and wooden folding chairs. Cold and harsh. Maura rose from her seat. The tension around her mouth conveyed concern, as if she really believed her client could harm himself.

And there he was. Tommy Ray Bruder. I gritted my teeth and felt perspiration form under my shirt. I caught his fleeting look of recognition before he lowered his gaze to the table. He knew I was the witness who saw him grab a girl.

Chapter Thirty-Five

I'd met Bruder years earlier, when I was a graduate student. Everyone in this room knew that. I'd discussed it on *Psi Apps*, especially once I'd launched into denouncing the efforts to free this jerk. I'd half expected Bruder to jump up and yell at me, but here he was, docile and depressed. Or acting like it. He'd gained some weight, his hair was shorter, and his face was pasty, but he still resembled the handsome mustached stranger who'd made two girls on a country road eager to jump on his bike. This time, he didn't smile.

Maura started to introduce us but stopped and waved her right hand as if to say, *whatever*. She had me sign an agreement to keep what happened here confidential. In her shoes, I'd have done the same. But I stipulated that my professional judgment might include a review with my team. She hesitated, then agreed. This surprised me. It also confirmed that something more was at stake than a clinical eval.

Monroe pulled out a seat for me opposite Bruder. I ignored him and walked around the table to sit close to my foe. I wanted to make him feel cornered by the one person in this room who'd seen what he'd done. He had to realize the discovered grave in Jasper County was just the first step in a process that would link him to more. Yet he seemed undaunted. We sat close enough for me to see details in the tattoos hugging his arms and climbing out of his orange shirt collar up his throat. One of those could show me where Hailey was buried. I wanted to rip open his shirt and demand to know which one.

Bruder stared at me, waiting.

I reminded myself to stay flexible. My ideas on this case had been upended several times. New elements had entered, which I hadn't yet collected into a theory, including his suicide drawing. Monroe slid it across the table near me. I made a mental note to study it so I could replicate it later if they wouldn't let me take it. Bruder glanced at it. I saw no ligature marks on his neck.

I leaned toward him. "You remember me?"

He nodded. Up close, he did seem distressed, as if he weren't sleeping well. The dark circles and red lids looked real. I smelled body odor.

"You know why I'm here today?"

He raised an eyebrow and flicked his brown eyes toward where Maura sat before he nodded once more. She couldn't see his face, but she leaned over the table catty-corner at his right, squinting with apparent concern.

I used my fingertips to pull the sketch closer. "Did you draw this?"

Bruder placed his entire open hand on it, then curled his fingers and used his index finger to tap four times on the written lines.

I tried again. "Is this how you feel?"

His eyes opened slightly. He tapped again, four times. His finger had landed on a phrase, *red bloom*.

"Is that the Oconee bell? The red bloom?"

A flash of exasperation crossed his face. He pulled on his right earlobe. I felt as if I were playing a game of Charades, something I wasn't good at. This was no suicide analysis, despite the façade. It was all I could do not to grab him around the throat and force him to tell me what I wanted to know.

I breathed out. "Is it the bloodstained flower? Where toothless men dance?"

His eyes went blank. He hesitated, blinked, then nodded once.

Something was off. He should have followed my lead. I decided on a direct approach. "Are you in danger of killing yourself?"

He made a chopping motion with his hand. Then he uttered his first word, in a raspy voice. "Maybe."

I pointed to the stick figure. "Is this you? Is it how you feel, or what you're planning?"

Monroe crossed his arms. I felt his impatience. I hated being watched. I had my methods, and they usually worked, but scrutiny made me tense. I looked at Maura. "Is there any chance we can be alone?"

She glanced at Monroe. He shook his head. I saw a flash of satisfaction on Maura's face. Bruder, too, indicated no. But did he mean he didn't *want* to be alone or that they wouldn't allow it? Something about this team didn't cohere. I stayed alert for micro-signals.

"I think Mr. Bruder will be more comfortable if I'm here," Maura said. "And he does need his attorney."

Bruder raised his left eyebrow, the one that only I could see, then dropped his gaze to the table. I looked at the drawing and wondered if Maura and Monroe were the two on the end of the ropes around the stick figure's neck. They were certainly connected to each other and seemed to be hovering.

I tried to appeal to Maura again. "I signed the paper, so he doesn't need an attorney. But have you administered any suicide assessments yet?"

"Of course. That's why I called you."

I began to think this wasn't an act. Maybe Bruder really was considering suicide. I recalled Jax thinking Bruder might be under someone else's control. And I had my own reasons for wanting him alive. I needed him to tell me what he'd done with Hailey. So I returned my focus to him. "Has something happened recently to upset you?"

This question seemed to surprise him. He leaned back, his eyes wide. "You!"

My heart quickened. I had an opening. I dashed straight through. "Do you mean me finding one of your victims?"

Monroe brought his hands down hard on the table. "Stop!"

I jumped. Bruder blinked but kept watching me. A slight movement of his eyes said I'd guessed right. Maura's face looked strained.

Monroe drew himself up. "There will be no talk of victims or murders or anything that implicates my client in a crime. Obviously, I need to stay in the room. You're here for one purpose only, Dr. Hunter. If you can't observe the limits of your role, I'll escort you out."

I flashed 3-M a nasty look. "If my activities are the cause of your client's depression, it's a fair question. I can't very well do an assessment if I'm boxed in."

Maura leaned toward Bruder. "Tommy, please tell Dr. Hunter what you mean. We want to help."

Bruder glanced again at the note. Then he rubbed the top of his left hand and raised it to graze over his earlobe. I noticed the image of a red flower in his tattoo. A recent tattoo, I thought. Vivid. A very red bloom.

But what the hell did it mean?

He leaned toward me. "Can't sleep. Have to stay alert."

"To what I'm doing?"

"It's deeper." Again he flicked his left ear.

I knew better than to lean closer. "Deeper *than* or deeper *in?*"

I felt Monroe bristle, but two quick blinks from Bruder suggested the latter. Or both.

"You should know…." He tapped the drawing, "this is what happens to—"

A guard rapped on the door. Monroe opened it.

"We'ah goin' on lockdown. We got a tornado warnin'. All inmates in their cells. All visitahs must leave. Y'all need to git tah cuvah."

While Maura and Monroe spoke with the guard, Bruder pointed to the drawing and whispered, "Next time, bring *candy*. Peanut butter." His index finger curved backward over his right shoulder, toward Maura and Monroe. Then the guard came over to cuff him and hustle him out. The look he gave me conveyed the impression he might never see me again.

Chapter Thirty-Six

I reached for the note, but Monroe snatched it.

"I need to study it," I insisted.

"No."

Maura looked peeved. I sensed the interruption was more than annoying. She'd had a plan. I leaned over the table. "I can't give you an opinion from just this interview. He does look depressed, but he barely said anything. If you show me your clinical notes and let me examine his—"

Maura frowned. "I'll be in touch, Dr. Hunter. Let's hope he can hold on for now." She walked out. Monroe gestured for me to follow. Maura disappeared. Her abrupt departure rattled me, but I wasn't about to ask Monroe about it. He turned me over to a guard, who showed me the way out.

Once I had my phone back, I went outside. A warm gust nearly blew it from my hand. I texted Ayden. The darkening sky had triggered lights to turn on. Monroe emerged. Without a word to me, he bent into the wind and strode toward the parking lot. Maura wasn't with him. I wanted to wait for her so I could ask her to let me see her files, but Ayden arrived. I looked back at the door. No sign of Bruder's psychologist, so I climbed into the truck.

Ayden did a drum roll on the steering wheel. "We got a tornado, Annie!"

"It's just a warning."

"Nope. Supercell with a funnel spotted southwest."

"Get us to a safe spot, then, please. I need paper. Where's your art pad?"

Ayden reached into a bag behind his seat and produced one. As an artist, he always has paper and professional pencils. I sorted through his drawings to find a clean sheet, then sketched everything I could recall from Bruder's note. Ayden took off. He made a quick turn, which made me make a mark where I didn't want it. "Easy, please. I need to get this exactly right."

"Copy."

I narrated the contents of the session to my phone with some commentary. When I felt the truck climb, I looked around. "Where are we going?"

"Best place I can think of."

"For what? Getting swept into Oz?"

"I scouted it, Annie, don't worry."

"I know you. I *am* worried. We should get inside."

Ayden raised a hand to assure me it was under control. "We have reservations, but there's a place we can get a view. This is so rare! We'll stay in the truck till we know it's not coming at us."

Brittle rain pelted the windshield with a sound like a crowd of people crumpling stiff plastic wrap. To my right, trees lost a flow of leaves as their branches snapped in fitful waves. I closed the art pad and sat back. I still didn't know quite how to think about what had just happened. I raised my voice over the noise. "Did you talk to Natra?"

"Hasn't called back. Jax said she left."

I picked up my phone. A text from her indicated she was heading to the town where Cassandra LaRue had abused the kids. She wanted to research the newspaper archives. In other words, she was in Keaton's territory. She knew to be wary, but I felt a hit of anxiety. I sent a text to urge her to call when she could and then described our situation. "What did Jax say?" I asked Ayden. "Any evidence of new digging at the site?"

"They walked around a wide area with the dogs but got nothing." Ayden glanced over. "So what's all this about peanut butter and red blooms?"

"I don't know. I need to sort it out."

"What was it like seeing him?"

I thought about this. "Not like I expected. He wasn't...arrogant, not like before. Maybe he's mellowed out. But I had the impression he expected me. Or, needed me. That's closer. He *needed* me. I think he was trying to communicate something but couldn't say it in front of the others."

"He remembered you?"

"No doubt about that. But he offered nothing to help us. And he didn't actually seem depressed. Disturbed, yes, but not depressed. I definitely wasn't invited for some specialized suicide assessment. And Maura knows I'd figure that out. I think she had something in mind, but maybe the weather crashed her plan. She'll try again."

Ayden pulled over at a lookout area where we could see lights from a couple of towns in the valley below. We were out of the rain. A gust of wind rocked us. I gripped my seat. "How far are we from the hotel?"

"Not far." He grabbed his weather radio from the back. Its static-y report warned us about severe storms. A siren's distant wail confirmed this.

Ayden called JoLynn and put the phone on speaker. "What do you see down there?" he asked.

I heard animated male chatter in the background as she answered. "We have two funnel reports near here, and a sighting north."

I gasped. "There are *three?*"

"Maybe more. People don't realize Tornado Alley's had an eastward drift. Twisters form here more often now, and where there's one, there can be others."

"Looks like optimal conditions," Ayden said. "Warm, humid air, with a cold front pressing in. Low clouds, lots of trees."

"Right. We see a potent line of thunderstorms west of you. If warm air causes an updraft, you could see a vortex. Let's hope it's not like the one that stayed on the ground for over two hundred miles."

I pulled needlessly on my already-tight seatbelt. "Sitting on a dryline is not where I want to be." I'm not the weather fanatic Ayden is, but I know that a shifting dryline that separates dry from moist air attracts storms. "What's the strongest tornado for this area?"

JoLynn checked with a colleague before she responded. "An EF4, nearly two hundred miles per hour, but it's not just about wind speed, Annie. It's also how far they travel, where they go, what's in their way, and how long they last. Each damage path has its own distinct characteristics. And you can

171

get micro-tornadoes inside the main one. In one event, we had an outbreak of nearly a hundred twisters across ten states. In another, three hundred and sixty popped up in just four days! One tornado endured for nearly four hours, killing over a hundred people."

I hugged myself. "Thanks. Now I feel safe."

She laughed. I didn't.

Ayden's eyes shone as he watched in front of us. The rotating clouds looked like muddy water circling a drain. Multiple bolts of lightning that blanched the greenish-yellow sky illuminated low-riding clouds. Another gust shook a tree near our truck. In the valley, a bright yellow flash snuffed a web of lights. When the wind shook a tree nearby, I hunched my shoulders. Hail pebbles smacked our windshield, and I smelled the scent of cut grass. My ears ached like I was on a descending plane.

Ayden pointed. "There!"

My heart raced. "Let's get to our hotel."

"We'll be all right. It's a ways away." Ayden reported the possible funnel location to JoLynn. The rain returned as a surge mixed with hail pebbles that blurred our view, despite the wipers going full force. A long roll of thunder overhead warned us away.

To my relief, Ayden backed out. But instead of turning right to retrace the way we'd come, he went left. I envisioned us going over a cliff. I pressed my left foot on an imaginary brake pedal. "You can't see. Where are you going?"

"Don't worry, Annie."

I held my breath. When the rain patter diminished, I breathed out. Ayden parked. We had a better view, but I've never liked front-row seats.

Ayden raised his binoculars, then shouted, "Look at that!"

I watched a building in the valley. A rush of water washed down a sloped roof, shearing off a line of shingles that flew into a spiraling maelstrom like a circling flock of crows. The top of a church steeple leaned, then snapped off. I blinked hard. "I can't see the funnel."

"Probably inside the rain. That's called a bear cage."

JoLynn's voice piped up from Aiden's phone. "Are you okay?"

"You should see this!" Ayden was giddy. "Wish I had a videocam, but it wouldn't show much. I'll grab some images on my phone when we get a better view."

"Listen," she said. "Be careful. An RFD, a rear flank downdraft, can come behind a tornado. It's very destructive."

"Copy."

Ayden handed me the binoculars. "We'll leave in a sec. Just have a look."

I adjusted them and watched a series of reddish sprites brighten the roiling, steel-colored clouds before a long horizontal bolt revealed a thick stovepipe twister. I jerked back. "My god! It's right there!"

More shingles and planks ripped off another roof while a brick wall gave way and punched a set of windows outward. An entire floor collapsed as items from inside went for a ride. A sudden shimmering eruption of light showed the dark Goliath hovering over a village of helpless residents. My mouth went dry.

Ayden shouted into his phone. "Jo, we can see it! We'll probably lose the connection, so meet us at the hotel. Over and out." He turned to me. "Let's go get closer."

Something large thunked against the window, shaking us. I flinched and grabbed Ayden's arm. The rain let up to reveal a better view.

Ayden seemed oblivious to the danger. "Just keep watch for other twisters. If we figure out this one's path and stay downwind—"

"No! We're not storm-chasers."

But he seemed transfixed on the valley. Then I saw why. The stovepipe had collected a whirling gray mass near its base that grazed along the ground. Debris blackened the hem of its undulant skirt. It turned in slow motion, sweeping up a semi and twisting it in the air before tossing it to the ground. Shrieking wind rocked us, and a torrent of hail nicked my window. Ayden swung his arm out to cover me.

Time for my boss hat. "Let's get out of here. Now!"

Ayden glanced at me. He knew I meant it. He nodded and peeled out. I looked back. The pale column had filled with dark shapes that emerged and submerged. Most, I thought, were pieces of buildings or branches stripped from trees. Pressure crushed my chest and popped in my ears in time to hear the noise that people describe as a rumbling train. We'd stayed too long.

Cars parked along the road blocked clear passage as people got out to gawk at the sky or get videos.

Ayden looked at me, and I nodded. This was a rare event, after all. He steered his truck off-road to pull around to give us one more view. Despite the danger, it was astounding to see the tall column sway its hips back and forth like a flirtatious woman. For a breathless moment, it seemed to stand still. But spinning items in its collar showed its furious momentum.

Ayden stared. "Look at that, Annie! Never thought I'd get this close."

I watched people shout and snap pictures. Ayden got out and held up his phone at Mother Nature as she chose her menacing path. I smelled sulphur in the air and stayed where I was. Ayden came back in and steered us eastward. "It's past us now," he said. "I'll find a hill. We can watch."

"Ayden…" I felt grungy from my long day on the road.

"We're helping Jo."

A crowd of cars blocked our way, but Ayden edged in to find a spot. The tempest still spun in front of us, wider now, and tossing lightning spears from its dusky skirt. Green and yellow sparks along its left cheered a transformer's demise. I followed the flight of a telephone pole that shot through the sky and pierced an airborne car.

Ayden raised his binoculars. "This is so awesome!"

"Not if the wind pushes us over." I gripped my seatbelt and tried to keep my breathing even. My skin felt clammy. I didn't have to tell my weather buddy how unpredictable tornados can be, but weather events like this were his cocaine. The whitish funnel sucked up another building and spat out bricks in all directions.

I thought of the prison and assumed the guards had herded the inmates into safe spots. Prisons have solid reinforced walls. They're considered secure, but a direct hit from a powerful cell could still do damage.

The tornado veered to the left and seemed to consider revisiting us. I tensed as I sensed it looking at me. But then it swung away, as if a sudden blast of sirens had deterred it. A couple near us hugged each other and exclaimed over what they'd seen. The sky cleared, yielding enough of the fading light to see glimpses of the destruction below: downed trees, piles of debris, broken fences, and flung vehicles. In one place, the skeletal frame of a big rig blocked the road. My eardrums ached.

More sirens cut through the air, along with flashing red lights. As Maura had said, if Bruder were truly suicidal, he could exploit the chaos to complete his plan. But chaos could serve him in other ways, too. I felt his eyes on me. He'd wanted something. I drew my arms together, aware he could carve out a more malignant damage path than this tornado had just done.

Chapter Thirty-Seven

I sat on a couch in Ayden's room and stared in shock at the news report. We'd sped southeast through spasms of blinding rain under the threat of more funnels emerging from the roiling clouds. Ayden's weather radio had spit out static-filled reports. When we finally arrived at the hotel, I was in meltdown. And then this!

A mile-wide possible EF4 had swept over the prison complex, slamming the building I'd been in, lifting part of the roof, and crumpling a tower. Several people were injured or dead. I held my breath. Ayden put his glee on hold to listen.

"We have reports of missing inmates," said a male anchor. "We don't know their names or what they did, but a spokesperson confirms that the location of at least a dozen is unknown."

"Not good," Ayden commented.

My heart pounding, I called Maura. I couldn't hear her phone ring. I texted, but my unsteady fingers failed, and I had to keep erasing. I knew she had to be as concerned about Bruder as I was. "Maura's not picking up. She stayed behind. I don't know where she had a room."

Ayden set his gun on the table. "Just in case. And you should stay armed, too."

I looked up at him. "Even if Bruder got out, he doesn't know where we are."

"He knows where we'll *be*. His buddy was at your place, right?"

"Okay, I take your point. We need to warn Natra and tell her we're okay."

"Can't get her, Annie. Or Wayne or Jax." He pointed at my phone. "Or

Maura, apparently. I think the cell tower's down. Can't get Jo, either, but she knows to come here."

I took a breath. I was tempted to just drive home, but it was dark out now, with inmates out there somewhere. Maybe more tornadoes.

Ayden rubbed his face. "Can't do much till we know more. At least we have power. For now. Let's look at your notes."

I turned off the TV's sound but left the picture on. Then I opened the tablet. I explained the context and let Ayden listen to the description I'd recorded of the encounter. Its brevity helped me recall the vital details. While he focused on the audio, I made a list of bullet points.

I showed them to Ayden. "These behaviors stood out to me. Bruder tapped on the drawing. Twice. Four times each, like Morse code. He made a cutting gesture when I asked if he were in danger of killing himself. He drew a triangle around a choking figure, and he wrote some cryptic lines. He also seemed concerned about me and something I'm doing. I thought he was about to warn me when the guard interrupted us and took him out."

"Warn you or *threaten* you?"

I shrugged.

"And what about the peanut butter?"

"That was odd. There's no real context or connection to anything else. He asked me to bring him candy next time, as if he expected me again. He specified peanut butter."

Ayden stared at my rendition of the drawing. "Seems like the red bloom is pretty important. We've seen that twice now, and you said it's on his hand."

"Yes, it is."

"And Airic envisioned a triangle, right?"

"Yes."

"Seems like there's lots of triads in this, with Bruder part of several. There's also our team, and Cassandra with the two kids."

I waved a hand to stop him. "Let's take it from the top. Maura calls to get me there. She doesn't really need a specialist, so she has some other agenda. She wants something from me or wants me to do something."

"Or to believe something."

"True. And Monroe's going along with it, 'though he was ready to block it. He didn't want me there, so he might not know Maura's full plan. And then there's Bruder. I thought he was trying to convey something he didn't want the others to know. His gestures and expressions were shielded from them. So, they weren't all in agreement about my presence."

"And *they're* a triangle." Ayden pulled the drawing toward him and tapped on the stick figure with the ropes around its neck. "Someone's caught in a bind between two...things. Are they people? Maybe. Wish we had the original." Ayden studied the written lines. "This could be a deflection. I mean, why would they let you see a poem after what we've used his poems for?"

"They might not know my part in the Jasper discovery. They do now, but not when I first went in. But that's still a good question. Why *did* they? Bruder's behavior suggests *he's* the one who's caught. He made this odd chopping motion when I asked if he was in danger of ending his life. It was like in Charades."

Ayden repeated the phrase and chopped his hand through the air. "In the game that means 'cut the phrase, you've said too much.' So maybe he's in danger. Period."

I sat back. "But why would he think I'd help him? And another thing of interest: I don't think he wrote the Devil's Fork poem. I have to agree with Jax. He's not the poet, not for that one. He didn't know the lines I quoted. He acted like he understood, but I could tell he didn't. So what's *that* about?"

"Didn't write it but knows who did, and knows why."

"So it could be Keaton. And if Keaton's his mentor, as we surmise, maybe Keaton showed him how to use cryptic poems to code their messages."

Ayden picked up a pencil and tore out a sheet from his tablet. "These are the capitalized letters. There are four of them, and Bruder tapped four times, so they're important. Nothing else in the drawing is related to four. Let's isolate them. E P L and H." He rewrote them in several combinations until he stopped and turned the tablet to show me. H E L P.

I stared at the message. "What the hell?"

"So he's the stick figure. Are the other two Maura and Monroe, or someone else? Are they the guys who harassed Nemeth? And how does Keaton fit in?"

I shook my head. "Seems too simple."

"The real question is, why didn't *they* see this message? It didn't take us long."

Ayden played with the other lines while I thought out loud about their meaning. "We've already seen the role of fire. We think that's Keaton's part. I can see him and Bruder laughing together if they're accomplices in murder. But what are the pieces? Maybe the missing fingers? I do see the word, 'three,' but it's split. Why? And what does the misspelled 'see' mean? Is a letter missing, or is the 'se' a set of initials, S.E.?" I stared at the lines, willing something profound to jump out.

fire buries Everything
in Pieces, they Laugh
Half asleep, th-ree se the red bloom of doom.

Ayden looked up. "Did you say he was pulling on his ear? Was there a tattoo there?"

"Not that I noticed, but it could have just been a way for me to see the tattoo on the back of his hand. The one on his neck was faded, and he didn't really point at it. So, we're back to the red bloom. What does he mean by 'doom'? And 'half-asleep'?"

"Near death, maybe? Or no one sees what's really going on?"

"He did mention he had to stay alert. Then said something about it being deeper *in*. I think. He was certainly conveying *something*. Specifically to me. I just don't know what."

"And you couldn't tell what the scribbles inside the circles were?"

"No. I didn't get to examine them closely. I needed a magnifying lens. But if we want to link Airic's triangle impression to this, his symbol could help. I'd have to look at it again."

Ayden grinned. "That's paranormal, Annie. Are we going there?"

I threw up my hands. "I don't know. We've got all this input, and some of it's been corroborated. Let's stick with this message for now. We should just study it, let it perk in our brains, and see if something pops. I've told you what Jax said, and you've done the research on Keaton Keller. We've got a lot to work with. We might be missing some ingredients, but I think we're close to making something edible."

A knock on the door made me jump. Ayden put his gun in his belt and opened it. JoLynn lifted a large white bag. "Thought you all'd be hungry. Just junk food, but better than nothing, right? And there's this." She held up a bottle of *Stormy Weather* Cabernet.

Ayden let her in. Despite my mood, I smiled. She was catching on. "Perfect. You're just in time."

JoLynn set down her goodies and went over to the TV to watch the storm update crawlers. "When the wind let up south of here, we sent out drones with cameras. You should see the nasty tracks these bad boys made. Whole streets knocked out in some places, and swaths of trees cut in two. We counted eight funnels between Chattanooga and where you were, with places that still need confirmation. But one was an EF4, for sure. Stayed on the ground about twenty minutes, and it had an RFD with some impact. People just don't expect that tail-end punch. We've heard about some fatalities."

"Any more info about the prison?" I asked.

She gestured toward the screen. "Just what you're already hearing."

While I poured the wine into plastic hotel cups, Ayden showed her the footage on his phone of the one we'd seen. She was impressed. With JoLynn in the room, confidentiality kicked in on the Bruder case, so we chatted over our makeshift dinner about her work here on the exhumed body. Her taphonomic background had given the investigators some science-based grounds for an arrest warrant.

I was impressed. "I'll have to hire you to give our team some lessons."

JoLynn smiled. "Well, Ayden here's a quick study. And he spotted some things about this case I didn't see."

He beamed at her.

I patted his arm. "He's my secret weapon, as long as I can get him out of the storm."

"We were safe," he insisted.

CHAPTER THIRTY-SEVEN

I rolled my eyes.

JoLynn set down her glass. "I do have some information about that dirt in the bag at your house."

I sat up.

"My lab buddy said they can't narrow down the area from the mineral content in the dirt, but they did find something unusual. There's ash in it, like from a burnt building. And from paper."

"Not a campfire?"

"This ash seemed to be integrated into the dirt, as if something had burned in the area before it was dug up. And there were traces of chemicals that suggested arson."

Ayden looked at me. The lines on Bruder's drawing had mentioned a fire. *Fire buries everything.* I nodded to indicate we'd discuss it later.

JoLynn opened a bag full of treats for dessert and dumped them out on the table. "You might also consider that there's a third grave. One where a fire happened before they dug."

"Well, there are certainly three. More than three. Hopefully, Natra's narrowed down the potential counties for another search. We've been lucky. We had some guidance, but if we don't get another poem or something like it, we can't search effectively. And we've got killers on the loose who know where the other graves are."

I suddenly felt exhausted. It had been a long day. Ayden and JoLynn launched into weather facts and figures, so I excused myself. "I have a very early flight back." I pointed at Ayden. "I'm afraid he's needed back home."

JoLynn tilted her head toward him with an exaggerated frown. "I'll get drone footage, don't worry." To me, she said, "And I hope to get back on your case myself. I'd like to work with Jax again. That session was awesome."

Ayden picked up a bag of peanut M&Ms and ripped it open. He froze. "Wait!" He grabbed his art tablet and flipped it around to show me. "This right here." He pointed at the third line on the drawing. "Peanut butter candy!"

I saw it before he said it.

"*Th-ree se.* Pull the 'ree' out and remove the space. Reese! Reese's *pieces.*

That's what he meant in the second line."

I held up my hand to stop him, but I knew where he was going: Reese was the girl we were looking for. Bruder wanted us to find her. Of course, he knew about her. He was Keaton's cousin.

We stared at each other. Then Ayden said, "I guess I know my next assignment."

Chapter Thirty-Eight

The Reese mystery had deepened. She figured into this. Bruder had pointed toward Maura, as if Maura knew her, too. Maybe Reese had been her patient. In any event, my cases had merged. I'd just seen two people who had Maura in common use cryptic communication. That was no coincidence. And I mistrusted her motives for pulling me into Bruder's case. She was angling for something. I wanted to go back and talk to Bruder, but the prison was on full lockdown. That had to wait.

Once we got cell service near the airport, we listened to the news about the prison situation. There were two deaths, multiple injuries, and half a dozen inmates missing. More had gotten through a damaged wall, but they'd been rounded up by midnight. The tornado had cut a devastating swath through that area. Ayden dropped me off, then took off to Greenville, where Natra had gone to do her research. If traffic were with him, he'd arrive before me.

A call from Maura before I boarded confirmed that Bruder had escaped. My heart sank. She sounded distraught. "I've been driving around the area, hoping he'd spot my car and come out of hiding. But he doesn't know me that well. He might not trust me."

I could understand that. I wasn't keen to side with Bruder, but the more I knew about this woman, the less I trusted her. I told her to keep me informed.

I called Natra, Wayne, and Jax to fill them in and urge them to be watchful. Wayne said he'd send a patrol to my house. He was home today with Kamryn, and Natra had dropped Mika off there on her way to her research destination, so they had a dog in the house to alert them.

I could hardly tolerate the length of the flight or how long it took to get back on the road. I looked forward to having my core team back together. It was like going out fully dressed…and armed. Keaton was out there, and now with his cousin on the run, he might close in. I watched for cars following me. I'd confirmed that the tracking device on my car was still in place. But there was too much traffic to spot a tail. I listened to the news reports out of Tennessee and hurt for all the injuries and lost homes.

Just before I arrived, Janissa called. I'd nearly forgotten about the phone store videos.

"Can you see who purchased the phone?" I asked.

"We got an image we think is the person. It's fuzzy. We enhanced it a little, and the buyer obviously didn't want to be identified. Wearing a hoodie and jeans, so we see nothing that clearly identifies him. No slogans or unique patterns. But this phone is still active."

"That's interesting. Why buy a burner if you're not going to dump it? Did you call my cyber guy?"

"I did. Joe said he has some equipment that could assist. He didn't say what it was. Do you think it's a Stingray, a cell site simulator? You can get those devices on the dark web."

"Janissa, I don't ask. Joe and Ayden work in legal gray areas. They don't break laws, but they probably strain a few. Often, they modify devices to work better, or for situations not necessarily intended by the designer."

"I see. I'll keep working on it."

"And can you set up another session with Amber? Maybe later in the afternoon? I might be able to encourage her to show me a little more."

"Another gray area?"

I considered this. "Everything I do has shades of gray, I guess."

"Whatever you want, Dr. Hunter. I'll make it happen."

Natra preferred library archives to newspaper morgues, because she could learn more about an area from other available resources—including librarians. They generally know quite a lot about a community. Ayden had already fetched detailed data about the LaRue/Keller case from the legal appeal, but we needed more from local coverage. Reporters liked to give their impressions. Sometimes they even revealed addresses, relatives, and associates.

I ran through Keaton Keller's background once more: he and Reese had lived with a sadistic psychotic predator who made kids beat other kids. They'd fallen under her spell. She might have exploited their youth and need, but I thought there had to be more. How had she gotten them to obey her, day after day, in brutalizing a young girl to the point of mutilating and killing her? Reese had done it till *she* was the target. So, her survival instincts had kicked in. She'd even gone back to get corroboration. That meant she was strong. I hoped Jax could get her records. But his assessment of Keaton as damaged goods was consistent with what I knew about male juveniles. Keaton had been reprogrammed, using sexual gratification as a powerful reward system. Shame and remorse had been effectively erased.

And where did the young Tommy Bruder fit? I knew his background. He'd never been homeless. He was Keaton's cousin but a few years younger. Why had he signaled me about Reese and pointed to Monroe and Maura? What kind of help did he need?

I tried several news stations but couldn't get much more about the prison situation. I finally arrived at my destination. Before I got out, I looked around for anyone suspicious and spotted Ayden's truck near Natra's Bronco Sport. I texted her and got directions to a nearby café where they were having lunch. I walked down the street, looking for the place. Then I stopped short. Not fifty yards from me, a familiar figure ducked into a red dot liquor store.

There weren't many men that short. But what could Pete the Panty Thief be doing here?

Chapter Thirty-Nine

I entered the store and looked down each aisle. I didn't spot him. Since the place was busy, there was no use asking the clerk if a scrawny man with a seedy reek had just come in. I walked down the vodka aisle and spotted a door at the back. I looked up another aisle, saw no one who looked like Pete, and went out the back door. I walked around the building to an alley. No one there. But I was sure I'd seen him. And he'd been close to the café where my team had chosen to dine.

I found Natra and Ayden at a table for four, with notes spread out. Odors of fresh-ground coffee wafted through the place. Natra had a mug of it ready for me. I sat down. "I just saw Pete outside."

Ayden's eyes widened. "You sure, boss?"

"I counted the roaches on him. Yes, I'm sure."

Ayden half rose, but I gestured for him to sit. "Let's think about this. He might have a legit reason to be here that has nothing to do with our case."

Natra squinted at me as if I'd just lost my mind. "Suddenly you like a coincidence?"

"No. And Jax does think Pete lied about why he sold us those maps. But we're at a disadvantage. We can't let him see that."

"What disadvantage?"

"I keep working on this puzzle only to find I'm putting in the wrong pieces. I don't know what to make of his presence here. The tracker is on *my* SUV, but he wasn't following me. He was here before I arrived."

Ayden sat back with a frown, his arms folded.

"It's not on you, Ayden. If they're setting us up, they're doing a good job.

You had no reason to suspect him. But now I wonder what else might be on that property. We have dirt from a grave with traces of paper ash. And we know Pete's stack of crap was torched. *If* it was even his crap."

I grabbed a pen and used Natra's notepad to diagram where Pete's property stood in relation to our known gravesites. "If we include where Bruder was arrested in Tennessee, as well as where he grabbed Hailey near Asheville, we have a fair sense of the corridor in which these guys operated."

"Their damage path," Ayden said.

I glanced at him. "We also have the other missing girls we've linked to them. And our geographical analysis puts them in this corridor. Pete's isolated property is a good place to bury a body. Or two."

Ayden sat forward. "Maybe someone burned it to get us to write it off."

"Maybe, but I want to go back. If there's time after you're done here, head over there, both of you. Take Mika. All of us have overnight bags, so let's just do it. I'll join you after I see Amber again this afternoon. I'll be done in time to put me at Pete's around five at the latest. Ayden, set us up with a place to stay for the night. Make it two nights, just in case. I'll eat the cost if we come back early. And talk to Wayne. See if the lab has turned up anything about the map drawings we gave them that contradicts what Pete told us. But don't give away our new suspicion."

"Copy."

I glanced from Ayden to Natra. "Look for trackers on your cars. I don't know Pete's role in all of this, but he could be a grunt guy who does what he's told. And even without cell service on his property, he could have some kind of surveillance system. Just watch your backs. We know he knows Bruder. Maybe he's being leveraged. And Bruder's out there, too. Maura called me. She's trying to find him."

Natra passed me a menu and raised an eyebrow.

I nodded. "Yes, I know. Maybe Bruder was with her when she called. I think she had some plan for me that got blocked. She won't stop. So I need to get Amber to tell me about this woman. I'm certain she knows something." I told them about the phone purchaser. "Someone called that girl. Someone *directed* her. Amber had a strong reaction to Maura's testimony. The more we turn up about Dr. Reynolds, the better our position."

Natra made some notes. "Any thought about remote viewing Bruder? Mind-to-mind communication?"

I cocked my head. "Meaning?"

"Just thinking about the CIA viewers who tracked down a fugitive. That guy who worked for the Customs Service in Florida. When they suspected him of taking bribes, he took off. You found that case."

Ayden nodded. "FBI's Most Wanted, as I recall. On the run for several years. And one of the RV assets located him in some small town in Wyoming."

Natra air-tapped her pen. "She said he'd be found at a campground with a rock at the entrance, near a Native American burial ground. Very specific. And also right. She even knew he was about to leave, like she could sense his intentions. They nabbed him just in time."

I took a sip of coffee. "Yes, a very unique case. But let's not forget that the other five viewers who were looking for him were way off the mark. The viewer who got it right seemed to be uniquely gifted."

"We have gifted viewers."

"To whom I already owe a debt. But I'll ask Jax what he thinks. Airic won't do it. He thinks we're bumping against dark energy. But Jax doesn't like Bruder being out here any more than we do. Hopefully, they'll track him down before he leaves the state. It's tough to survive the wilderness with no resources."

"They've rounded up all but three," Ayden said.

Natra touched her pile of papers. "Speaking of Jax, he gave me a contact for accessing some of the older juvenile records, which I've been doing. Reese Wendham's are sealed, but I found the name and current address of her former caseworker. She lives near Wayne, so I could stop there when I pick up Mika."

"Good idea. Anything else?"

"I pieced together some items about Keller. He'd gotten into some trouble, and each time, there was additional news coverage. I even found a news clip where he comes out of a courthouse and sneers at the camera."

I placed my lunch order for she-crab soup before I asked, "Any articles about him attending Bruder's hearings?"

Natra shuffled through her papers and pulled a copy. "This one includes the details Ayden uncovered about him being this abused juvenile. And then, after Cassandra LaRue's death, a reporter tried to interview him. Apparently, he was seen near Cassandra's house several times before she died."

"That's weird. But Jax did say Keaton thought he'd done nothing wrong, despite killing a girl. LaRue had sexually groomed him. Bonds that form under those circumstances are tough to break, especially if he's unstable to begin with. She also used cognitive tools that can disintegrate a kid's fragile sense of identity."

"And maybe he *did* kill her," Ayden said.

"True enough. So they both stayed in the same town where the original crime happened. Cassandra was released, and Keaton either watched for the chance to get his revenge or sought some sort of continued relationship with her. Any ideas on that?"

Natra pulled out another page. "Jax helped me with this. Once out of juvie, he lived under supervision in a group home at first and got a job fixing motorcycles. No college courses. He stole a van, torched a couple of buildings, and robbed some places. One criminal incident involved the sexual assault of a young girl."

"Interesting. Did his criminal record ever coincide with Bruder's? Like they engaged in illegal things together?"

"Can't get Bruder's juvenile record yet. I have some chronology from coverage when he was arrested and some from your files, but in the legal statements we have, he never mentioned his cousin being involved."

Ayden lifted his steak sandwich to take a bite, then paused. "Maybe Keaton went to his trial to intimidate him, so he wouldn't."

I hadn't thought of that. I looked from him to Natra. "Jax would love to hear me say this, but it really does look like I might be wrong about Bruder. I need to rethink this."

Natra smiled.

I continued. "Here's what we know. When Bruder was 17, he snatched my friend Hailey, age 13. Later, he was arrested with a near-victim the same age in a van. In a deal, he led police to the grave of another girl. He went to prison. He's suspected in other disappearances. He seems to be exploiting all this recent true crime fascination to get someone to take up his case. He claims he wasn't the killer. We've had mixed messages from these poems, but they've led us to victim burial locations. Or, to one and possibly to another. He—or *they*—use codes. We suspect Keaton's associated with him, and perhaps he penned one of the poems. Also, we received some significant puzzle pieces from Pete, who's suddenly turned up within steps of us. If Pete's involved, then the maps are meant to lead us. Maura fits in, too, as Bruder's therapist. Maybe more."

Ayden held up two fingers to indicate he had something to add. "Speaking of her, Cole Cheney's parents told me this morning they gave his journal to an attorney when they considered a lawsuit. They were waiting to see what happened at Amber's trial. That's how Janissa knew about the kid. The attorney still has the journal, and I have an appointment with him in twenty minutes. I told the parents we might be able to help. Hope that's okay."

I nodded. "Give it a try. I'll dig into Maura's background. I've read her bio, so I'll corroborate that info, maybe look for some of her colleagues." I pointed at Natra's paper. "Make two columns for our two distinct lines of inquiry, with Maura in both. Bruder's our immediate concern, which means we focus on Keaton and possibly Pete. Do what you can with your current leads but get over to Pete's as soon as you can. It's about two hours away from here."

Natra pushed her salad bowl away. "I'm ready."

Ayden held up a hand. "Just need to finish my sandwich. I'll look around town for our panty thief."

As I grabbed the bill, I glanced across the café and out the window before I said to Ayden, "I just thought of something. Remember when we were at Nemeth's? He didn't invite us inside his trailer, and I was glad he didn't. But while we were talking, he did look over at it. Did you notice that?"

Ayden nodded. "Yeah."

"And I sensed someone watching. Jax thinks someone else knows about the maps he gave us. Now that I've seen Pete here, I think he might've been putting on an act. Maybe someone else was there, listening."

Chapter Forty

I'd half-expected Amber to decline to meet with me. When she entered the room and took a seat, I noticed she looked thinner. Her hair was stringy now, and she wore no make-up. I asked some general questions about how she was, but she made it clear she wanted no chitchat.

"Did you do it?" she asked. "Did you see the ghost?"

"No, Amber, I didn't. Apparently, you're the only one who does."

Her upper lip curled. "You didn't try."

"Did *he* tell you that?"

She leaned back in her metal chair and pointed her chin.

I still couldn't tell if she really believed Trevor's ghost had approached her, but I decided to use it. "I came because I have an idea. I know a way we might be able to communicate with Trevor together. If you see or hear him, I'll be a witness. Interested?"

Her green eyes narrowed.

"It's called automatic writing. Here's how it works." I produced a pad of paper and a pencil, which I shoved toward her. "It's pretty simple. The idea is for you to relax and allow the spirit to use your hand to write a message."

Amber frowned. "Now? In here? It's not even dark."

"It works anywhere, any time. It's been successful in helping people who've crossed over to communicate."

She squinted.

"You'll be in a relaxed state. You don't have to do anything but hold the pencil. I'll use hypnosis to—"

Her eyes went wide and she jumped from her seat. "No!" She backed away toward the wall and looked at the door. "No! That's how *she* does it."

I stood, my heart beating. "How who does it?"

Amber shook her head. Her mouth formed a hard line. "I don't want to do this. I don't want to talk to you anymore."

I held up my hands. "It's all right. We don't have to. I just wanted to find a way to contact Trevor, since you think he has a message for me."

The girl trembled. Her face flushed red. "I can't tell you anything. Did *they* send you here? To see if I'd talk? Are you trying to trick me?" She looked around as if for hidden cameras.

"Amber, relax. It's just an idea."

She breathed hard and watched me like a cornered animal. This wasn't going well. But her reaction supported my suspicion that someone had manipulated her.

I opened my hands in a gesture of friendliness. "Amber, let me tell you something I know. While you were talking to Trevor on the day he died, someone called you. They gave you an instruction."

She paled and shook her head. Her jaw clenched as if in an effort to prevent her from blurting out something. "No one called me. That's not true."

"I have the text and phone records. Someone called. And you took the call. You talked to them."

She looked around the room and up at the ceiling as if expecting a drone to be filming her. Her hands clenched, the way they had during her trial when she'd watched Maura talk about her.

I took a risk. "It isn't true, is it, that you canceled Trevor's appointment with Dr. Reynolds. She lied, didn't she?"

Amber froze. She stared at me. I'd hit the mark, so I kept going. "She's holding something over you, isn't she?"

I smelled perspiration. Amber looked ready to run. I sensed her teetering on the razor edge of a decision: trust me or get the guard to take her out. If she chose the latter, I knew she'd never speak with me again.

I held out my hand as if to pull her to safety. "I can help you. What happened in court isn't the real story. I know that."

193

Amber breathed hard. In a small voice, she asked, "You know her?"

"Yes, I do. And your attorney told you Trevor wasn't the only one, didn't she?"

I saw a slight nod of her head. Her shoulders dropped a little. Progress.

I drew a finger across my lips to show we should be careful in this room. "The person who called you that day directed you to do something you didn't want to do. It wasn't your idea, but you didn't have a choice."

I gestured for her to return to her chair. She looked at it and then at me. But she went to sit down. She stared at the pad of blank paper. Then she reached for the pencil.

I sat across from her. "Just let him speak. He wants me to know something. He can do that through you. Do you understand?"

She nodded. I hoped she'd see this as a way to convey what she knew without putting herself at risk. She leaned over the pad as if to shield it from cameras while she worked. It didn't take long for her to produce a rough drawing. She turned it toward me. A figure with a hairstyle like Amber's appeared to be inside a jail-like room with an open door. Another figure, less defined, stood outside. Then I saw the hangman's noose inside. Amber watched me. I must have looked confused, because she grabbed the pad and drew someone sitting on a dock with what looked like a fishing pole. She circled the hook and drew a squiggled line inside.

In a low voice, I said, "You were bait."

She nodded.

"Not his girlfriend."

She gave a tight shake of her head.

Now it made sense. She'd been used to ensure Trevor would kill himself. She'd misjudged the potential consequences.

I leaned toward the girl. "I need to know who directed you, and why you were told to say the phrase you repeated to Trevor."

Amber watched me as if she didn't quite believe I could—or would—do anything for her. Finally, she said, "The one who lied."

I nodded to show I understood. She meant Maura, who'd said that Amber had canceled Trevor's appointment. *And* said she didn't know the girl.

Clearly, she did. "Why would she do that?"

Amber shrugged. "Secrets."

"The boys were part of those secrets?"

She nodded.

I wondered if this was why Maura "specialized" in troubled boys. When they killed themselves after whatever she subjected them to, she could insist she'd tried her best. They'd just been too lost. But what had she been doing with them?

"How did she get you to do it?"

Amber started to rock. She shook her head and glanced at the door.

"Okay, Amber. I think I know what was going on, and how it was done. I'm trying to get some proof. When I do, that could make a difference for you."

"Just stop her." She pushed her drawing toward me, rose, and went to the door to get the correction officer's attention. I grabbed my items and followed her out. I touched her shoulder briefly to assure her I'd try. She flinched.

Back on the road, I called Janissa. "That burner phone will lead you to Maura, even if someone else purchased it. I don't know what she was doing with Trevor, but she lied on the stand. She not only knows Amber but used her to get Trevor to kill himself. The phrase she texted was part of a hypnotic suggestion. Trevor was primed for it."

"Amber told you this?"

"She told me enough to be able to figure it out."

"So, it's just what you thought. That helps pin it down. I think the phone's been turned off, but it shows recent activity. We'll see if it's related to her office or residence. We can't get a warrant to search, but maybe I'll drive by and see what we're up against."

"She's in Tennessee."

"Good. She won't spot me."

"Be careful."

I ended the call. A text from Natra got me on the phone with her. "Are you at Pete's yet?"

"Soon. Half an hour. Didn't find the case worker."

"Are you with Ayden?"

"No. He took a different route. We'll get there near the same time, give or take. But FYI, I checked Carly's site, in case she heard from Bruder. Figured she wouldn't keep that a secret."

"Good thinking."

"She's being coy, but she's hinting he had help getting out. She's posing as if she knows a big secret. Hold on. I'm pulling over." I heard her fumble with something before she came back on the phone. "She posted a video apparently meant for him, should he have the means to get on the Internet. She seems to think she'd be his point of contact. She had a little poem, which I assume has a code. Afraid I haven't had a chance to figure it out yet."

Natra played it for me, but I could barely make it out. "What's she saying?"

"I think she's giving a location and time for where to meet her. In the style of his poetry, but short and sweet."

"Good lord! That girl's an idiot. Can you send it to me?"

"I sent it as an email. I also sent it to Wayne and Jax."

"Carly's linked to 3-M, and he was at the prison when Bruder escaped. He hasn't called me, which suggests he knows something, too. Did Ayden tell you anything about the Cheney journal?"

"No. Just told me where to park."

"Okay. I'll get there when I can. There's no cell service there, so we won't connect till I'm there. Go ahead and take Mika onto the property."

I pondered this new information. How would Carly have known how Bruder escaped unless someone told her? Had it been pre-planned? That would certainly implicate 3-M. But why would he do it and risk everything? For that matter, why would Maura help Bruder? And why had she brought me there? Whoever had been Bruder's facilitator in the escape hadn't planned for a tornado, but it had worked to their advantage.

These thoughts occupied me the entire way to Pete's. When I arrived where Ayden and I had parked before, I saw Ayden's truck. He wasn't in it. I couldn't text him, so I got out. I remembered the way, but I didn't want to get near Pete's place without one of my team nearby. Then I saw Ayden running toward me.

"Go back!" he yelled. "Get in the truck!"

I did as he said. When he jumped in, he slammed his door and locked us inside.

"What's wrong? What's happening?"

"Someone was here. They must have been watching us!"

"Ayden, what are you talking about? Where's Natra and Mika?"

He looked at me, panting, his eyes wide. "I don't know, Annie. She's missing. They're both gone."

Chapter Forty-One

Ayden showed me the small, embroidered case Natra had made for dog treats. "They were here. She's in trouble! I was twenty minutes behind her, Annie, I swear!"

I held up my hands, partly to stave off my own panic. My heart was in my throat. "Okay, let's think. Maybe she went to a different part of the field."

Ayden shook his head. "I told her to park here. And she did. I saw tire tracks that match her Bronco. And there *was* a tracker on her car. We checked. We left it, like you said, so they wouldn't know we were on to them. Someone must have followed her. I should've—"

"Any other tracks?"

"Several. But hers ran over theirs. Someone was here first."

"Could be cops. There was a fire."

Ayden's anguished face quashed my attempt to explain. I swallowed hard. Who could she have encountered? I looked at my phone. No signal. Ayden stared out the window. I knew he felt responsible. I wanted to get in my car and go look for her, but that was just reactive. We needed a plan. I took a breath. "Ayden, what did you see? When did you last hear from her?"

His jaw muscle tensed. "She called about fifteen minutes out, right after she talked to you. I let her know where I was. I told her to wait, but she said she wanted to get on the field. When I pulled in here, I didn't see her car. I walked over to Pete's place. The trailer's still there, but it's charred. I hollered for Natra. When she didn't answer, I looked for her." He shrugged. "Didn't find her. I came back here and saw the tire tracks. I couldn't text her, so I walked into the woods. I kept calling, but she didn't answer. Then

I found the bag."

"You didn't see anyone? No cars on the roads near here?"

"No. Someone must've already been here."

"But if she'd seen a car, she wouldn't have gotten out of hers."

"Pete could've parked somewhere else. The Firebird's gone. And we don't know how many acres he has."

"But *why* would he take her? And how did he get past Mika? She'd have attacked him."

Ayden shrugged. "Maybe he had his dogs. Or someone else was with him. But that treat bag wouldn't just come loose. She left it for us, to tell us."

We looked at each other. "Bruder," I said. "I bet he was here. He knows Pete, and he knows it's a good place to hide."

"But how'd he get here?"

"Hijacked or stole a car. Or maybe 3-M brought him. Natra told me he might've had help getting out. That person would've had a car. We need to call Wayne. Let's get some cell service, see if Natra texted us, and then come back. Maybe there's something else here that will help."

Ayden drove us out the way we'd come until I got phone reception. We both checked for messages. Nothing. Ayden called Joe to get him to track Natra's phone. I called Wayne, told him what happened, and gave him our coordinates. We returned to Pete's. On the way, Ayden told me about Cole Cheney's journal.

"The attorney said the kid was struggling over his mother's drug use." He looked at me. "He thought Cole either had a fantasy about Maura Reynolds or was involved with her."

"Involved? *Sexually?*"

Ayden shrugged. "Maybe. Cole liked how nurturing she was and how she listened and made him feel good. He had a friend who told him there'd been other boys, too."

I blinked. "Did you get to see the journal?"

"No, sorry. But Janissa has the info."

"I need to read the actual entries."

"Thought of that, boss. I asked if he'd copy the pages and send them to her. So, you'll get them from her."

"Good work. Maura has secrets, that's for sure. God, I hope she wasn't seducing those boys!"

We pulled in. There was no sign that anyone had come while we were gone. I gestured toward the property. "Let's check that trailer."

With guns drawn, we left the truck. We knew Pete might have a surveillance system set up and could be watching us. Without the Internet or cell service, it could be limited. We stepped cautiously. I saw the empty spot where the Firebird had been. They'd taken Natra's car and had another, so that made two people, at least.

Our first stop was Nemeth's former abode. The lean-to, with its stacks of magazines and newspapers, was now a pile of rain-soaked ash with a few scorched chunks of wood. I wondered how many roaches had lost their homes. Shielding my mouth and nose against the smoky stench, I nudged the mess with my foot while Ayden tried the charred trailer door. The frame had buckled from the heat, and the door wouldn't budge, but a hole exposed the inside.

Ayden peered through it. "You were right about one thing. Hoarders don't burn their stuff. This place looks cleaned out. I guess the stacks out here were just a hiding place."

I leaned in to see for myself. A back window on the other side offered light. I narrowed my eyes. "Something's in there, something not burned. Let's go see if that window opens."

We circled around to the back. Ayden pointed to a shovel that leaned against the trailer. "Red dirt!"

I bent down to scan it. "And no damage, so it was placed here after the fire." I looked for a hole nearby, but weeds blocked my view.

A wooden box sat under the window, as if used to climb inside. I stepped on it to see. In the middle of the floor were a crumpled sleeping bag and a pile of clothes gathered into a pillow. I got down to let Ayden look.

"Has to be Bruder," I observed. "Who else would sleep here? Maybe Natra surprised him, and he got the jump on her."

Ayden looked toward the woods. "He had a gun, then, because he wouldn't have got past Mika."

I took some hope in the fact that we hadn't found her body. Her abductor might use her as a hostage. He'd want something. He'd communicate. "So, Nemeth's presence in Greenville was no coincidence."

Ayden nodded. "Looks like he might've dug up the dirt that ended up in your yard."

"And that dirt had a decomp odor. There must be a burial site here somewhere." I looked around. "Where'd you find the treat bag?"

Ayden pointed. "Over there. Down that path into the woods."

It didn't take long to come upon a hole, three-foot in diameter, with one area going down deep. It was twenty yards from where Ayden had found the treat bag. Around it, we found a light layer of ash. Not far away was another burn site, topped with fresh ash.

I stood over the hole and shook my head. "We're at least two steps behind these guys. Mika must have run right to this spot. And whatever was here is gone, taken or incinerated." I looked around and saw a familiar tree. "There's another blackjack oak. I remember JoLynn pointing out the rough bark." I went over to see if it was marked but found nothing like the 'K' symbol we'd seen on the other tree.

We ventured further into the woods, unsure where Pete's property ended. We found Mika's footprints in some dirt, so we kept going. The path took us to a clearing. Across it stood another blackjack oak. About twelve feet up, it split into two trunks, as if once hit by lightning. One trunk leaned almost at a right angle, allowing a spot to seat an old deer blind.

I pointed. "I wonder if Pete was up there, watching them."

Ayden surveyed it. "Think there's a connection with the Jasper site?"

"I wouldn't rule it out, but oak trees aren't unique. The carving on the other one made it significant."

"This one's on his property. He wouldn't need to mark it."

I nodded. "There's that. But unless he had some reason to go dig up that body in Jasper, why'd he mark the tree at all?"

Ayden kicked at a rotting log. "Maybe it's time."

"For what?"

"For what Natra said. RV. Whose eyes are better to see through than hers?"
I considered this. "We'll tell Jax. He can arrange things. But there's something I want to check. I think Carly tossed us some breadcrumbs."

Chapter Forty-Two

We arrived at the cottage Ayden had booked. There were no messages yet from Joe. I texted him to tell him we were in cell range again. I realized that Bruder had likely tossed Natra's phone or made her turn it off, but I wanted to hope there was a way to find her. I rejoined Ayden in his truck and pulled up the poem Natra had grabbed off Carly's website. I read it out loud.

"Get a ride at Stoner side
Where Devil Diver Opens Fire
The girls in red await at 45 till 8.
For Whiskey and a Berrie."

We looked at each other.

"No idea," I said. "Natra would've had it solved." I stared at the lines. Then I remembered. "She sent it to Jax. Maybe he worked on it." I called him.

He didn't even greet me. He just asked, "Have you figured it out?"

"The poem? No. I just now read it."

"I'm on my way to Aiken."

"Aiken? What do you need? We're south of it. We rented a cottage for the night."

"Text me the address. I think there's a meet this evening."

"In Aiken? When?"

"If the poem is right, at 7:15."

"That's soon! Are you that close?"

"No. I hit traffic. But can you make it? There's a museum for thoroughbred racing. Carly used names of horses in the Hall of Fame there. I suspect she hopes to get Bruder to meet her."

"How would he know the names of horses?"

"Don't know, but it's certainly a signal. Just go."

"On it, but Jax, Natra, and Mika are missing. We think someone grabbed them at Pete's place."

Silence on the line told me he hadn't heard from her. Then he said, "I'll meet you when I can."

Ayden put the Thoroughbred Racing Hall of Fame address in his GPS and started to drive. I called Wayne to describe what we'd seen at Pete's. "I think Bruder was there," I added. "Any news on his status?"

"Still missing, Annie. You two, go home. I'll send someone to check the place."

"He's not there. He's in Natra's car. Anyone seen it yet?"

"Not yet."

"Natra sent you the poem from Carly Krebs' website, right? We think she's communicating with Bruder."

"We're working on it."

I told him what we knew and what we were going to do.

"Annie, do not confront him."

"Then get someone over there. We need to find Natra." I ended the call. "He's so aggravating."

But aggravating or not, talking with him had offered a moment of relief. I knew Natra could handle almost any situation, and she'd know we'd be looking for her, but I still worried. I could only hope she was too valuable to her kidnapper to harm. I felt the same flood of guilt I'd experienced the day Bruder had snatched Hailey right in front of me. Was he taunting me? He might know that Natra's every bit the sister-friend Hailey had been.

Soon, Ayden turned off the highway and rolled down a busy street. He followed the GPS directions to the target building. We cruised slowly to look at the grounds. Two large horse statues framed the front entrance, but the place looked quiet. I shook my head. "It's closed. And I don't see anyone in red."

"It's not 7:15 yet. And we don't know if it's tonight or tomorrow. Morning or evening."

"True." I pulled out the poem and called Jax. "We're here. No one dressed in red that we can see. Is anything in the poem *not* a horse name?"

"The last line. Whiskey and Berrie. I noticed a bar on the map less than a mile away. That could be the whiskey."

"So we should go there?"

"You have the poem, Annie. It doesn't give directions."

"Wait. Whiskey." To Ayden, I said, "We're on Whiskey Road, right?"

"Yup."

I told Jax I'd call back and punched the map app. I made it larger and moved it around. "There's a Berrie. It joins Whiskey."

"I see it."

Ayden turned right onto Berrie, a narrow road with no place to park. He found a turnaround and drove back. A long fence lined Berrie to our right, perhaps to block a home from road noise. Aiden pulled over onto a bare stretch of ground and turned off his lights but left the engine running.

"We can watch the intersection," he said, "but it's not promising for covert observation."

"Your windows are tinted. That helps." I grabbed one of Ayden's baseball caps and pushed my blond curls up into it.

Ayden breathed out. "Annie, no one dressed in red's gonna stand around on this road, waiting. There's not even a sidewalk."

"The poem fits."

He shrugged. "We should be looking for Natra."

"We are. If we find Carly, she might lead us to Bruder. And we have no other leads. Let's just see what happens at 7:15. If no one comes, we'll leave."

I didn't want to admit he was right. This seemed an unlikely way to find Natra. And if Bruder was meeting his next ride, Natra might be instantly expendable.

I looked at my watch. Five minutes to go.

Joe called. My heart raced as I answered. "Phone's off or busted," he said. "I got her to where she probably went out of range up at that property, and that's it. Sorry."

"I was afraid of that. But keep trying, please. Maybe it'll come back on at some point."

"I do have something. Natra had a tracker put on Mika's collar. It's trickier to track, especially far away, but we'd modified the GPS for better range. Ayden should be able to tune in if he's close."

"Do whatever you can, Joe. We'll do the same." I ended the call.

Ayden tapped my arm and pointed. "Red car." I caught a flash of red moving fast on Whiskey, past Berrie. We looked at each other. I hadn't thought of the 'girls in red' meaning girls in a red car.

"I hope we didn't miss them!"

"Should I follow?"

I froze. Stay here, or go. I didn't know.

"Boss?"

My heart pounded so loud I couldn't hear. Then we saw the car again. It slowed down, then turned onto Berrie. The red Mazda CX-30 drove past us. I pressed back against my seat. The driver and passenger both wore lidded hats that obscured their faces, but they had on red shirts. They kept going. Ayden watched in his rearview mirror. Seconds ticked by. I looked back. No sign of the car.

"Annie!"

Ayden stared ahead, his eyes wide. A lean man with short dark hair stepped onto the road and looked our way.

I shrugged. "It's not Bruder."

Ayden nodded. "I know." He looked at me. "I'm pretty sure that's Keaton Keller."

Chapter Forty-Three

A chill hit me. To this point, Keller had been a phantom, a character in a bizarre horror story. Now he was close. I readied my phone camera. The red Mazda returned and swept passed us. I took a series of shots to get the plate number and the man on the corner. He raised his right arm as if he knew them. The car stopped. He spoke to the driver, then got in.

Ayden sat up. "He's got a gun!"

"Stay on them."

The Mazda pulled out and turned right. Ayden moved into position but had to let a blue Ford Escape drive past before he could pull out.

I pointed. "That car will buffer us."

I checked my photos for a clear one and texted it to Wayne with a message, "Bruder's cousin entered this car at Berrie and Whiskey in Aiken, heading south. He's armed. Two females possibly in danger."

His return text didn't surprise me. "Don't tail them!"

He knew we would.

I texted Jax: *Keaton with Carly. We're following.*

I wanted Carly to speed up to enhance the chance she'd be pulled over. But if Keller had a gun on her, he'd likely ordered her to drive with care. I mentally urged Wayne to get patrols on the lookout.

They continued south on the same road. "Stay back," I told Ayden. "Just keep them in sight."

The car between us turned right, leaving a clear view of our truck. If any of them had noted the truck parked by the fence, they'd realize they were being followed. I texted Wayne about their course.

"Keller's no fugitive," I said to Ayden, "so their meeting's not breaking any laws. That's a problem. We can't prove he intends them harm."

"Carly's a person of interest."

"Let's hope we see a cop soon."

We drove past farms and through a small town. They kept going. "I wonder if he's going to Pete," I said. "He could get there on this road."

Suddenly, they slowed and pulled over into a driveway. We had no choice but to drive past them. I watched in my side mirror to see their next move. "Damn! They're turning around."

"Keller must've figured he should lose us."

"Or they missed a turn. Let's go see if there's a road."

Ayden U-turned and drove for ten minutes before it was clear they were gone. We did find a crossroad but couldn't tell in which direction they'd gone. We went to the left for five minutes but saw no one else. "He must've decided to take back roads. That won't be good for cops looking for him." I texted Jax that we'd lost them and were heading to our rental.

"At least Wayne has the info," I said. "I'm not sure what I'd've done if we'd cornered them somewhere."

Ayden glanced at me. "If Keller knows Carly, he probably knows who you are, Annie. And Jax says he's dangerous."

"Right. We need a new plan. But the poem doesn't take us anywhere else. We don't even know who they meant it for. Maybe Keller's taking them to Bruder."

"Or taking them hostage."

"Okay. Joe said we should try to track Mika's GPS."

Ayden nodded, but I sensed he didn't see this as a good option.

I felt exhausted. I sent Wayne a text about our setback.

It was darker now, but visibility was still fair. The cottage Ayden had booked was down a lane on a larger property, but the place was close to a busy street. I surveyed the cars parked along it and saw nothing unusual. Ayden went to open the place and check inside while I walked over to my SUV to fetch my overnight bag. I opened the door and grabbed it.

"Dr. Hunter."

The male voice made me pivot so fast, I dropped my bag. Within six feet of me was 3-M. My heart raced. "What are you doing?" I demanded. "Are you following me?"

"We need to talk. It's urgent."

I took a step toward him. "What happened at that prison? Who helped him get out? Where is he? Is he with you?"

"No, he's not." He looked around. "Can we talk inside?"

Ayden strode toward us. "Annie!"

I held up a hand. "S'okay." I looked at Monroe. "*Where* is Bruder?"

"I don't know. But I do know something you should hear."

"Are you aware that your buddy, Carly, is with Bruder's cousin, Keaton Keller?"

His eyes went wide. "Keaton? You saw him?"

"What's going on?" Ayden asked. My PI, ordinarily boyish, can be menacing when he wants to be.

Monroe's hesitation made me realize they'd never met. I gestured toward 3-M. "This is Monroe, Bruder's attorney. Also known as the Murder Mentalist." I looked at Monroe. "The one who wouldn't give me the suicide note."

Monroe crossed his arms and leaned toward me. "For a reason. *I* wrote it!"

Chapter Forty-Four

Ayden retrieved a pad of his drawing paper for recording information before we gathered at the dining room table inside the cottage. I disliked having this pretender in my space. I sensed Ayden ready to spring into action if Monroe made any false moves. Monroe had assured us he wasn't armed. Ayden had searched him, anyway. As we sat down, Monroe pulled a piece of paper from his inside jacket pocket and placed it on the table. It was the suicide note I'd seen in the prison. I showed it to Ayden.

"You wrote this," I said. "Why?"

"It was Maura's idea. She wanted to get you to the prison. She arranged it all, bribing guards, greasing wheels, claiming you were a suicide specialist. That's how you got in so easily. And *she* got Tommy out. She hadn't expected it to happen so fast, but the tornado strike helped. She'd planned to set you up for his escape, but they haven't realized yet he didn't go out with the others. When they do, she'll point them toward you."

"Poor plan. I had no prior contact."

"Like I said, she wasn't ready."

"Were you helping her?"

"I was helping Tommy. He thought she'd get Keaton off his back. He told me her plan. He went along with it because he's scared his cousin's trying to have him killed and he wanted to get out. Keaton's the killer. He wants to silence Tommy. For good reason. Tommy knows things."

"Why'd he wait so long to claim he's an accomplice?"

"He *didn't*. Someone else wrote to Carly."

"Someone besides him wrote that poem? Why? Who wanted that body found? Who else knew where it was?"

"Look, it's all gotten complicated, and Tommy's in trouble. I want to find him before he gets hurt."

"He kidnapped my assistant. And he's a fugitive. Cops in both states are looking for him. I'd say he's in trouble."

"Bigger trouble."

I glanced at Ayden, hoping to keep him quiet about Pete's place. I turned back to Monroe. "So, Maura helped him. Where'd they go?"

"I don't know. She didn't tell us the full plan."

"And why's Keaton in this area, if not to meet up with him?"

Monroe shook his head.

"I thought you could read his mind."

His face hardened. "He's protecting himself. Tommy's escape threatens him. So, he's dangerous to all of us."

"You don't need psychic powers to figure that out."

Monroe tapped the table. "I need help, and so do you. I have information, but I also have a price for it."

I sat up. "*What?* You're negotiating?"

"You want your assistant back. I can help. But I want you to publicly apologize for your comments about me. I want your endorsement."

Ayden got to his feet. "Annie won't support fraud, buddy!"

I gestured for Ayden to stop. He sat back down, but his face remained fierce.

Monroe watched him warily. To me, he said, "I can help you."

I mentally reviewed my options. Monroe might be able to locate Natra. I could play along if he claimed he "knew" this supernaturally. But a public affirmation of his tricks risked my reputation. I tried an end run. "You're an officer of the court. If you're a party to—"

"I'm not." Monroe cocked his head. "I don't know where he is."

Ayden bristled. "We're wasting time! Where's Natra?"

I glared at Monroe. "Here's the deal. You tell us what you know. If it helps us locate my assistant—safely!—I'll let you prove yourself. If you impress me, I'll have you on my podcast."

Monroe shook his head. "I can't guarantee anyone's safety." He crossed his arms.

That sounded ominous. Ayden snorted.

I took an alternate route, hoping to ferret out what he knew. "So, it was Maura's idea to fake a suicide note as bait for me. But we both saw Bruder in that room. He was trying to convey something he didn't want her to know. Was that part of her plan, too?" I slid the note toward him and tapped it. "We've got a central figure in front of a burning house, two figures with ropes around his neck, a triangle, and a three-line poem. Who are the people with the ropes?"

"Tommy drew the images."

"What does the fire mean?"

"Keaton burns things."

"And the red bloom of death?"

Monroe touched his ear. "Maura's earrings. Poppies. She wore them at the trial. She had them on in the prison. You didn't notice?"

"Poppies?" I looked at the images again. "Why didn't *she* notice this reference in the note?"

"She didn't see it. I wrote two notes, one for her and one for you. She thinks you read the one she saw."

This guy was clever. "Why didn't you let me have it, then?"

"Couldn't risk her grabbing it from you. She thinks I'm on her side. I want to keep it that way."

I pointed to the last line in the poem. "You must know who Reese is, then."

Monroe frowned. "You don't? You haven't figured it out?"

"I know that Reese is Keller's former partner-in-crime. I think Maura has some connection to her."

Monroe's eyes widened.

In an instant, multiple mysteries dissolved. Reese, a damaged young victim, had grown up to victimize others—including Trevor, Amber, and Cole. She'd known Keaton, leading her to his cousin, Tommy Ray Bruder.

I sat back. "*She's* Reese. Maura Reynolds is Reese Wendham."

Chapter Forty-Five

This was a revelation. I had to absorb it. But I still had questions. "How did Bruder know I've been looking for Reese?"

Monroe leaned in. "The court case. I was there to support her. He knew her, and thought we could get her to persuade Keaton to back off. She agreed to help, but she had her own agenda, namely to kneecap you. Our simple plan got messy fast. She knew you were talking to that attorney for Amber and might look into her work."

"And did she tell you why? That she was seducing depressed boys whom she knew she could trigger into suicide if they gave her trouble?"

Monroe looked from Ayden to me and shook his head. "I didn't know that. I... It was her idea to help Tommy escape. But he'd planned to ditch her as soon as he could. He thought she was going to get him out, kill Keaton, and set him up for it." He held out his right hand. "Do you have a pen?"

I squinted. "For what?"

"You like remote viewing. You talk about it. Tommy knows it, too. And he's gotten pretty good at it."

I felt as if my home had just been robbed. "Why?"

"He has a lot at stake. Like it or not, he *was* just an accomplice. And he's heading to where he can get the evidence to prove it. He's been trying to find the sites, too. You gave him the idea."

"He told you this?"

"You know about these master-apprentice relationships," Monroe said. "You discuss them on your podcast. I don't know why you find it so hard to believe about Tommy. He was just a kid. You seem to acknowledge mitigation for other teenage offenders. Just not him."

He had me, but I wasn't about to admit it. I deflected. "He's basically admitted to murder. We know about three graves and potentially four different sites. We have one set of remains. We'll find others. With the poem and tattoos, we can nail him, unless there's clear evidence to the contrary. What do you bring to the table?" I bit my tongue to try to stay open to his supposed abilities.

"I've been working on Tommy, what he's thinking."

"Too vague. Give me something specific."

Monroe blinked. He looked down the way mediums do who claim they're getting information, but he didn't close his eyes. Then he looked up. "It's the dog. He needs the dog."

I narrowed my eyes. "So, he was at—" I'd nearly said, "at Pete's place."

Monroe beat me to it. "An ex-con he knew was supposed to retrieve him from a rendezvous spot. Maura arranged it. But she didn't tell me where it was."

"What do you know about the ex-con?" I asked. "A name? What was he in for?"

Monroe shrugged. "Tommy said the guy knows his cousin."

"Can you read *him*?" I asked. Obviously, he might know Pete really well and just pretend to read him, but it would still get us information.

Monroe slid a pad of paper over to himself. He looked at me. I didn't sense any nervousness. He was used to being on the spot. That's how he impressed people.

He made a quick sketch, a circle with spikes coming out of it and an odd little cap. "It's a flower, I think," he said. "I'm not an artist. But it's something he can see, something he likes to look at." He pointed to the cap. "That's purple."

Ayden spoke first. "So, you know him. Anyone who's met him would've seen that—"

"Ayden!"

"We're wasting time, Annie. If he's got something to tell us that can help, he should just say it. That would impress me more than him drawing Pete's tattoo."

Monroe drew another piece of paper from his pocket. He kept it in his hand as he looked squarely at me. "Tommy has something specifically for you. And if you accept my terms, I'll show you."

My heart stopped. It had to be about Hailey.

A shout outside interrupted us. Ayden rose and drew his gun. Another shout had me on my feet. That was Jax. I strode over to shut off the light while Ayden went to the back door. He opened it with caution, checked, and then exited. I stayed in the front, peering through the window blinds. Jax came toward the porch, so I opened the door. Ayden came around to the front.

"Back inside, Annie," Jax said. "Someone's out here."

I let Jax in. Ayden looked around, but only a dim light in the small parking lot illuminated our vehicles. He came in, and I closed the door, locked it, and turned on the light.

"Annie!" Ayden yelled. "He's gone!"

Chapter Forty-Six

Monroe's chair was empty. Ayden ran to the back door.

I shouted, "Don't go out! You don't know who's out there."

He stepped back inside but kept his weapon ready. "He was playing you, Annie. Didn't you see it?"

"Maybe." He'd been about to give me a message from Bruder that might have led me to Hailey. That's the only thing Bruder knew that would matter to me. "Lock the door."

"Who's gone?" Jax asked.

"Monroe was here. That attorney for Bruder."

Jax looked surprised. "Here? Why"

"Claimed he could help us."

"Did you tell him anything?"

"No. But he told us some things."

Ayden shut the door, locked it, and came back. "Can't trust 'im. He might've been lying."

I held up my hands. "Maybe. But he does know about Pete. And whether he meant to or not, he revealed things." I gestured for us all to sit before I asked Jax, "What happened out there? Why were you shouting?"

He leaned on the table. "When I pulled in, I saw someone near Ayden's truck."

Ayden's eyes widened.

"Could you see who?" I asked.

"No. Just a small figure, bent over."

"Female?"

"Couldn't tell, but I thought it was a male."

"Pete's short."

"What was he doing?" Ayden asked. "Trying to break in?"

"He was on his knees, so possibly planting a tracker."

Ayden made a move toward the door, but I held up a hand. "Not yet. If it's a tracker, it'll stay there. We can check when we're sure we won't be shot."

I could tell this didn't sit well with my PI, but he nodded, grabbed a pad of paper from his pack, and said, "I say it's time for some viewing. We got three. Let's do it."

"Let's try to put this together first," I said. "I'll assume for now that Monroe told us the truth. It fits with what we know. He said Maura helped Bruder escape." I looked at Jax. "She's Reese. So now we know where Reese has been. She transformed herself into a therapist, and she's just as dangerous as Keller. *He* took off with Carly and another girl, probably her podcast buddy. We don't know if they're intentionally together or if he took them hostage. Monroe told us an ex-con picked up Bruder, probably Pete, because we think Bruder was hiding out on his property. We saw Pete earlier today in the same town we were in. Maybe he planted the tracker on Natra's car, leading him to where we were. We left it on the car to try to discover who might follow us." To Ayden, I said, "I'd guess they want one on your truck now, too. I think Bruder saw Natra's car at Pete's and acted on an opportunity. He took her hostage and made her drive him somewhere. If these people are now trying to track Ayden's truck, maybe Bruder removed the tracker on Natra's car, and they don't know where he is."

"And neither do we," Ayden added.

"But they know we might get leads."

"Where's Monroe's car?" Jax asked. "How'd he get here?"

"I wondered the same thing," said Ayden.

I shrugged. "I didn't think about it. He was just *there*. I mean, he could've parked on the road and walked over. But now I wonder if he was supposed to deflect us to shield the outside work. He's a mentalist, after all. Sleight of hand. From your description, the person outside is probably Pete, so Monroe might know him better than he admitted."

Jax nodded. "I agree. As you know, I don't think it was Pete's idea to give you the maps. I'd thought it was Keaton, but Reese has some connection with him as well."

"With Pete? How so?"

Jax gestured for Ayden's pad of paper. On it, he drew some figures. "Let's get some context. When Cassandra LaRue was arrested, Reese and Keaton went into the juvenile system. Around a decade or so later, when Cassandra died, we have this series of vanishing girls." He pointed to me. "From your list. The ones you think could be related to Bruder. But he was an adolescent. It's more likely that Keller's the primary predator, acting out. Your panty thief tattooist comes into the picture, seemingly as a fellow con who can draw the tattoos. But he's more significant."

I nodded. "If Pete picked up Bruder from Reese, he must want to help him."

"Or he's being coerced. Why'd he draw tattoos that could implicate Bruder in four murders? And also say so in an interview? And then give you the original maps? That sounds more like Pete's working *against* Bruder."

Ayden held up a finger. "When we first met Pete, I had the impression someone was watching."

I nodded. "Me, too."

"What's at stake then?" Jax asked. "Who would benefit from heaping all the responsibility on Bruder?"

Ayden and I said it at the same time. "Keller."

"So, he must have leverage over Pete. But you think Pete picked up Bruder from Reese and hid him. And that Bruder abducted Natra when he might have just killed her and taken the car. So, he wants something."

"Monroe said he wants the dog. Mika."

Jax considered this. "If so, then something's buried somewhere. That's where they're going." He tore off the top sheet of paper, took another, and passed the pad back to Ayden. "Let's get started. Annie, can you dim the lights?"

I did so, as Jax gave us direction. "All phones must be off."

I placed a protective hand on mine. "But we might get—"

His expression told me to follow directions. He looked at Ayden. "I assume you know about this method."

Ayden nodded. "Never done it, but I've listened to Annie's podcasts. I'm ready."

"It requires focus, but first-timers can achieve good results. It all depends on how you connect. You're an artist. That's an advantage. But looking for a missing person is tricky. We don't know if they're moving around or holed up somewhere. That means we could all get different impressions from the person's route."

Ayden passed me a sheet of paper and a pencil.

Jax continued. "Forget about whoever might be outside. No distractions. Our main goal is locating Natra. She's our outbounder, so to speak. She'd expect us to be looking, so unless she's blindfolded, she'll pay attention to things that could work for this. She'll show us where she is. Be open to anything—an image, a fragrance, even something tactile, like feeling cold or being in water."

Ayden nodded. "Just record whatever comes?"

"Yes. Don't think about whether it makes sense. Remember Airic's drawing of the symbol. We saw it later on the tree. We didn't know what it was at first."

"Poppy!" I covered my mouth. The other two looked at me. "That's what was on Airic's triangle drawing, the one JoLynn brought us. Monroe said the red bloom of doom is the poppy. One species of poppy produces opium, related to both sleep and death, mentioned in the suicide note. Maura—Reese—wears earrings that look like poppies. And she uses hypnosis, which poppies are related to. It all connects to her."

"Makes sense," said Jax. "And the image or impression can happen just like that, as an aha! moment. Let's start. I suggest we go into separate rooms so we don't distract each other."

Chapter Forty-Seven

I stayed in the main room. It was difficult to focus. My jaw hurt from worrying about Natra. Mika would protect her, but only if that was even possible. I kept defaulting to the tattoo maps and the possible places Bruder might take her. Then I remembered that maps can assist remote viewing. I retrieved them from my pack with a regular map and the photos of Bruder's tattoos and spread them out on the table.

We'd identified just the two counties so far: Jasper and Oconee. We could add the county where Pete's property was located. I looked at each of the maps he'd given us. None looked like his county. That was a puzzle. I was either wrong about the bag of dirt being from the hole there, or he'd been selective about the dumpsite maps he'd given us. That chilled me. There could be more than four victims. Had Bruder stayed *there* to look for something buried? Had we left that place too soon?

I pushed the maps away. I was trying to use logic. That's not how this worked. Stay open, Jax had said. Pay attention to whatever comes, even if it makes no sense. I wasn't good at meditating, but much was at stake.

The house was quiet. I hoped the others were doing better. Ayden's mind was more distractible, but he'd been keen to use RV, so he'd focus.

I looked out the window toward our cars. Everything seemed quiet. I took the paper and pen over to a couch to get more comfortable and closed my eyes. I recalled how I'd done this before. I'd been upset then, too, but I'd managed it. I'd drawn shapes that had meant nothing to me. The first time, I'd been with Puca, in his underground chamber. I'd drunk some special tea. I'd gotten sick. I didn't even remember drawing anything. Maybe I hadn't. Puca had given it to me, but the contents had been meaningful only to me. The second time, I'd been with Airic. He'd probed my mind and cleared me of the suffocating guilt that had blocked me regarding Hailey. It hadn't helped to find her, but it had provided images that showed us the location of crucial evidence. And the success of that session had renewed my commitment to Hailey.

I breathed deeply to steady myself. I thought I saw a number, 4. Or, a 2, possibly a 3. I wasn't sure. Not much to go on. I felt a sharp pain in my right earlobe. I rubbed it.

Jax walked into the room and sat on the couch. The light in his eyes told me he had something. Ayden must have heard movement, as he came from down the hall. We returned to the table.

Ayden slapped down his drawing. I blinked at it. This wasn't his usual work. He was a skilled artist. This looked like a primitive depiction of a square face with round eyes and a snouty triangular nose over an open mouth—something a child might make.

"That's all I got," he said. "I guess I'm not very good at this."

I shrugged. "I think I got a number. I'd say it was a 4. I can't tell what it means. And I felt a stabbing pain, but that could just be me."

"I had only an impression," Jax said. "But it was vivid. The smell of fresh dirt."

I sat forward. "Maybe they're digging. Monroe said Bruder wants the dog. He's looking for another body! Or he found one." My shoulders slumped. "But where?"

Jax studied Ayden's drawing. He grabbed his phone, turned it on, and tapped it a few times. Then he laid it down next to the image. We both leaned in. Ayden pointed at the phone. "I've seen that building. It's near the Jasper site."

Jax nodded. "Yes. It's not a face. It's the way the windows are set. They look like eyes. I hadn't noticed when we were there, but your drawing caught the primary features. I think it's this building."

Ayden looked surprised. "So, this worked? I viewed something?"

"We had a little help. Airic likes Natra. He agreed to assist if we had three together and it was brief."

Ayden pulled his drawing over to study it.

I looked at Jax. "I think I know the source of the disturbance Airic's getting, the thing that gives him the creeps. Monroe said Bruder's been doing RV. Maybe they're crossing paths."

I grabbed my phone and turned it on. "There's a message from Joe." I read it. "He got something from Mika's GPS. It's just a blip, though. Too far out of range. The best he can tell us is that they went south from Pete's." I tapped Ayden's drawing. "JoLynn said there's more there. They must have gone back here, to the exhumation spot."

Ayden rose. "Let's go, then."

I held up a hand. "Wait. I looked at the tattoo maps. Pete didn't include his county, but a body—or *something*—was removed from that property recently. Maybe they stayed there. We just didn't go far enough."

"All of our intel says Jasper," Jax said. "We go there."

Ayden nodded. "I agree. I wanna see where this takes us. We'll take my truck."

Jax shook his head. "My Jeep has no tracker. We don't want to be followed. And they might be watching this house. If I leave, it makes sense. I'd just be going home. If your vehicles remain here, they won't know you have a lead.

They'll think you're staying here for the night. We need to get out without anyone realizing we're on to something." He pulled my piece of paper closer. "This number might be part of a coordinate, like she was looking at a map. Or maybe an address, or road number."

"Let's just go," Ayden said. "They have a big head start. Even if they're not still there, we'd know if they'd been there, right? Maybe Natra dropped something else. If there's nothing, we can eliminate it and go to Pete's tomorrow."

I gave in. It was time for action.

Chapter Forty-Eight

I t was dark out, but a light from the main house on the property threatened our plan. We decided to make it look as if we were just getting things from the truck. Ayden fetched a pack filled with stuff he thought we'd need. Jax blocked me with his body while I slipped into the back of his Wrangler. Ayden walked back toward the rental and went inside. Jax drove to the other side of the house, where the back door was in shadows. Ayden came out and jumped in. We didn't know if we'd fooled anyone, but I watched behind and saw no one following us.

"Should we call Wayne?" Ayden asked.

"He already sent a patrol that way, and I'm not telling him we got more info with a method he'd dismiss. They're looking for Natra's car. If they'd found it, we'd know."

We stayed on back roads to make it easier to see if someone followed. Natra's car might still have the tracker on it, but we didn't know who'd put it there. Could've been Keaton, Pete, Reese, or any combination. I sensed no honor in *this* gang of thieves. Each seemed to have reason to undercut the others. Joe sent a message that he'd tracked some intel about Pete on the dark web and was learning about his connections.

Trees rose on both sides, making me feel isolated. I mentally willed Natra to connect. But the closer we got to our target destination, the more I worried about the complications. "We need a plan. It's dark. That could help, but it could also hinder us."

Ayden handed me a small flashlight. "We should split up. We all know where the site is. We can each approach from a different angle. Bruder probably has a gun."

"Not a bad idea," Jax said. "But won't Mika bark and alert him?"

"All the more reason to do it this way."

Jax glanced at me. "I should drive right up to the site as if I'm checking it. I've been there several times. I'll drop you two off first. If it looks suspicious, I'll stay in the car and text you."

While Jax and Ayden discussed logistics, I checked my email. I had something new from Janissa—a warning. "Annie, I received Cole Cheney's journal from the Cheneys' attorney. He hints at finding something at Maura's house that made him think she'd killed someone. He was scared. He thought she knew he'd snooped. It's not proof of anything, but be careful of her."

I read the email to the others. Ayden nodded. "She doesn't know Maura's Reese."

"Nothing could have come from Cassandra's sick influence but sheer malignancy. Reese and Keaton were both damaged goods. One of them most likely killed her. My money's on Reese. I wonder where she went after she left Bruder with Pete. And where's Keaton Keller?"

I asked Ayden for his pad of paper. I tried to sketch out the relationships based on what we'd discovered. Thinking out loud, I said, "Reese and Keaton were associates, but not tight. We haven't seen them together, and Reese allegedly wants to use Bruder, Keaton's cousin, to bait him. According to the note, Bruder apparently felt squeezed by Keaton and Reese, at least, that's Monroe's interpretation. Reese helped Tommy escape, and Pete picked him up, so Pete and Reese are associates." I paused, then added, "I think her attempt to set me up for his escape is just a side issue to distract me from tracking her patient abuse. I'm just a fly on a rhino. Monroe's another side issue. He seems unrelated to these earlier relationships. So, we're focused on Reese, Keaton, Pete, and Tommy. Pete placed the tattoos on Tommy, and he or someone else wanted us to have the maps of the gravesites. And whoever wrote the Jasper poem to Carly, which apparently wasn't Bruder, wanted her to find the grave. Pete or Tommy kidnapped Natra to keep looking for something."

"Seems like Pete's a central character," Ayden said.

"We should've checked him more thoroughly," Jax added. "We might have to figure out his association with Keaton or Reese."

I scanned my notes. "And we should've looked into how an ex-con with seemingly no financial means acquired that piece of property. He's definitely part of a cover-up. Joe's looking for info now."

Ayden tapped his leg. "So, Pete had the original maps, and he did the tattoos. He picked up Bruder and let him hide there. But he also said in that interview that the tattoos were related to Bruder's victims. That's what got me interested in him."

I had a thought. "Where'd you get that article about Pete? Did you dig that up yourself?"

Ayden went quiet for a moment before he said, "Natra got it from one of the chats on the *Killer Hooks* site. Someone posted a note about it, and she found it. That's where she got the tattoo photos, too. Some groupie said she'd taken them when she visited Bruder."

Jax looked at me. "I have a feeling the groupie is actually Pete with a smuggled phone."

We discussed a variety of possible scenarios, but each had holes. I just wanted to get to the site to see if we were right about Natra's location. That Pete had duped us stung a bit, but we'd had no reason when we met him to think he'd put on an act. Aside from one thing: he'd called himself the camouflage king.

A flash of light from behind us made me look back. "We might have company."

Chapter Forty-Nine

When he could, Jax turned right onto a dirt road. The car sped past. I made out a black Ford SUV, not a vehicle that concerned us—unless Keaton had made a switch. Jax pulled to the side and turned off the lights. "We're close," he said. "You can walk from here to get to your positions." He pointed. "There's another road up ahead that goes left, which should give you some cover."

From his stash, Ayden handed out penlights and two-way radios. We all checked our weapons.

"Maybe you should stay with me, Annie," Ayden said. "At least until we're closer."

I shook my head. "That's duplication of effort." To save time in an emergency, I turned off the password protection on my phone. "Keep your phones on mute but check them regularly. No one enters a situation without backup."

They both looked at me.

"I know, I know. I don't take my own advice. But we've got several dangerous people who've managed to find us, and we don't know where any of *them* are. Maybe we'll get lucky, and one of them will kill another before we arrive. Seems like they're each gunning for someone else in their pack."

Jax assigned a direction to each of us and provided a sense of where we were relative to the target area. "I'll drive by and have a look, but Annie, you'll arrive at the site next. I'll park beyond it and come in from the south. If Bruder's alone with Natra, wait and alert us. If Mika barks, just stay still.

Shooting in the dark is the last thing anyone wants."

I nodded. "I want Bruder alive. He needs to tell me where Hailey is."

"Eyes and ears open," Jax said, "weapons ready."

We parted ways. I went down the dirt road before I found an opening on my left into the woods. I followed parallel ruts on a seemingly disused road or driveway. I looked back. Jax and Ayden were gone. I felt instantly vulnerable. As I went under the trees, darkness pressed in. I used the penlight to keep from stumbling over logs or breaking my ankle in some random mole hole. I listened for noise and heard only the typical night sounds. Part of me wanted Mika to bark, to help us locate her, but part of me wanted her to stay quiet.

I watched for the clearing where we'd exhumed the remains of a young girl only a few days before. We had one victim location; we knew of possibly two more. If we captured Bruder, we might be able to persuade him to interpret the tattoo maps. After about ten minutes, I paused to check my phone. No messages. My compass said I was moving in the right direction, but I feared I might be lost. The track kept going.

I took a step and froze. I thought I'd heard a muffled bark. I listened. Then I moved to my right, toward it. The lane went in that direction. I walked as quietly as I could. Soon, I saw the dark bulk of a small building. I slowed down and crept closer.

It looked like someone's dilapidated house. This wasn't exactly backwoods, not like Pete's set-up, but in this area, an older shack wasn't a surprise. Wayne had mentioned a couple of abandoned properties. I stepped around it, listening. The place was silent. It smelled old, as if no one had been here in a while. I brushed away insects and used the penlight to explore. A dark BMW parked in back alerted me to someone's presence who didn't live here. No resident of this shack drove a BMW. But Reese did. On the other side, I saw what I was looking for: Natra's Bronco.

They were here. At least, Mika was. But she hadn't barked again. I stepped close to a grimy window with a crack down the center and saw a dim light inside—a camp light, like the kind Natra carried in her car. Flickering told me there were also some candles. I reached for my phone. To Jax and Ayden,

I typed, *Follow road I took to shack in woods.* Before I hit 'send,' I pondered what to add for better directions when someone behind me knocked my phone from my hand. I heard a woman's voice. "Nice of you to join us, Dr. Hunter."

I spun around to face Maura Reynolds, aka Reese Wendham. She gestured with the barrel of a nine-mil. "I'm sure you're armed. Toss your weapon over there."

I seethed. I wanted to jump at her and pummel her face for what she'd done to her young male patients. Instead, I pulled out my Glock and placed it where she'd pointed. She kept her weapon on me and picked up my gun and phone. "Now, go inside."

I stepped up to the porch and saw the number: 143. I opened the front door and entered. The place smelled of layers of dust mixed with mold. Mika barked in another room, and Natra shushed her. Relief flooded me. They were alive. I entered the room, lit by camping candles, and saw them. Natra looked surprised. To my right, Bruder leaned against a table, holding a handgun. He'd replaced his prison garb with jeans and a blue shirt. From Monroe's message, I'd thought he'd gone his own way, but clearly he was still with Reese.

Mika whined. I went over to calm her and asked Natra, "You all right?" She gave a curt nod. I hoped I looked reassuring. I knew we could both be dead before Ayden and Jax realized they should start looking for me. I hadn't sent my directions, but eventually, they'd notice my absence. I had to figure out a way to warn them to be careful.

Reese placed my phone on a table near Bruder. I stared at it. Bruder noticed. He picked it up and looked, then glanced at me. Reese grabbed it. She read the message and snorted. "Let them come. We'll take care of them." She looked at Bruder. "That'll give us a car no one's looking for."

I nearly gasped. I'd inadvertently baited a trap. I had to stop this. When her thumb moved to press *send*, I launched myself and slammed her against the wall. It knocked the phone from her hand. Behind me, Mika went into a barking frenzy. I hit Reese in the face as hard as I could. Mika was there, growling and biting her arm. Reese cried out, "Tommy!" She shielded

229

herself against the dog and knocked me in the jaw. I tasted blood.

Natra yelled at Mika, and I felt hands grip me and pull me away. Reese recovered, got up, and held up her gun. Her shirt was torn, and her nose was bleeding. I saw blood where Mika had bitten her. I backed off, struggling to break the grip that held me. "You killed those boys! Trevor and Cole! We know who you are, Reese! It's over. The cops are coming for you." Turning, I saw that Bruder had grabbed me. "For you, too! They know about this place. I've told them I'm here." I swung around to strike him, but he blocked me. Natra pulled me away.

Reese wiped her nose and shouted, "Get her under control. And shut that dog up!" She handed Bruder the gun and entered an adjoining room. He gestured for us to move over to the wall. Natra made Mika stop growling. I looked on the floor for my phone, but it was too dark to see. I had to get it. I'd heard it hit the floor. Possibly it had slid under a chair, but I couldn't get down to look, or Bruder would realize what I wanted to find. I couldn't let them send that text.

Natra came close behind me. I felt something slide into my back pocket. I breathed out. She'd grabbed the phone.

Reese came back in and looked around. "Where's that fucking phone?"

To distract her, I shouted, "You don't have a chance. Cops are crawling through this place, looking for you. Both of you. They know you broke him out of prison, and your partner just kidnapped two girls. *Everyone's* on this!"

Reese looked at me. "What girls?"

"Your buddy, Keaton. He took hostages."

Reese looked at Bruder. He shrugged. She grabbed a candle to search for my phone.

"Don't call 'em here," Bruder growled. "We got 'nough with these two. We need ta split. Now!"

"They're looking for my car!" She gestured toward Natra. "And hers."

"They know mine, too," I said. "You won't get very far, and it's parked at least a mile from here. It won't—"

My two-way crackled. I grabbed it to silence it.

Reese looked startled. Then her expression brightened. To Bruder, she said, "Get that!"

He looked at me and held out his hand. Pursing my lips, I took it from my waistband and handed it over. Ayden's voice came through.

"Annie, come in. Where are you? The red car's at the site, empty. Keller's here."

Chapter Fifty

Reese beckoned for Bruder to come over to her. She said something in a voice too low for me to hear and handed him my Glock. Natra signaled to me to be patient. I took a breath and leaned down to Mika while I searched for a way out of this mess. Not responding to Ayden would alarm him and possibly lure him into danger. I had to warn him.

Reese took the two-way and went outside. Bruder closed the door. He crossed over to the window and moved the tattered curtain. Mika whined. I heard a car engine. The BMW. Reese was leaving.

"What's the plan?" Natra asked Bruder.

"She wants Pete to bring Keaton over, then ambush 'im."

I looked from Bruder to Natra. They were acting like *friends*. "What's going on?"

Bruder laid my gun on a table. I was tempted to lunge for it.

Natra put her hand on my arm. "Annie, it's all right. This will sound crazy, but we were looking for evidence. And we found it."

"*We*? You and *this* guy? This *fugitive*?"

"Sorry. I couldn't call. Pete followed me to his place. He took my phone."

"Pete?" I looked at Bruder. "But you were there, too, weren't you? That's where you were hiding out, in Pete's trailer."

Bruder nodded.

"Whose side's Pete on, anyway? Is he helping you, or is he setting you up?"

Bruder's gaze darted around as if he expected Reese to return any second. "Don't matter. He's bein' squeezed. Reese and Keaton both have somethin' on 'im. He's jus' tryin' ta survive. He's a fuckin' chameleon. Goes whichever way works. So, you figured out the note."

I stared at Bruder. "What are you doing? Why'd you leave the prison? Why are you with this woman?" I almost said *she's a killer,* but so was he.

"My cousin's tryin' ta snuff me. Thinks I'm leadin' that crazy radio girl to his ...*spots.* He wants ta shut me up. I had ta get out."

"He's not wrong. That poem you sent to Carly gave it away."

"Didn't send 'er nothin'. Pete was tryin' ta get 'er to find somethin' *he* hid without it comin' back on 'im." Bruder gestured toward Natra. "We got no time ta talk. She's comin' back. An' now Keaton's here. Pete musta told 'im."

I went to the door and forced the rusty lock into place. "Reese isn't getting back in here."

"Can't do that. She thinks I'm with 'er."

"Tell her we rushed you." I gestured to Natra. "We're leaving."

Bruder shook his head. "She can't go. She knows where it is."

"That only helps you," Natra said.

"'Less you nick it." He glared at her and gestured toward me. "She's got reason ta hurt me."

"Where's this evidence?" I asked. "What is it?"

Bruder turned on me with fury in his eyes. "This is your fault! I was fine servin' my time till you stirred it all up. You made Keaton mad. An' he's *crazy!* He don't even know I seen Reese kill that woman. He'd skin 'er alive if he knew. I don't know why he's comin' after me! I done what he said. But yur makin' it look like I didn't. Like I *want* you to dig up these girls. Jus' leave 'em be!"

"Then why'd you get those tattoos, like some kind of boast?"

Bruder strode over to me, his jaw tight and his eyes blazing. Mika growled. He stayed focused on me. Standing over me, he said, "Think I'm stupid? *Pete* put 'em on me. *They* tell 'im what ta do! These tats was ta remind me ta keep it buttoned up. Pete shouldn'ta said nuthin', either."

What he'd just conveyed floored me. He'd seen Reese kill Cassandra. He'd been forcibly tattooed. He hadn't corresponded with Carly.

I raised my chin. "Well, Pete did talk, we figured it out, and I intend to find my friend, the one *you* snatched. It was you, on a bike. You took her.

Tell me where she is. Show me which one of your stupid tattoos will lead to her grave. Then we'll leave."

"No." He moved his head toward Natra. "She ain't goin'. She knows where it is."

"Why didn't you grab it when you found it?"

"We did," Natra said. "But Pete's unpredictable. We didn't want to risk him caving in to Keaton and handing it over, or Reese getting it, so we moved it till we could go back for it."

I looked from one to the other. "What is it? What did Pete have?"

"He was the 'ridg'nal one," Bruder said. "He grabbed girls for Keaton. An' he recorded stuff, 'case he needed it. But no one came fur him, not fur that, so he laid low. When you people started focusing on me an' thinkin' I done these murders, he got nervous. An' he feels guilty 'bout gettin' me involved."

I took a stance. "Where did you bury my friend?"

"You're not getting' nothin' till I have what *I* need. An' then yur gonna help me."

"*Help* you?"

"You talk about it, what happens to kids who get forced into this. It's not their fault. You help 'em. I seen somethin' you wrote about it. The court, they'd listen to you. Then I wouldn't go back ta prison. I served my time."

"You're going back, Bruder. You killed people. Girls!"

"I didn't kill nobody! Jus' picked 'em up and brought 'em. I didn't know any better."

I didn't buy it. "For three years?"

He shrugged.

"Why didn't your attorney say that?"

"Keaton woulda killed me. He's crazy. Better ta be locked up."

I wasn't sure I could argue with that. I changed the subject. "What did you write on that note for Monroe to give me? Was it a location?"

Bruder shook his head. I didn't know if he meant he didn't write the note or wouldn't tell me. And he wasn't ready to follow my lead. "Keaton killed 'em. He made me bring 'em to please that dead guy. I didn't know that's what he was doin'."

"What dead guy?"

"Pete's dad. *Pa!* He's…" He grimaced, as if recalling something revolting.

Mika jumped up, her fur raised, and barked. She shook herself, whined, and pushed her nose against Natra. I wondered if Ayden was close.

"It's smoke," Natra said. "Can you smell it?"

Chapter Fifty-One

I sniffed the air. "I do."

Bruder went to the window and looked outside. "Shit! He's here. He's burnin' us out."

I grabbed my gun off the table. A loud rap sounded on the door, like a forceful kick.

"Natra, go!" I ordered.

Someone slammed against the door. Natra took Mika out the back door, where her Bronco was parked.

I heard a loud *crack!* The doorframe broke, and the door burst open. I flattened myself against the wall. A man came in, gun raised. I'd seen that slender figure before. Keaton! He aimed for Bruder. I fled. Shots rang out behind me from two different guns. A bullet *snicked* into a wall near me. Bruder yelled, like he'd been hit. I made it to the back door.

Natra was in her car, ready to go. I ran to her window. She rolled it down. "Get Mika away," I said. "Ayden and Jax are out here somewhere. Text them to stay back. Then call Wayne."

"No phone."

I handed mine over. "Use this. It's unlocked."

"You can't stay!"

"I think he was hit. We can't lose him. Unless he told you—"

"He didn't."

"Do you have your gun?"

"Bruder has it."

I felt a rush of searing heat. Thick smoke told me the far side of this shack

236

was burning fast. "Go! Get away from the fire and wait. I'll come as fast as I can. Watch out for Reese."

She handed me a baseball cap and a bandana for protection, and drove off. I took cover at the side of the house and wrapped my face. Smoke-thickened air made me cough. I edged around to the side where flames licked up the side of the shack. Keaton, the burner. The place would go fast. It was nothing but dry wood, surrounded by a thick bed of dead pine needles. This entire area was threatened. I looked through the window but saw no movement. Taking a breath, I raised the bandana over my nose and went through the open door.

Bruder sat slumped against a wall. Keller had seemingly left. Bruder coughed. He was alive. Taking a candle to him, I saw blood on his shirt, right shoulder. I looked around. The curtain! I ripped it down to get a piece to use to apply pressure to his wound. Not the best, but nothing in here was sanitary. I wasn't about to take the shirt off *my* back for this guy. Dark smoke billowed in and flowed across the ceiling.

"Come on," I urged. "Don't let Keaton win." I needed this guy alive. "Keep your hand pressed on this. I'll help."

I got him almost on his feet before he went to one knee and cried out.

"Come on. *Now!* Stay with me."

I hated having to save this guy. I hated him, period. But he was a human being. I wasn't leaving him to perish horribly in a fire.

I got him up again, got his arm around my shoulder, and half-pulled him out the door. We were both coughing from the acrid air and flying ash, which left a sour taste in my mouth. Outside, Bruder stumbled and went down again.

"Get up," I shouted. "We're not safe ye—"

My head was yanked back, and intense pain shot through my scalp as someone pulled my hair and knocked off my cap. I let go of Bruder. The hard muzzle of a gun pressed against my skull. I braced for a shot, but then heard Mika's fierce growl as she flew at my assailant. A shot went off, but she continued to growl and bite. I saw a figure roll and try to crawl away. Keller! I looked for my dropped pistol. A glint of light reflected from the fire showed its location. I reached for it, but my hand landed on Bruder's. He pulled the gun away and aimed at his cousin. I grabbed his arm to keep him from shooting Mika. He pushed me and tried again.

Natra ran up and shouted for Mika. Behind us, a loud roar and a burst of heat told me the roof had caved in. The walls would go next. We'd suffocate. I felt like we'd been trapped in an oven turned up to broil.

"Car's over here!" Natra pointed to her right.

Keller, facedown, shielded the back of his neck. I couldn't see his gun, but I assumed he had it. His hands and shirt were bloody from Mika's attack. Natra dragged her away.

Bruder aimed my gun toward Keller, but his hand shook. I took the weapon. He was bleeding badly. We had to get him to a hospital.

Natra brought her Bronco over. Ash rained down, some of it white-hot. This whole place could ignite. We had to leave.

I went to Keller. "Get up!"

He didn't move.

"Get up now!"

Keller rolled over and threw a handful of pine needles at me. I shielded my face. He darted into the woods. Furious, I went after him, but he got away. I couldn't see very far, and he had a gun. I got behind a tree to look for him, but he was gone. By now, the house was engulfed in flames. I grabbed the cap to protect my hair while I helped Natra get Bruder into the back seat of her car. I got in next to him to buffer him from the dog, and Natra drove us away.

In the back compartment, Mika licked her paws. She'd gotten some burns. I grabbed Natra's first-aid kit. It was for the dog, but I could use some for Bruder.

Natra handed me my phone. "Calls are in. Jax said to meet him at the site. Cops should be here soon. Also a fire truck."

Bruder reached for the door handle, but I put a hand on him. "You're not going anywhere."

"We need to get to—" He coughed.

"On our way," Natra said. "I think Pete knows where we went."

CHAPTER FIFTY-ONE

"If he knows," Bruder added, "then *she* knows."

Chapter Fifty-Two

I looked at Natra. "What are you talking about?"

She glanced in the rearview. "What Pete has on Keaton's in a leather pouch. We moved it so he couldn't get it if Keaton bullied him. It's what he was trying to lead Carly to."

"We can't get it now."

"We have to. I forgot about the tracker on my car. Pete put it there, and he could figure out where we went."

I shook my head. "Pete doesn't know a damn thing about technology. He doesn't even have a cell phone."

Bruder snorted.

I recalled his reference to Pete as a chameleon. "What?"

Bruder sneered. "He played you. That guy's a wiz. You should see his vault. Got stuff strung up all over the place. Cell jammers. Cell simulators. Satellite phones. Hacking tools. He's a survivalist."

"He smudged my surveillance camera. Not very sophisticated."

"'less he wanted to get you ta think one thing while he did another. But I doubt it was him. He'd a been in an' out 'thout you knowin'. But he's weak. If Reese or Keaton catch up to 'im, either of 'em could get the pouch from 'im."

This was important new information. I motioned with a bandage. "Let's attend to your wound."

He leaned back. I unbuttoned his ripped, bloodstained shirt and saw that Keaton's shot had scraped across his chest and arm, leaving a bloody groove. He'd need stitches, but he'd survive. He had to. I cleaned the area the best

240

I could. The intricate tattoos on his muscled chest reminded me of my mission. He looked at me through reddened eyes as if to say *I knew you'd help.* "You get me that pouch," he said, "I'll tell ya what ya wanna know."

"What's in it? You said Pete recorded something."

"Fingers, ears, whatever he cut off," Bruder murmured.

A chill ran through me. Robin Dahl's fingers. That's why Bruder had needed Mika—the decomp scent.

"And an audiotape," Natra added. "Keaton made Pete record torture sessions. Pete made copies."

I couldn't argue. We couldn't let Keaton confiscate proof of his bloody deeds. He'd destroy it. "How far is it?"

"Not far."

I tore the wrapping off the bandage and applied it. When I tried to move my gun from under his belt, Bruder put his hand on it and flashed me a warning look.

"Who made Pete do these tattoos?" I asked.

"Keaton."

"And the interview?"

He nodded. "Also Keaton. Ta keep me shut up."

"You mean silent or shut up in prison?"

"Both."

"And all you did was bring the girls."

"Couldn't do the rest. Couldn't bury 'em." His mouth clenched, and his eyes watered.

"Why not?"

"Got claustrophobia. Couldn't go in the vault."

"What's in the vault?"

Bruder's eyes widened. He looked at me as if he thought I was dense. "*Him.* The dead guy. Pa! Keaton tortured the girls in front of 'im, an' he beat 'em an' cut off parts, an' then buried 'em alive. Like Pa sposably wanted. Think I ain't 'fraid of *that* kinda crazy? I was *glad* ta get locked up away from him. Don't even care if Reese kills 'im an' lays the blame on me. Least he'd be dead."

I tried not to think about Hailey. Buried alive. Carly had been right, except "Captain Kidd" was Keller, not Bruder. And Keller was repeating his act for Ma, under the imaginary Pa's direction, like sealing that first girl alive in the wall. How had the juvenile system missed his dangerous delusions?

"Where's this vault?" I asked.

Bruder lifted his chin. "Said 'nuff. I get what I need, you get what you need."

Natra maneuvered the bumpy lane. Bruder grimaced as I taped the bandage more firmly in place. He watched out the window. His face showed his pain.

I got in the back and worked on Mika. She licked my hand the entire time. At least *she* was grateful.

I came back to the seat next to Bruder and checked my phone. Texts from Ayden and Jax had gone unanswered. I had to respond. I started a text when Bruder pulled the phone from my hand.

"Not yet," he growled.

I reached for it, but he withdrew my gun.

I made a face. "You're gonna shoot me now?"

He turned the muzzle toward the phone screen. "Back away, or it's gone."

I held up my hands.

He tapped something on the screen. "We'll call Pete." He gestured toward Natra. "He has her phone."

"He turned it off," Natra said.

"An' I turned it back on before he left that shack an' stuck it in his car. He'll hear it."

Natra stopped the car. She turned around in her seat. "Don't call. We're close. Maybe we shouldn't drive right up to it."

It was too dark for me to see anything. "Where is it?" I asked. "I'll get it."

"Nope." Bruder shook his head. "She goes."

"I'll be all right," Natra assured me.

"And you'll be back," Bruder added. The implication was clear: He had control of Mika and me.

Natra got out and closed the door.

Chapter Fifty-Three

Mika whined. I quieted her. I thought I might be able to overpower Bruder if I slammed something against his wound. I wanted to grab my gun. As if reading my mind, he turned the weapon on me. Mika growled.

"What did you give Monroe to show me?" I asked.

"You saw it."

"Not the suicide note. The other one."

Bruder looked confused.

"The note for me."

"He has all my papers. Could be anything."

"Was it about my friend? The girl you snatched."

Bruder's eyes went right, as if he'd realized something.

"Did he read your mind?" I asked. "That's what he claims he can do."

Bruder sneered. "He's a convenience, that's all. He got Reese. I needed her, but I didn't 'spect her ta want you involved."

"So she'd planned to set me up for your escape."

"That's her bizness. So, I used it for *my* bizness."

"And what you drew on that suicide note. That was you trapped between her and Keaton, right?"

Bruder stared at me. "It's *Pete*. Thought you figured it out. Keaton burned his place. That was the fire."

"And what was the message?"

"They're both squeezin' him. Ya can't trust 'im. When he's with one, he does what that one says. Then he switches. If Keaton threatens him, he'll give over the pouch ta save 'imself. I wuz warnin' ya that Reese was right there and she had hold of Pete just as much as Keaton did. Doin' you a favor."

"How does Pete even know Keaton? Why would he pick up girls for him?"

"It was somethin' they done together. It was Pete's idea ta get me into it. He thought girls would go for me. I wuz jus' bringin' 'em back, not knowing what wuz up till I saw one in a hole at Pete's."

"How many are there?"

He shrugged. "Don't know. The dead guy's Pete's ol' man. Starts with him. Don't know who killed 'im, but that's how Keaton made Pete do stuff."

"So, everyone's got something on everyone else."

"'Cept me. What I know don't mean nuthin'. I need that pouch."

Natra came back and got in. She shook her head. "Can't get it. She's here. Spotted her car. I think she's waiting for someone to show up."

Bruder sat up. "Fuck!" He opened the door and got out. I made a grab for him but missed. He strode into the darkness.

I scooted toward the door. "We can't let him go!"

"I don't have a gun," Natra said.

"He's got mine, too, and my phone. Keep Mika quiet and the engine running. I'll be back."

I stepped out, slammed the door, and ran after Bruder. I heard yelling and recognized Reese's voice. I moved toward it.

Car headlights illuminated two figures in a clearing, Bruder and Reese. I ducked behind Reese's BMW. She held something dark and boxy against her, which I suspected was the coveted pouch.

"I need this," Reese said. "Pete told me what it is."

Bruder had my gun on her. "*I* need it!" He reached for it, but she pulled away.

"You can't do anything!" Reese shouted. "You show your face, you're going right back inside. We have the same goal. I'll take it to help us both."

"Yur goin' ta prison, too. You killed those kids, an' they know it."

"She was lying. I haven't done anything wrong but help you, and you won't be telling anyone about that. Put down your gun, Tommy."

"No!" He grabbed the pouch.

I considered getting into Reese's car and driving at them if I could, but then I saw Pete. That scrawny little tattooed guy watched from the edge of the clearing where Reese and Bruder bickered. Was he there with Reese... or Keaton? I saw a shadow move on his other side. Keaton would've needed a ride to get here from that shack. So, Pete was with *him*.

Reese struggled with Bruder and got the pouch back. She strode toward her car—and me. I crouched into the shadows.

"Stop!" Bruder yelled. "Now!"

This scene, I knew, was a reckoning, like the movie monsters Godzilla, Mothra, and Ghidora about to clash. Reese, Tommy, and Keaton were all in the same place, but Reese and Keaton were the primary foes. They were the vile blooms on Cassandra's toxic vine.

The dark shadow moved. The lights revealed Keaton. A glint in his hand showed a gun. "I'll take it."

Reese stopped and turned. "I was bringing it to you. I knew Tommy would use it against you."

"Bitch!" Bruder turned toward his cousin. "She killed Ma! I saw it. She hit 'er an' pushed her down the stairs. An' she wants ta kill you, too, an' hang me up fur it."

"He's lying," she shouted. "No one was there!"

Silence. Even the night bugs went mute. Bruder backed away. I leaned in for a better view.

Keller aimed at her. "If you know he wasn't there... you must've been. Always thought it was you. Drop the pouch."

Reese waited for a tense moment. Then she sprinted in my direction. Keller shot twice. I flinched. Reese went down. The pouch flew from her hands toward me. It was just a few yards away. I tensed, about to run for it, when I heard Pete shout, "No!" Keaton shot again. Bruder went down.

I gasped and held my mouth. Keller looked in my direction, as if he'd heard me. I turned and ran.

Chapter Fifty-Four

J umping into the Bronco, I yelled, "Get out of here!"

Mika barked. Natra took off. I related what I'd just seen.

Her eyes widened. "Bruder's dead?"

"I don't know. But I would've been if I'd waited to find out." I looked back. Reese's car was there, but Keller would need to locate the key or go back to whatever car he and Pete had. That bought us time. Bruder had my phone, and Pete had Natra's, so I couldn't alert anyone.

Natra tore through the way we'd come, steering to avoid ruts. I looked at her. "You know where we are?"

"Pretty much. Compass right there." She let go of the wheel briefly to point. "We need to go southeast."

Mika whined and made her way to the seat where I'd recently tended Bruder, so I calmed her. My own heart beat so fast it blocked my breath. "It's okay, girl." It wasn't. Bruder couldn't be dead, murdered right in front of me. That would snuff my hope to find Hailey. And my phone and gun were on him. I could see Keller spinning this double homicide against me.

I sat up. "Do you see that? Ahead of us."

"The light? Yes. Someone's coming, but it can't be them. They couldn't get over there that fast."

"Let's hope it's Jax. By now, they should've tracked my phone." I peered through the trees. "It's a light color SUV. It's not Jax."

Natra slowed. "What should we do?"

I looked at her. "You called the cops, right?"

"I called Wayne."

"Then he sent the cavalry."

Two sets of lights approached. Natra stopped. I gripped the seat. The lead car pulled up, and a man got out.

"It's Tim." Natra breathed out. "From Wayne's team. The one who likes Mika." She rolled down her window. From the back seat, Mika barked.

Tim walked up. "So, they found you. Glad to see it. Are you two all right?"

I pointed behind us. "They need help back there, but they're armed. Two were shot. One's the fugitive from Tennessee."

Tim turned and strode back to the second car. In a moment, they were on their way. He returned to us. "We got an ambulance close by, another on the way. You're sure you're all right? Dr. Hunter?"

I realized I probably looked like I'd been rolling around with some wild animal. My face felt swollen where Reese had slugged me. "I'll be fine. Banged up a bit but not shot. How'd you get here so fast?"

"Oh, I came down on my free time when I heard your partners here'd gone missing." He gestured toward Mika.

I liked this guy. Natra rolled down the back window so he could pet her. "Have you seen Ayden?" I asked.

"Yes, ma'am. He gave us your coordinates."

"Do you know about the fire?"

"We're on it."

Another set of lights shone from the east.

"That'll be the paramedics," Tim said. "I should go help."

"Thank you. We'll get out of your way. Oh, and if you find a leather pouch, handle it carefully. It's evidence. And my phone's back there on the guy who's shot."

"Yes, ma'am. Copy that."

I didn't expect the pouch to still be there. Surely, it was now in Keaton's hands.

Natra found her way back to the main site. Ayden came to open my door.

"What happened, Annie? Are you all right?"

"Long story. I need your phone. Mine's gone."

I called Wayne to fill him in. He seemed to sense how tired I was. For once, he didn't scold me. He didn't even remind me I'd have to give a statement. I asked him to keep me informed about Bruder. I thought he might be dead.

Jax stood close. When I ended the call, he hugged me tight. "I'm glad you're safe," he said. "We had no idea where you were. We'll head to my place, get some space from all this."

I pushed away. "I have to stay close. Bruder was shot."

"I'll find out the status."

While paramedics checked me out, I watched for Tim's return.

Ayden's phone rang. He nodded to me and listened. When he hung up, he said, "One dead, one wounded, no one else there. Bruder's alive. They're taking him in, but he took a bullet to the head. Looks bad."

"So, Pete and Keaton got away."

"They must've. Tim said there wasn't any pouch, but he found your phone. They'll keep looking. He wants you to give a statement if you're up to it."

I nodded. Weariness had settled in, along with a headache. Jax helped me over to his Jeep. "Bruder will be in surgery for a while, Annie. You need to rest. Natra's telling Tim what he needs to know for now. You can talk to them tomorrow."

Ayden was antsy to get back to his truck, but since it was late and Jax's place was closer, he agreed we should go there. I reminded him that Pete and Keaton might try to ambush us at our rental. I'd seen Keaton shoot down two people tonight. He wouldn't hesitate to kill us if he thought we were a threat.

And we most definitely were a threat.

Chapter Fifty-Five

At the ranch, I cleaned the smoke residue off my face and arms and had my burns treated. Despite exhaustion, I knew I wouldn't sleep. My mind was as active as Ayden's foot when he's ready to get into action. In the library, surrounded by the comforting scent of books and leather, we debriefed. Natra created a timeline so we could collect our respective accounts in one place. Mika and Digger snoozed together in a corner.

We'd removed the tracker from Natra's car, although I doubted anyone would have followed us onto Jax's property. He had a sophisticated security system. I felt good about our decision to stay here tonight.

Jax went first. He described stopping at the exhumation site. "I saw multiple tracks, but it was hard to tell when they'd been made. JoLynn had been there, and cops've been in and out. Otherwise, it looked deserted."

"We were near there," Natra said, "but we didn't drive right to it."

"How'd you even get there?" Ayden asked. "How did I completely miss you?"

Natra took a breath. "When I got to Pete's property, I took Mika out. She alerted on the hole you probably saw, where I tossed her treat bag. Hoped you guys would see it. Pete was there in a tree, watching me. He'd put the trackers on our cars, and he'd tracked us to where we had lunch, like you thought, Annie. Then he got back to his place ahead of me, because I'd stopped to get Mika."

I squinted. "But you were with Bruder."

"Yeah. He was there, too. He knew Pete had stashed evidence against

Keaton in Jasper, cuz it was away from the property. Reese knew it, too, so he wanted to get it before she did. He figured it was near the grave we dug up. Tommy told Pete to go try to delay Reese. When Pete left, Tommy had me drive him. He thought we might need Mika, but when he said it was near a tree, I knew it was the oak with the K cut into it. That's why it was marked. The pouch was buried between the roots, under that root that was sticking up. Remember how Mika and Digger kept sniffing around there? We thought the roots had absorbed decomp, but something else was there. The leather muted the odor, but they did indicate."

"That's over an hour's drive from Pete's," I said. "Did Bruder talk to you?"

"Yes, some of the same stuff he told you. I tried to work him, but he was jumpy. And armed. He had my gun. I picked up that Keaton thinks Pete's *his* partner or accomplice or whatever. So, Pete was pretending to keep tabs on us for *him* but also trying to help with Tommy. Like Tommy said, Pete was Keaton's original procurer. Keaton had something on him. He'd make Pete bring redheaded girls that he'd then hold captive to torture before he killed them. Sometimes he made Pete do it so he could watch, like Cassandra's fetish had rubbed off on 'im."

I cringed and pushed the image from my mind. "What was that story about Pete's father?"

"He didn't tell me that part."

To the others, I said, "From what I made out, Pete or Keaton killed Pete's father. I had the impression Keaton thinks he was Pa, the imaginary partner behind Ma's abusive behavior. If I understood Tommy correctly, the body's preserved in a vault somewhere." I grimaced. "Like he's still directing them to kill."

Ayden grimaced. "That's sick."

"I've seen worse delusions but not much worse. With no mental health resources to keep Keaton in check, he's free to be bat-shit crazy."

"It makes sense," Jax added. "He'd bought Cassandra's claim that Pa was out there, watching, making them abuse the other kids. Keaton resisted therapists' efforts to free him from her influence."

I told Natra to continue.

She hugged herself, as if grateful to be safe. "Pete tried to get himself out of it by recruiting Tommy Bruder. Tommy was fifteen. Pete gave him a motorcycle as incentive. Tommy picked up some girls, including Hailey, but got busted with one. By then, he was eligible for adult incarceration. Keaton scared him into accepting the conviction and going to prison. I guess that's why he showed up at Tommy's trial—to make sure."

"What's the evidence?" Ayden asked. "What's in the pouch?"

"I didn't see it, but he told me it had body parts, items from victims, and an audiotape of Keaton torturing a girl."

I made a face. "The missing fingers."

"Maybe."

Jax leaned in. "Who wrote the poems?"

"Tommy said Pete wrote the Jasper poem. And it wasn't to locate the body; it was to go find the pouch. He gave Carly instructions that she kept to herself. He thought she'd just follow the clues to the tree. He picked her because she's such a fangirl. He wanted her to use the pouch to nail Keaton. At first, Tommy didn't want him to do it, but Pete told him Keaton was worried about the podcast's attention to Tommy and had told Pete to set up a hit. Pete figured if the pouch got Keaton arrested, that would help Tommy."

Ayden cocked his head. "If you were with him, how'd you end up with Maura...I mean, Reese?"

"Not sure, but it's likely Pete told her where we were, since she'd had him track us. So, we ended up all meeting in that shack where Annie found us. Pete went to get the pouch, but by then, we'd moved it. I figured when he realized that, we'd be in trouble. That's when Annie came."

"Right." I looked around. "I went into the woods near where we parted and found an overgrown lane. It brought me to the shack, and I saw Reese's car, then Natra's. I was about to text you two—" I pointed at Ayden and Jax "—when Reese grabbed my phone. Things happened fast. Pete either discovered the theft or ran into Keaton, so Keaton knew where to find us. He shot his cousin and torched the place."

"We got away," Natra added, "but we had to go get the pouch because

Pete could've tracked us to where we'd hidden it. And he had. I don't know whether he told Reese or Keaton, or both, but you all know what happened in the shoot-out at the OK Corral. Now *they* seem to have the pouch."

Ayden held up a finger. "I just want to add that we went in the right direction to find Natra, thanks to remote viewing."

"And to Mika's GPS," I said. "Your phone was off, Natra, at least when we first ran the search. Tommy said he turned it back on, but I guess that was later."

"Where I went," Ayden said, "I saw the red Mazda parked behind bushes. No one was in it, but the license plate was right. So, if you saw Keaton but not the girls, I wonder where *they* are."

I nodded. "And if they're alive."

"I'm still confused about the tattoos," Jax said. "They're on Tommy Bruder. Don't they show the victim locations?"

Natra took this one. "Keaton made Pete do the tattoos. Pete had the maps he gave us because he knew the locations. Just before we found the first body, Pete had gotten Reese involved, and *she* made him give us his drawings. She wanted the bodies found and linked to Keaton."

I shook my head. "This sounds like a circle shoot. Everyone has a gun to another one's head."

She nodded. "It's complicated, but here's the nutshell: The pop culture attention to Bruder stirred things up. He's just trying to stay alive. He agrees with Pete that the best way is to reveal what Keaton did. Reese also wanted this. So, Pete's the hub."

"Sounds like he also betrayed pretty much everyone," Jax observed.

"That's why we moved the pouch. Wayne won't be happy we handled it, but we didn't want Pete changing his mind and handing it over to Keaton or Reese."

Jax frowned. "He'd go to all this trouble only to surrender it?"

I held up a finger. "Bruder said Pete's a wild card. Leveraged pretty much by everyone. In short, he serves the one he's with. Keaton wants him to kill Bruder, and Reese wants him to kill Keaton." I folded my arms and asked Natra, "Did Bruder give you any clues for interpreting the other tattoos?"

She shook her head. "I tried to get that out of him, but he wouldn't say. He mentioned he'd been trying to conjure images. He said he made a drawing he was going to give you to get you on his case."

This surprised me. "He meant that? Like I'd testify for him?"

Natra shrugged. "You do advocate for forced accomplices."

I bit my tongue. There was no point in debating it. I'd never support him. "That drawing must be in his cell. And it might depict what he actually witnessed because he was there. We need to get it."

"He gave it to Monroe."

"Oh, right. Monroe was about to hand it over."

"Pete's property should be searched," Jax said. "That's the next obvious step. You should suggest this to Wayne."

I nodded.

Ayden leaned in. "How did Pete get involved? Was he at Cassandra's?"

"Tommy said Pete and Keaton met in juvenile detention."

"So, after Cassandra was exposed."

"Yes. Pete was in for beating up his abusive father. Keaton made a deal that he'd help kill Pete's father if Pete helped him kill Pa as payback for Cassandra. When they couldn't find Pa, that plan fizzled. But obviously, Keaton followed through, if the dead guy in the vault is Pete's dad and Pete owns the property."

I hugged myself. I didn't want to think about Hailey being paraded in front of a moldering corpse.

"I'll do some research," Jax said. "But the police have this case now. There's not much else we can do."

"There's one thing I can do," I said. "I can find Monroe."

Ayden shook his head. "Don't make that deal, Annie."

"I might have to. He's got Bruder's drawing. I need to know what it is."

Chapter Fifty-Six

We were nearly back to our rental the next morning when Wayne called to arrange for our statements. He was at a command post in Aiken, so he agreed to come to us. Bruder had made it through surgery, he told me, but he was in a coma.

"You're not getting near him, Annie. The police presence's intense."

I heard myself say something stupid: "If I hadn't gotten this ball rolling—"

"I know. And I'm aware of what you want. I'll keep that in mind, but if he didn't tell you when you had him, he won't say anything in front of us. Anyway, you're not getting him alone, maybe not for months."

It was a nasty setback, worsened by Bruder's precarious condition. Wayne was right. I'd had my chance. I'd blown it. I could've softened up, given Bruder a chance to talk, made a deal. And I was partly responsible for him getting shot.

I still had two potential routes to information: I could get that pouch from Keaton or that note from Monroe. Well, maybe I had just one route, but Monroe had nearly handed it over. I'd left him a message about Bruder on the number I found for his podcast, but he hadn't called back.

"Any word on the girls?" I asked Wayne.

"Not yet. No one came back to the Mazda, so we left it there, under surveillance. We don't know how Keller and Nemeth got away."

"Whatever Pete was driving, I'd say."

"Did you happen to see what that was?"

I gave this some thought. "I noticed a car missing from his place. An old Pontiac Firebird. A dark color, maybe black. We know Keaton rendezvoused with Pete somewhere along the way, maybe to hand off the girls. If you get Pete, he'll cave. He's a double-dealer. He saves himself first."

"We'll get 'im."

"What about Reese Wendham?"

"Two bullets in the back, one through the heart. Body's in the morgue. And you witnessed that, right?"

"I did. She was running with a pouch, the one everyone's after. If no one found that, I'd say it's gone. And she had a car there. A BMW. A coupe, I think."

"I'll see if it's in the report."

We arrived at our rental cottage. Ayden checked his truck and found no tracking device. "If Pete was here, he didn't finish the job. Looks like he was trying to get inside the cab. The lock's scratched."

"Maybe Jax scared him off in time."

My car seemed undisturbed. I went inside to call Janissa to tell her about Reese.

"I'm stunned," she said, "and relieved, I confess. I expected an awful legal battle and threats to my life."

"She wouldn't have much of a chance. They'll trace her bribes and her assistance to a fugitive. Heads will roll."

"Was she even a real psychologist? Sounds like she faked her way through life."

"She was. I checked her out. But she entered that profession as a manipulator. She just got better at it. There could be more victims like Travis and Cole."

"I'll check. It looks like we'll get that call to Amber traced back to Reese. With her gone, Amber will probably tell us everything, and I can request a new evaluation of her case. Do you want to tell her, or shall I?"

"Please go ahead," I said. "You stuck with her. She'll be relieved. A kid who's been coerced through intimidation has a good case for compassionate treatment."

Even as I said it, I remembered Bruder claiming that he did, too. I mentally willed him to hang on.

Wayne looked tired when he arrived, and I guessed he'd been up all night. He'd brought a drawing for me from our daughter, who'd also sent kisses to Mika. He made a face. "Not kissin' a dog."

"I'll do it."

"I know."

Ayden went first, because JoLynn was on her way to Pete's property with her drone. She'd left Chattanooga early that morning. An official dog handler was also on the way. As soon as Ayden was done, he prepared to go help. I reminded him about deer blinds and cameras in the trees. "Watch for Pete."

Wayne wouldn't let me listen to Natra's statement, though I'd already heard her account. While they talked in another room, I tried to think of where Carly and BH could be. During the time we'd been forming our plan, Keaton could've hidden them or handed them off and gotten to Jasper in their car. But why had he even gone there? Pete must have told him Bruder and Natra were there. Or Reese. I sure wanted another chance at Pete.

Natra emerged to say Wayne was ready for me. "I'll take Mika for a ride and pick up lunch. Be back in a bit."

I entered the room. Wayne was checking his phone. "Nothing's changed," he said. "But just to bring you up to speed, the bag of dirt dropped in your yard did contain human biological traces. Handwriting analysis of the letters from the *Killer Hooks* website show they're not consistent with Bruder's. Content analysis of the poems suggests different authors. The Jocassee hole seems to have been a grave, as you thought. We have shoeprints there consistent with a short male."

"Pete Nemeth." I resisted telling Wayne we were steps ahead of him on these items. "So, if he was *there*, he probably wasn't in my yard."

"Can't rule it out, since we don't know *when* he was there."

"Bruder said he's a cyber and electronics wiz, so he wasn't tampering with my surveillance in some amateur way. I'd say someone else was there—someone who'd been on Pete's property, because that dirt no doubt came from the hole we found there."

Wayne held up a hand. "We'll test it." He took a swig of his coffee. "We need at least two statements from you, Annie. We got a dead woman who had some dealings with you, and we got a killer, maybe two, on the loose, and one in the hospital. You're our primary witness."

"And I saw one of those killers with the missing girls."

"Ayden gave us the photos. But, yeah, you're in the middle of this mess. As usual."

"And without me and my team, you'd have few, if any, leads on a major case. I appreciate Tim's help last night, but we did the heavy lifting, so why don't you treat me like a *valuable* witness? Turn on your recorder."

By the time we were done, I was spent. I'd told Wayne most of what I knew, excluding Monroe's possession of that note from Bruder. That was for me, until such time as I thought it was evidence. Wayne checked his phone and informed me that JoLynn and Ayden had arrived at Pete's. They were setting up. He'd head over there.

I collected the coffee cups. "Just let me know about any change in Bruder's status, please."

"Going home?"

"We've got this place for another day. I'll wait for Ayden."

Wayne cocked his head. "Why do I think you're up to something?"

I shrugged. But he was right. I had to find Monroe. He knew about this place. He had unfinished business. He might come back.

Chapter Fifty-Seven

Natra was gone, and Ayden was beyond cellphone range. I wished I were there on Pete's property, too, watching JoLynn's drone in action again. I had a feeling she'd get some hits. I'd told Wayne about the alleged vault and the dead guy.

The image of the shooting last night flooded back. Keaton, in the shadows, coldly gunning down his cousin. That guy was like a venomous spider on your ceiling that calculates its best chance to drop down and sting. And Pete, with his pseudo-loyalties. I wondered how he felt about his part in easing Keaton's access to his targets. He didn't want Keaton to get the pouch or kill Bruder, and yet he'd put him in prime position to do so.

My main concern was Monroe. The tiniest shred of hope I still had for finding Hailey was that Bruder had written or said something to him. He still hadn't called back.

I stepped outside to look around. Behind the cottage was a wooded area. I didn't see an opening for a pathway. I went out to the road to look at the parked cars. None looked familiar. A black Ford Escape, a gray Porsche Cayenne, a silver Honda Accord, and two white SUVs—a Range Rover and a Subaru. No muscle cars. Further down was a darker car. I was about to walk to it when Natra texted she was on her way back. I returned to the cottage to set out lunch plates. As I reached to pull the screen door closed, Keaton Keller yanked it open, held up a 9-mil to force me back, and stepped inside.

Up close, his arched eyebrows and squinty dark eyes looked demonic. He was tall enough to make me look up. His tight black T-shirt stank of stale sweat, and the beard stubble suggested he hadn't seen a sink in three days. His mouth formed a hard thin line. His eyes had that intense sheen typical of a man with a delusional mission.

I backed away. My heart raced. This guy was barely in touch with reality. And a good shot. But I had to stay calm. "What d'you want?"

He raised an eyebrow. "The tape."

I frowned, then grasped what he meant. The tape of his torture session from Pete's pouch. "I don't have it. I wasn't even near Reese when you shot her."

"So, you *were* there. Thought so. 'S Tommy dead?"

He didn't know. I had an advantage.

"We saved him," I said. "He's talking."

Keaton's eyes widened, and he took a step toward me. "Don't matter. Get me the tape."

"I told you, I didn't—"

I suddenly realized Pete had the pouch, and Pete was no longer with him. I raised my chin. "I want those girls returned alive. I know you were with them."

He sneered. "They wanted this game, they got it."

"They're just kids. Let 'em go."

I was sure my trembling was obvious. I hoped Natra would be back soon. I had a .357 in my bag, but it was in the bedroom. I saw a twitch on Keller's face. His eyes brightened. I knew my next move was risky. "You know this isn't what Pa wants."

His nostrils flared, and his finger moved toward the trigger.

I had to make this work. "They're not the right girls. You know what Pa wants."

"Shut up! You don't know 'im."

"Reese told me. She knew how to contact him. And now you've killed her and kidnapped the wrong girls. He's not pleased."

He shook his head. "She didn't understand him."

"You have to go see him. He has new orders. You're the enforcer. He has something for you to do."

Blood drained from Keaton's face. He turned his head. I heard it, too. A car coming.

"That's our patrol," I said. "Cops checking on me. Pa won't be happy if they catch you."

Keaton looked desperate. "Get me that tape!"

"I want the girls. Alive!"

The car stopped close to the cottage.

"Get it!"

He strode past me and out the back door, slamming it shut.

Chapter Fifty-Eight

I breathed out and ran to get my .357. Natra came in with a bag, and Mika raced to where Keaton had gone, barking. I called her back.

"Keller was here," I told Natra. "He just left. He must've been watching for Wayne to leave. Pete absconded with the pouch. Keller wants me to get it. Wait here." Holding my gun ready, I stepped outside. I saw no sign of him. Mika came out, but I stopped her from chasing him. He'd have shot her without a thought.

My hands trembled. I could still smell his body odor. I'd taken a hell of a gamble, but I'd baited a trap. We locked the doors and pulled the curtains, but I still felt naked. I called Wayne to alert him to what had happened. He said he'd circle back.

"No," I told him. "He's gone. We're okay. But I'm sure he's heading to wherever this vault is."

"See what he's driving?"

"Wait!" I told Natra to cover me and ran out to the street to look at the cars. The dark car I couldn't ID was gone. To Wayne, I said, "I think he has Reese's BMW. Was that car in your report?"

"Tim said there was no car where the shootings happened."

"Then he's driving a dark color BMW, probably registered to Maura Reynolds."

"Copy. I'm sending a patrol over to you."

"Don't waste it on us. You've gotta find him. And put an extra guard on Bruder. Keaton knows he's alive. He might show up at the hospital to shut him up."

"Copy that, Annie."

I went back in. Natra urged me to sit down. I drank some water and brought my trembling under control. While Mika licked my hand, I repeated what Keaton had said.

Natra raised an eyebrow. "You told him Pa—?"

"Yes. Because of what Jax said about his delusion. Tommy confirmed it. Keaton's scared of Pa, but he obeys him, and he doesn't know what Reese might've said. And I told him Bruder's talking. The pressure of getting caught might provoke him to make a mistake. Either way, he's desperate, so he's vulnerable."

Natra shook her head. "I don't know if that's the smartest thing you could've done, or the dumbest."

"Me, neither."

"Do you think he killed the girls?"

"I didn't see any signal from him like that. He's excitable, so probably a bad liar. I think the girls are too valuable as hostages to kill them. Grabbing them wasn't about his compulsion. He probably thought they'd lead him to Bruder, but obviously, they were trying to get Bruder to come to them. Keaton seems to believe if he gets the tape that implicates him, he's home free. So, he'll use the girls to negotiate."

"They gotta be on Pete's property. Where else could he stash them?" Natra got out her laptop. "Sounds like Pete's made another twist."

"Yeah, but where would he go? He hinted he had a hiding place from *them*. He must've meant Keaton and Reese. I saw a deer blind in a tree, but it didn't look stable."

"I saw it, too. That's where he and Tommy stopped me. But Pete *wanted* the pouch found." She looked at me. "He could just turn it over."

"He didn't want it linked to him. And we can't go chasin' a guy who's brilliant with surveillance and has more resources than we realized." I gestured toward her laptop. "Let's rethink this. We need to change our analysis. We thought Pete dropped off the bag of dirt, and Keaton was in Oconee. But *Pete* was at that hole on the Oconee Trail. He dug up whatever was there. Since he wrote the Jasper poem and someone else wrote the

Oconee poem, I'd guess Keaton dropped the bag of dirt. But why? Makes no sense. We might not have even made the connection."

"Could've been Reese. Maybe she wrote the poem, too."

I rubbed my face. It still throbbed where Reese had hit me. "I hadn't considered that. She had it in for Keaton. There must be something important on Pete's property."

"A dead guy in a vault?"

"Yeah, maybe." I hugged myself. "Wayne said they'd check out the whole property. He's got a survey map. I wish I'd paid more attention when we first met Pete there. Back then, he seemed like a minor player."

Natra shook her head. "He's like one of those illusion paintings that changes whenever you move."

"Yeah. Being everyone's handyman had its advantages. He knew all the moves."

"Including ours."

I crossed my arms. "We have to find Pete. We need *him*. The best way to catch Keller is to make him think Pete's offering him the tape back. But I don't have a clue where he is. I doubt he stayed at his place once he saw police activity." I pulled out my phone to check for updates. "Something from Joe. I didn't even hear the text tone."

I called him. "What's up?"

"Just checking in. I found out from some dealers what kind of equipment Pete Nemeth purchased. He's got law enforcement-level cell phone jammers, so he probably gets reception himself when he wants. He's also got some crypto accounts. And the cellphone purchase you were inquiring about can be traced to him, even if he wasn't the guy in the store, but it stayed in the area where it was bought."

"That's because he gave it to a woman who used it to goad a girl to participate in a crime. She probably told him to get rid of it, but he didn't. Maybe he hoped it would get her arrested. Seems like Pete's brilliant at tech but not so great at setting things right."

"Do you still want info on Natra's phone? It's back on."

"Oh, we found her. She's right here. So's Mika. But, yeah, we'd like to get

263

it—" I stopped and looked at Natra. "Didn't Tommy say he put your phone in Pete's car?"

She crossed her arms. "Yes."

I returned to Joe. "We want that location. Her phone was stolen. What can you tell us?"

Chapter Fifty-Nine

Together, Natra and Joe mapped what seemed to have been Pete's route. From where I'd last seen him watching Reese in the clearing, he'd gone north. He seemed to have been in the vicinity of our rental before he'd headed west. The trace ended abruptly, as if he'd entered the no-cell zone near his property or the battery had died. Joe said he'd keep working on it.

"I bet he wanted to give us the pouch," I said to Natra. "But we went to Jax's place. I can't believe we missed it."

Natra looked thoughtful. "Maybe we didn't. Let's get Mika out."

I kept watch while Natra took Mika around the cottage and a short way into the woods. The dog sniffed and looked at us as if confused. We took one more run around the cottage before we let her rest. I was disappointed. We sat on the porch to consider our next move.

"If he left it here," I said, "he hid it too well."

"She'd find it."

"Unless he dumped everything but the tape."

"It would still retain the odor."

"So, he probably took it with him."

We sat quietly, each absorbed in our own thoughts.

I spoke first. "You weren't here, but last night Jax saw someone about Pete's height near Ayden's truck. Jax pulled up and shouted at him."

"But that was before he got the pouch."

"Right, but Pete knew where we were and saw the truck earlier that evening. When we came back this morning, Ayden said someone had tampered with the lock on his cab."

"But he didn't break in."

We looked at each other.

"Ayden's out of range," I said. "One of us should go. If there's *any* chance that pouch was placed in or attached to his truck...."

"We stick together. It's not that far. I'll drive."

On our way, I called Jax to update him. He had news, too.

He said he'd talked with someone familiar with Pete's stint in juvenile. "Pete's mother and father divorced. He ended up with his father, who was arrested several times for assault. One day, the guy disappeared. They thought he'd left to evade a warrant. Pete was 18 by then, and he took over the property. There wasn't any suspicion of murder because no one ever looked for his father. I guess he didn't have many friends."

A call from an unknown number interrupted. I ignored it.

"So, presumably, Pete's father was murdered," I said. "If we can believe Tommy Bruder, the body's preserved in a vault, and Keaton's made it a 'Pa' proxy. He seemed to accept the idea of Pa giving him orders." I told Jax what I'd said to him.

"That was risky, Annie."

"I've seen lots of delusional offenders. You buy into it, they're so pleased someone believes them they tend to go with what you're saying. And he needs me to get the tape; he wasn't going to kill me, at least not till after I deliver it. Anyway, Wayne has a BOLO out for Reese's car. If Keaton's in it, they'll locate him. Hopefully, they'll just follow him till he leads them to the dead guy or the girls."

"Let me know what happens."

"I will. I have another call. Gotta go."

I had a message. We were getting close to where I'd lost service before, so I told Natra to pull over. She found a spot. I listened to the message. It was Monroe. He gave me a new number to use to call him back.

Service was weak, so I got out and found a spot at the back of the Bronco where I thought I'd keep reception. I called him back.

"Dr. Hunter?"

"Monroe. Did you get my message?"

"I'm at the hospital. They haven't let me see him."

"How is he?"

"I don't know yet."

"Do you still have that note?"

He didn't say anything.

"Monroe?"

"It's not a note. It might not even mean anything."

I closed my eyes. *Be patient.* "Was it meant for me?"

"It's from his remote viewing."

I had to stay open. "So, it's an image? He drew it and asked you to give it to me?"

Again, Monroe went silent. I hate these psychic games, but I had to let him go through the motions.

"Dr. Hunter, I know you think I'm a fraud, but—"

"Monroe, okay. I'll have you on my podcast. You can describe how you extracted this from a killer's head—"

"He's not a killer."

I was losing it. "What do you want, Monroe? How can I get that drawing?"

"I can't bring it. I'm not leaving the hospital. I don't want cops talking to him if he wakes up, not without me there."

"Do you have the note with you?"

"Yes. I left last night because I didn't want them to get it."

I took a breath. It was hot. A fly buzzed near my ear. I swatted it away. "Monroe, Reese is dead. Keaton shot her, too. He's on the run. In fact, he might show up there. We still don't know where Carly and her friend are, and I think that note might help."

Silence.

"Monroe?"

"I don't see how it could. It's not a location. Anyway, I can't leave to bring it... Hold on... They're walking over to me. Maybe I can see him now. I'll call you back."

He ended the call.

I nearly tore out my hair.

Natra got out and came over to me. "What's wrong?"

I told her.

"Why doesn't he just photograph it and send it? You've agreed to the deal."

"I was about to suggest that when he cut me off. I can't leave till he calls."

"Text him. Tell him to send you the image."

I started to type that into my phone when it rang.

"Monroe? You need to—"

"He's gone." His voice was thick. "Tommy didn't make it."

I froze. My stomach lurched. "What? No, no, no, no, no!" I put my hand to my mouth and gave Natra my phone. "Tommy Bruder just died." My eyes teared up. I had to lean against her SUV. I barely heard her talking to Monroe. I hadn't anticipated this. I'd been sure he'd make it. I started to rock. I wanted to retrieve the past two minutes, start over, not hear Monroe say those chilling words. *He's gone.* My hope had crumpled. Now I'd never know.

Natra put her hand on my shoulder. "Annie, look at this."

I shook my head.

"You need to."

I blinked back the tears and wiped my face. The image on my phone was a blur. I wiped again and focused. Then my heart raced. I gasped. "Oh, my God!"

There was no mistaking what it was.

"We have to go," Natra said. "Now!"

Chapter Sixty

I could barely talk as I absorbed the sudden loss of Bruder and the task that lay ahead.

"I hope we're right about this," I said in a thick voice. "What did you tell Monroe?"

"Just told him to take the photo and send it. He seems genuinely broken up, by the way."

"I can't even talk about it. And, yes, I was wrong about Tommy Bruder, and I feel awful that this is what happened."

I grabbed Natra's computer and found the file with Pete's maps. Her analysis of the drawings did not list the county where Pete's property was located, and yet Bruder had given us that location. "Pete duped us. The camouflage king. He made sure we focused elsewhere, not on him. I was so relieved at his willingness to hand over the maps I didn't suspect his deception. The spotlight of focus. It'll always blind you."

"My bad, too," Natra said. "I should've researched him, especially knowing how we got the newsletter with his article."

We arrived at Pete's. Ayden's truck, Wayne's SUV, and a cop car took up the small clearing. Natra squeezed in. I wiped my face again.

"We have to let a cop search Ayden's truck," Natra said. "Not us, not Ayden."

"I agree."

We headed for the area around Pete's trailer. I heard the buzz of JoLynn's drone before I saw the crew. JoLynn's van was there. They had a table set up with the items she'd used before. Tim Wheeler and Debra Goldsberry watched the drone. Ayden and Wayne stood talking. Wayne noticed us first. He waited for us to approach. I knew he wasn't happy.

I tried to talk but couldn't get the words out. Natra glanced at me, then told him. "Tommy Bruder died."

Ayden looked shocked. Wayne strode toward me and hugged me. He'd been with me since grad school on my search for Hailey. He knew what Bruder's death meant.

"Sorry, Annie," he said.

He'd made me cry again. I nodded, thanked him, and pushed away. "We're here for another reason."

As JoLynn guided her drone back in, I said, "There's a tree here." I gestured west. "It's down that path. There's a deer blind or surveillance seat, something like that."

Ayden nodded. "I remember it."

"We need to check that blind."

Wayne watched me. I knew he wanted to ask the source of our intel.

I held up my phone to show the photo. "Bruder drew this. He told his attorney to give it to me. There aren't many trees with this kind of deformity. I don't know what's there, but we need to check." I looked at Ayden. "And also, we think Pete left the pouch, or at least the tape, somewhere on or in your truck. Mika can probably find it, but we want police oversight."

Wayne went into action. He used a two-way to call back a team he'd sent to search the property. He told Goldsberry to go with Natra and Ayden to check Ayden's truck and had Wheeler wait to direct other cops while he went with me to see the tree.

"I should go, too," JoLynn said. "I have tree-climbing equipment."

"All right. Let's leave the drone for now."

JoLynn got out her gear and distributed it in pieces to Wayne and me for easier transport.

"I'm so sorry, Annie," Ayden said.

"Let's not talk about it. I need to keep it together. And maybe he did tell me what I needed. We'll see when we get there."

At the split tree, JoLynn examined the bark. "Another blackjack," she said.

"And I see climbing spikes installed. Not good for the tree, but good for us. I won't need spiked gaffs."

Tim Wheeler arrived with a dog handler. He said they hadn't found anything yet. Wayne told him to assist JoLynn with getting up to the deer blind. I could barely stand the suspense. I half-expected Pete to come out from the trees to blast us with some military-grade firearm. He'd see this as violating his property. I wondered if he was watching from some remote place. I looked around for cameras.

JoLynn unpacked ropes, goggles, a helmet, carabiner clips, and what she called a saddle with leg loops. She put two ropes around the tree to assist her with climbing and then hooked up a lifeline to throw over a strong branch when she got higher up. Tim helped her put on a backpack, in case she found something to bring down, and made sure she was "bucked in," as she called it. She asked Tim if he could tie a Blake's hitch, and he said he could.

"There's no obstruction from small branches," JoLynn observed, "so I won't need a saw." To Wayne, she said, "Okay to just use my phone for photos?"

He looked up to consider this. "Depends on what you see."

"Copy." She braced herself against the ropes and started to climb. With the footholds she got from the embedded spikes, she made quick progress. At the deer blind, she threw her lifeline over the tree's crotch and let one end come down to us. Tim tied the knot.

"There's room for just one up here," she called down. "Shall I proceed? I see what looks like a cut in the floor and some hinges, like a trap door."

"Gloves on," Wayne said. "Take photos before you open it."

"Copy."

I'm not scared of heights, but it was difficult to watch her. When she went onto the platform, she opened the trap door and used a flashlight to explore. "There's something here." She took more photos. "Looks like they built this blind over a hole in the tree."

I took a deep breath.

Wayne's two-way crackled. He walked away to answer it. I saw him look back up the path we'd just come down. "Bag it," he said. "Carefully."

A chill raced up my spine. I knew he wouldn't reveal anything, but I guessed they'd found the pouch.

JoLynn, on her stomach, reached into the hole. She pulled something out and placed it into her pack. Then she went back in. After she stowed the second item, she searched the space. Finally, she climbed off the blind by using her system of ropes until she found purchase again on one of the spikes. She used the lifeline to steady her descent. I thought I'd burst from the suspense, because I really wanted this to be Bruder's redemption. On the ground, she handed Tim the backpack.

"Let's take it back to the table," Wayne said. "We can't afford to lose anything. In fact, we should just get it to the lab."

"What if it's a map?" I asked. "What if it can show us what's on this property and help us find the girls? Or find Pete's hideout? We have to find Pete."

Wayne nodded. "We'll open it on the table. But you'll need to stand back."

We met Natra on the way back, and she confirmed they'd found a tape. "Not the whole pouch, but the tape. It's a cassette, so they'll need special equipment. He stashed it inside the grill shield. The pouch probably didn't fit."

"At least we have that. If it's not damaged."

Ayden helped JoLynn put her equipment back in her van. I took a seat on the ground, away from the table, while Wayne organized his team and had them carefully open the first box from JoLynn's pack. The dark gray item resembled a cash box. I watched Wayne's body language to try to interpret what they were finding.

Tim snapped photos with a Nikon DSL-R camera, and another officer made an inventory. At one point, Wayne looked intently at something. He used a pen to move it. Then he stood straight and looked over at me. I felt cold. Tears burned my eyes. I'd always known but didn't really want it confirmed, not here. Not this way. Wayne gestured for me to come over.

"Don't touch anything," he warned. "Just tell me if you see something familiar."

On a white sheet of paper, I looked at a row of items—a killer's trophies: IDs that featured girls, a heart on a necklace, a couple of rings, and some earrings. A package of yellowed cling wrap seemed to contain soft clumps of reddish hair. I didn't want to see any hint of a braid. I glanced at Wayne. He looked away, uncomfortable, and cleared his throat. I stopped at a silver chain bracelet with a flattened nameplate. I touched my own identical one and nearly lost it. Wiping my eyes, I looked at Wayne and nodded. I couldn't speak. The nameplate, scratched and tarnished, was still readable. It bore the name that confirmed the fate of my "wrist sister." *Hailey.*

Chapter Sixty-One

The rest was a blur. Natra, Ayden, and JoLynn all spoke to me, but I felt numb. I now knew without a doubt that Tommy Bruder had brought Hailey here for whatever terrible treatment Keaton had devised. She'd been forced to look at that preserved body—Pa. I sat down and just stared. I heard the cops talking about the other discoveries, but I barely processed their comments. Some of them left. I don't know how much time passed, but I sensed it was nearing dinnertime. The skies had clouded over. I heard car engines. JoLynn commenced her work with the drone. Wayne's radio crackled.

He came over to me and knelt down. "Annie, we found the vault. It's buried underground."

I stared at him. "Pete's vault?"

"We think so. We found a diagram of the property with its location and some detailed plans to build a dungeon inside a shipping container. If the girls are in there, I want some psychological support for them. Can you handle that? I have a social worker on the way, but I need someone now."

I could hardly believe Wayne wanted to use me in an official capacity. I swallowed. "I can do that."

I got in his SUV. He explained that the property had two parts, divided by a road. His team had found an abandoned cabin, along with more junk cars. As we arrived where several cop cars were parked, I got out and followed Wayne to where they'd uncovered a camouflaged opening to a set of steps that went down to the vault. It had a rollup door. Tim Wheeler and Debra Goldsberry were trying to cut the heavy locks at the bottom.

"I hear something," Tim said. "Someone's banging in there."

Wayne raised a hand. "Careful, then. Maybe it's the girls or maybe someone with a gun."

I looked around. Pete had to have surveillance on this. I scanned the trees for any sign of an observation post. He could easily pick us off from up high. He'd given us the tape, but it didn't lead back to him the way items we'd found here did. We were about to trap a man who'd made an art of eluding his foes.

I stepped back to survey the scene. Wayne's team was focused on the vault. Two wore bulletproof vests, but two did not. Wayne didn't, either. I felt uneasy. Wayne glanced at me. He gestured that I should return to his vehicle. He felt uneasy, too. "Okay," I said, "but please put on your vest."

He went with me to his car, got his vest, and told me to keep the car door shut.

He returned to the vault. A few minutes later, I saw movement to my right. Pete came out from between two cars. He held an assault rifle poised to shoot.

"Git off my land!' he shouted. "You got a warrant?"

Everyone turned. Tim and another cop drew their guns, but Wayne held up his hand and identified himself. "Nemeth," he said. "Put down the weapon."

"Ah'm warnin' ya, leave mah property!" He moved toward them.

"Stop there!" Wayne repeated. "Put down your weapon and get down on the ground!"

I feared this was a suicide-by-cop. Cornered men with a lot to lose will make such moves. A muffled yell came from the vault. Pete kept walking. Wayne drew his Glock. Pete was less than thirty yards from him. I saw Debra move to a strategic position. I got out of the car and yelled, "Pete! Tommy's hurt. You gotta help him. He needs you."

He hesitated and looked toward me. It gave Debra a chance to maneuver.

"Weapon on the ground, Nemeth!" Wayne shouted.

Debra announced her presence behind him. "Drop it!"

Defeated, Pete lowered the rifle.

"On your knees," Wayne ordered.

Pete went down. He placed his rifle in front of him. Debra stepped in to handcuff him while Wayne removed the weapon. Tim took it from him.

"I don't know nuthin'!" Pete yelled. "Twern't me. Keaton shot 'em. He kidnapped them girls."

Wayne stood over him. "You have a key to this vault?"

Pete shook his head. Debra got him to his feet.

Wayne held out his right hand. "Hand it over."

"Don't go in there!"

"Now! Before I knock you down and search you myself!"

Pete buckled. "In my pocket," he said. Tim retrieved the key and went to open the two steel locks. As soon he rolled up the door, Carly and BH, dressed in red, ran out, screaming. Wayne gestured to me.

A stench from the vault nearly knocked me back. The girls went to their knees, coughing and retching. I went over to Carly. Her T-shirt and face were smudged and dirty. Both girls were crying. I gave each some tissues and a bottle of water. Carly moaned, "I'm so sorry. We just wanted to help Tommy."

Two cops moved Pete toward a car to transport him to a detention cell. The girls watched him with wide eyes.

"He was gonna kill us," Carly said. "That other guy. He was gonna leave us in there with that…that…." She retched again and put the tissue to her mouth.

I urged the girls to come to Wayne's car, partly to get away from the reeking vault. I saw Wayne go down the steps to enter it. I already knew he'd see whatever remained of Pete's father's corpse.

"Is Tommy okay?" Carly asked. "Did they catch him?"

"Carly, I'm sorry. The guy who kidnapped you shot him. He's gone."

"Oh, no!" She put her face in her hands and wept. "No, no, no!" BH frowned at me as if I were to blame.

"Can I call my mom?" BH asked.

"When we get to town, but I'm sure the officers are already on it."

Wayne came back, looking pale. He gestured for me to talk to him away

276

from the car. I told the girls I'd be right back.

"Is it bad?" I asked.

"Yeah." I thought he was close to vomiting. "This kind of crazy shit's your area. Who keeps—? Whatever. Those girls are gonna have nightmares. *I'm* gonna have nightmares. Paramedics will be here soon, and a social worker." He gestured with his head toward his car. "Then you can go. I know it's been a hard day for you."

"Just tell me one thing, Wayne. You said you got a diagram of this place. Were any graves marked on it?"

He seemed to get what I was asking. "There were markers. We'll get this asshole to tell us what they mean."

I suddenly remembered Keaton. "Pete's useful. You need to have him reel in Keaton Keller. He's out there, and he'll soon know his cousin's not talking. If he thinks Pete still has the tape, you can bait him."

Wayne closed his eyes. "Annie, I'm running this."

"Just an idea. You wanted my expertise. Pete's a deal maker. He preserves himself first. Believe me, with a little pressure, you can get a lot from this guy."

"I s'pose you want to coach the interrogation."

"Wouldn't hurt. No charge."

He waited a beat. "I'll let Tim decide."

Wayne went back to divvy up duties for the night. When the paramedics came, I made sure Carly and BH were okay. Carly looked at me through her tear-streaked makeup and mumbled, "Thank you." I gave them my number.

Tim drove me back to my team. He liked my idea about using Pete to trap Keaton. By the time he dropped me back at our starting point, it was getting dark. The evidence had been removed. Ayden and JoLynn had gone to get dinner. Only Natra remained.

She handed me a water bottle that contained a dark liquid. "It's from Puca. He gave it to me last night and said I'd know when to give it to you. It's now."

I took a drink. I'd had his concoctions before, and they'd settled me.

Natra touched my hand. "Let's do a ceremony. The cops are busy. They won't notice. I think you need to commune here with Hailey. She got you here. Your journey's over."

"Not yet. We don't yet—"

"It is. She's here."

I felt my shoulders relax. I nodded. "Okay. Good idea."

"I have the stuff ready. We can't light a fire, but we can use this."

She handed me a white candle, lit it, and urged me to go be alone. "I'll keep watch. It's peaceful now. This is a good time."

I agreed with her. Hailey was here. I walked to a spot and stood still. I recalled memories of our good times and our closeness, how she'd laughed and shown me a level of boldness that had influenced my career. Around me, in the weeds, fireflies sparkled.

That's when I got an idea.

Chapter Sixty-Two

Tim Wheeler accepted my offer to consult. He recognized that we knew much more about Pete, Reese, and Keaton than he did. To form my strategy, I collected the questions my team wanted answered. I even let 3-M have some input. The most important question for me was the location of Hailey's remains.

When offered a deal, Pete agreed to lure Keaton with the promise of handing over the tape. He also told a sordid story. He said his father, a survivalist, had created the vault as a shelter. When Keaton saw the acreage, he thought it would be a perfect burial ground. During a freakish delusional episode, Keaton sealed Pete's father into the vault and left him to die. He insisted the corpse was Pa, and they had to please him by tormenting girls in front of him, especially redheaded girls, just like the first one he'd killed for Pa. Over the years, the father's body became mummified. Pete did what Keaton demanded, but to get himself out of it, he recruited Tommy to pick up the girls. When Tommy saw what Keaton was doing, he resisted. Keaton threatened him by saying he was already implicated in multiple crimes.

I'd pieced this part together myself. Tommy had taken the fall, probably to get away from his demented cousin. He really had been just an accomplice. Only Pete knew where most of the bodies were buried because after the first couple, Tommy had refused this duty. More recently, when Keaton wanted to kill Tommy, Pete had tried to get Carly to find the pouch, but we'd intervened and found the body. Keaton got mad and wrote the Oconee poem to implicate Pete in that burial, but Pete had seen it and removed the remains. He didn't understand my question about the berries left there, so

I assumed that was Keaton's flourish. Pete had also been at the other two sites that matched the tattoos. He'd reburied all of the victims, aside from the one we'd found, on his own property. And there were others. He agreed to show us where to dig.

In response to my specific questions, Pete said Reese had caught him digging up a set of remains on his property. She'd collected a bag of dirt and left it at my place as a threat to him. It wasn't meant for me at all. She'd wanted him to think I could trace it back to him. She also made him place the trackers on our cars. Pete admitted he'd enlisted Reese to try to protect Tommy from Keaton, but she'd seen this as an opportunity to kill Keaton and set Tommy up for it. She'd made Pete give us the maps as part of that plan. He'd left out his own county. He'd also written most of the letters that passed as Bruder's on the auction sites, although Tommy had helped with a few.

We'd missed some things but had done a pretty good job of piecing this case together. My team debrief took place that evening at the lake house. These are always reserved for just Natra, Ayden, and me. My PI brought *Two Sisters* Pinot Noir. "Seemed appropriate," he said.

We gathered on the screened porch and lit some candles. I thanked them both for all they'd done to bring this case home. Then I summarized Pete's tale.

"So, they're setting up a sting?" Ayden asked.

"Already in motion. I wouldn't be surprised if Keaton's caught tonight."

"Insanity defense, no doubt," Natra commented.

I nodded. "I hate what he did, but I also hate what was done to him. He was psychologically vulnerable to start with. That's how Cassandra was able to reshuffle his psyche the way she did. He was fertile soil for her poison."

Ayden leaned in to fill his plate with the goodies we'd set out. "Are you really putting Monroe on your podcast?"

"I am. Because honestly, I don't know how he got that image of the tree. Probably it was just something Bruder saw and drew, but Monroe can tell whatever story he wants. I figured it's a platform for him to talk about Bruder in a positive light, which seems fair."

Natra raised an eyebrow. "You'll admit you misjudged 3-M?"

I nodded. "I sort of did. I don't think he can read the minds of murderers, but he accepted that Tommy might have used remote viewing, so he did get the drawings. He'll describe them on the show. That'll be interesting. And I've also decided to work on clearing Tommy's name. I misjudged him, too. I have Pete's statement to confirm it, and Monroe will help. That's a way to honor Hailey as well. For all I know, she gave me the idea, because I thought of it when I lit the candle for her out there."

Ayden cocked his head. "So, did I succeed at RV? Was I guided by some force?"

I smiled. "You did it right. Whether there's some force involved, I don't know. But, yeah, you should practice more. You can draw. Go for it. I'll be your outbounder any time."

"Do we have any ghosts in this one?"

Natra raised her glass. "Yes, we do. Thank you, Hailey. And Tommy. And Cole. And Trevor. And the ghost of Lake Jocassee."

I clinked my glass to hers. Ayden joined us.

My phone rang. "It's Wayne." I picked up.

"We got 'im, Annie. Keller's in custody. That was a good plan."

Chapter Sixty-Three

I held my own "wrist sisters" bracelet as we watched JoLynn direct the painstaking exhumation on Pete's property. It was the first of several in this area. It was the only one I'd attend.

Keaton had been "stung." Carly had begun recounting her ordeal on a new series of her podcast, and Pete had agreed to testify against Keaton Keller, should he ever be deemed competent to go to trial. I doubted that would happen. The preserved corpse, his bizarre experience with Cassandra, and his long-documented resistance to therapy gave Keaton's defense attorney plenty of ways to keep him in a psychiatric facility.

I'd paid for Tommy's cremation myself, since his family had shunned him.

On my return to my home on the Outer Banks, I stopped near Asheville to see Hailey's mother. I told her we'd found Hailey and I'd deliver the remains when I could. I offered her the bracelet. She wouldn't take it.

"You keep it," she said, with tears in her eyes. "You promised to find her, and you did. She'd want you to have it."

I thanked her and drove home. Thanks to JoLynn, we already had a new case.

Acknowledgements

I thank Lee Lofland, who invited me to write short stories about my Nut Crackers team for two anthologies, *After Midnight* and *People Are Strange*. "Natra" introduced me to sniffer dogs, and cyber security specialist Joe Pochron became my go-to for all things digital. My agent, John Silbersack, gave me priceless guidance, and Verena Rose at Level Best Books has been an enthusiastic editor. Susan Lysek, Sally Keglovits, Ruth Osborne, and Dana Devito read the early drafts and became my cheerleaders.

About the Author

Katherine Ramsland has played chess with serial killers, dug up the dead, worked with profilers, and camped out in haunted crime scenes. As a professor of forensic psychology and a death investigation consultant, she's vigilant for unique angles. The author of 71 books, she's been a forensic consultant for *CSI, Bones* and *The Alienist* and an executive producer on *Murder House Flip* and A&E's *Confession of a Serial Killer*. She's become a go-to expert for the most deviant and bizarre forms of criminal behavior, which offers background for her Nut Cracker Investigations.

SOCIAL MEDIA HANDLES:
  Blog: http://www.psychologytoday.com/blog/shadow-boxing
  Facebook: **https://www.facebook.com/Kath.ramsland/**
  Twitter: **https://twitter.com/KatRamsland**
  Instagram: https://www.instagram.com/katherineramsland/

AUTHOR WEBSITE:
  www.katherineramsland.net

Also by Katherine Ramsland

I Scream Man, Level Best Books

How to Catch a Killer, Sterling

Track the Ripper, Riverdale Avenue Books

The Ripper Letter, Riverdale Avenue Books

The Blood Hunters, Kensington

The Heat Seekers, Kensington

Confession of a Serial Killer: The Untold Story of Dennis Rader, the BTK Killer, University Press of New England

Haunted Crime Scenes, with Mark Nesbitt, Second Chance Books

Blood and Ghosts: Paranormal Forensic Investigators, with Mark Nesbitt, Second Chance Books

The Mind of a Murderer: Privileged Access to the Demons that Drive Extreme Violence, Praeger

The Forensic Psychology of Criminal Minds, Berkley

The Devil's Dozen: How Cutting Edge Forensics Took down Twelve Notorious Serial Killers, Berkley

The Human Predator: A Historical Chronicle of Serial Murder and Forensic Investigation, Berkley

The Criminal Mind: A Writer's Guide to Forensic Psychology, Writer's Digest

The Forensic Science of CSI. Berkley

Printed in the USA
CPSIA information can be obtained
at www.ICGtesting.com
LVHW091653070923
757245LV00009B/1052